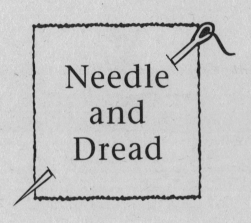

Needle
and
Dread

Elizabeth Lynn Casey

D0311095

BERKLEY PRIME CRIME, NEW YORK

BERKLEY
PRIME
CRIME

An imprint of Penguin Random House LLC
375 Hudson Street, New York, New York 10014

NEEDLE AND DREAD

A Berkley Prime Crime Book / published by arrangement with the author

ISBN: 978-0-425-28256-4

PUBLISHING HISTORY
Berkley Prime Crime mass-market edition / April 2016

PRINTED IN THE UNITED STATES OF AMERICA

10 9 8 7 6 5 4 3 2 1

Cover illustration by Mary Ann Lasher.
Cover design by Judith Lagerman.
Interior text design by Laura K. Corless.

Penguin
Random
House

Praise for the
Southern Sewing Circle Mysteries

"Sweet and charming . . . The bewitching women of the Southern Sewing Circle will win your heart."

—Monica Ferris, *USA Today* bestselling author

"Filled with fun, folksy characters and southern charm."

—Maggie Sefton, national bestselling author

"[Mixes] a suspenseful story with a dash of down-home flavor . . . Visiting with the charmingly eccentric folks of Sweet Briar is like taking a trip back home." —Fresh Fiction

"I love the setting and the coziness of the town. I've loved getting to know each and every one of the characters . . . and I've loved the murderous predicaments they've all found themselves in. But the camaraderie between the ladies is what makes the story so much fun!" —Marie's Cozy Corner

"Tori is fun, sassy, smart, and crafty in more ways than one . . . I like feeling the connection to the characters, like they are old friends coming into my home for the night to sew and solve mysteries together." —Two Lips Reviews

"This series has its own brand of charm, intrigue, and unique characters." —Once Upon a Romance

"An excellent read for crafters and mystery lovers alike. Elizabeth [Lynn] Casey has a knack for threading together great story lines, likable characters, and surprises in every page."

—The Romance Readers Connection

*For all those readers
who have sent me such encouraging notes
over the last few years.
This one is for you!*

Acknowledgments

When I'm knee-deep into the writing process, I often feel as if I'm in some sort of personal Batcave—just me and my computer. And while that describes a lot of my days, it doesn't describe all of them. Certain people always make their way into the Batcave with me via an encouraging email, a post on my Facebook author page, etc. That said, I need to call out a few specific people who made the writing of this particular book all the more fun for me.

First up: a huge thank-you goes to my dear friend, Joe Richardson. Brainstorming with you, Joe, is always a hoot.

Next, a big thank-you to my friend, Lynn Deardorff, who, once again, answered my SOS about the sewing project for this book.

And, finally, my family . . . for tossing an occasional candy corn in my direction whenever I got really stressed. I love you all.

Chapter 1

"I reckon, Victoria, if I don't quit pinchin' myself every time I look through this window, I'm gonna be black and blue b'fore long."

Tori Sinclair glanced over her shoulder at the polyester-clad sixtysomething she'd apparently been too distracted to notice, and smiled. "You must be awfully light on your feet this morning, Margaret Louise."

"Why, I think that might be the first time anyone's ever said that to me." The grandmother of eight lifted her ample weight up on tiptoes and directed Tori's attention back to its original starting place. "It don't matter how many times I've stood in this same spot over the past two weeks, I still can't believe my eyes."

She wanted to argue, to say it all made perfect sense, but the sight of Leona Elkin and Rose Winters—standing side by side behind the sparkly new register—defied everything Tori had come to know as reality where the two nemeses were concerned.

Sure, Margaret Louise's svelte and stylish twin sister had pulled the proverbial hatchet out of Rose Winters's back long enough to walk together, side by side, down the aisle on Tori's wedding day a month and a half earlier, but that truce wasn't expected to hold beyond the last note of the last song at the reception that followed. The fact that it had not only held but had also actually grown stronger was more than a little unsettling.

"I know it's wrong, but I keep waiting for the other shoe to drop," Tori murmured just loud enough for her friend to hear. "But it's not."

"*You're* waitin'? Why, Victoria, I've been walkin' 'round with my shoulders hiked clear up to my ears just waitin' for the *kaboom*. Only there ain't been no kaboomin' yet."

Tori stepped back just enough to afford a clear view of the newly hung shingle above their heads, the colorful trio of spools depicted in the bottom right-hand corner drawing her attention first to the turquoise-colored thread that spilled out from the center spool and then up to the shiny needle in the upper left corner. Between the pictures, and in bold, silver-etched black lettering, was the name the normally feuding duo had come up with (sans argument) over tea and pastries: SEWTASTIC.

Below that, in slightly thinner writing, was visual confirmation that hell had officially frozen over—at least as far as Sweet Briar, South Carolina, was concerned: LEONA ELKINS & ROSE WINTERS, PROPRIETORS.

"My Jake keeps sayin' all that thunder we've been havin' is really just the sound of our daddies and granddaddies turnin' over in their graves." Margaret Louise tightened her grip on the platter of finger foods in her hands. "I told him he was bein' silly, but Victoria, it's hard not to wonder. I mean, we *are* talkin' 'bout my twin and Rose. Them two are like Lee and Grant . . . like the Hatfields and McCoys . . . like Paula Deen and The Food Network . . . like—"

Clasping her hand over top of her friend's forearm, Tori did her best to stop laughing long enough to speak. "Okay, okay, I get it. And you're right. So let's enjoy whatever this strange phenomenon is before the bullets start flying, shall we?"

Without so much as a word, Margaret Louise shrugged her broad shoulders beneath her non-jogging jogging suit and jerked her chin toward the freshly painted shop door. "I'm ready if you're ready, Victoria. 'Sides, if I don't put these buttermilk hushpuppies down, I'm gonna start eatin' 'em right out here on the front porch."

Tori reached around her friend and yanked open the door of SewTastic, a medley of enticing smells rushing onto the porch in greeting. Instinctively, Margaret Louise's nose lifted into the air. "Mmmm . . . pumpkin. Cinnamon. And . . . nutmeg. Who made a pie?"

Leona tucked a strand of her salon-softened gray hair back into its stylish bob and made a face at her sister. "No one made a pie. Those are the scented candles I placed around the shop."

"We found them last night at Turner's Gifts 'N More," Rose interjected from her spot beside Leona. "They had a whole section of autumn- and holiday-scented candles."

"Y-you two went shop-*shopping* together?" Tori stammered.

Tugging her cotton sweater more closely against her frail body, Rose slowly made her way around the counter to hug Tori and then direct Margaret Louise and her platter of hushpuppies to a linen-covered card table in the back corner of the main room. "Of course. We had some last-minute touches to attend to before today's festivities, isn't that right, Leona?"

"A person only has one chance to make a first impression." Leona followed her sister across the store, waited for her to place the platter of food down on the table, and then proceeded to swap the item's position with one further back. "You were fortunate with Milo in that regard, dear."

Any question as to whether Tori had just been insulted by Sweet Briar's resident male-magnet was quickly wiped away by Margaret Louise's narrowed eyes. "Twin, you take that back."

Leona stopped fiddling with the assorted platters and plates and met her sister's gaze over the top of her chic glasses. "I didn't insult Victoria, Margaret Louise. In fact, my statement merely speaks to her ability to land a man like Milo Wentworth even under the direst of circumstances."

"The *direst of circumstances*?" Tori echoed.

Leona tidied up the already pristinely stacked napkins on the left-hand side of the table and then straightened to her full five-foot-seven, stiletto-enhanced stature. "Yes, dear. You weren't wearing makeup when you met Mr. Wonderful, remember?"

Before Tori could respond, Leona continued, the click clack of her heels as she made her way around the store serving as background clatter to her usual no-

nonsense voice. "The bus should be arriving in a little over thirty minutes, and Debbie still isn't here with the cupcakes and cookies I ordered."

"The cupcakes and cookies *we* ordered," Rose corrected as she returned to her post behind the counter. "You were worried about Victoria and your sister not getting here right up until the moment they walked through the door. And before that, you were convinced Charles was going to forget to turn on that ridiculous bunny-cam of yours. I'm quite sure Debbie will—"

"You find something *funny*, dear?" Leona snapped, shifting her focus from Rose to Tori.

Uh-oh . . .

Tori traded glances with Margaret Louise. "I, uh, take it my giggle just now wasn't as silent as I imagined?"

Margaret Louise shook her head.

Shifting her weight from one foot to the other, Tori swallowed. "I—um, well . . . I guess the bunny-cam thing just caught me off guard." At Leona's quickly rising eyebrow, she continued. "I guess I just expected Paris to be here. With you."

Like a balloon pierced by a pin, all fight left Leona's artfully nipped and tucked body. "One of today's crafters is allergic to bunnies."

"And you know this because . . ."

Charles sashayed into the room from the shop's back hallway and air-kissed Tori's left cheek. "Because at my suggestion, Leona included the question on the tour's sign-up sheet. These days, everyone is allergic to something. My next-door neighbor, Gladys? Her great-granddaughter is allergic to *chocolate* of all things. Can you imagine? And Douglas-John, my palm reader? He is allergic to silk."

"*Silk*?" Leona gasped.

Charles pursed his lips. "I *know*. Can you imagine carrying *that* curse?"

Leona tsked away the horror and then rested her hand atop Charles's pencil-thin forearm, batting her mile-long eyelashes at their young friend as she did. "How *is* my precious angel doing? She must be positively distraught without me."

"When I checked your computer just now, she was sleeping in her box, nestled up with your red satin bathrobe." Charles lifted Leona's hand to his lips and kissed it reassuringly. "If she needs anything during this soiree, I'll break away and attend to her needs. You have my word on that, gorgeous. In the meantime, I'll go peek at the screen again right now just to be sure."

"Have I mentioned yet this morning how badly I want you to leave New York for good and come live here with me?" Leona followed her own question with a dismissive flick of her hand. "Then again, this is Sweet Briar. Asking you to leave civilization for the epitome of hillbilly central would be grossly unfair of me. And if there's one thing I'm not, it's selfish."

Tori glanced at Rose and waited. But thirty seconds later, the comeback that would have undoubtedly followed such a boisterous claim six weeks earlier remained unspoken.

Stunned, Tori gathered the underside of her wrist between her thumb and index finger and pinched.

Nope. I'm awake . . .

Leona strode toward the window only to stop

midway, her brown eyes large with—uncertainty? "Victoria, dear, does everything look okay?"

"Everything is lovely, Leona."

"You didn't even *look*." Leona threw her perfectly manicured hands into the air and marched back to the food table. "I asked you if everything looked okay, and you just answered . . . like it doesn't matter. But it does. Very much."

Taken aback, Tori glanced at Margaret Louise for help but got nothing. "Leona, I—I—"

"Don't you fret, Victoria," Rose said. "Leona has been like this all morning. I keep telling her it's just nerves and that everything is going to be fine, but it's like talking to a brick wall."

Leona narrowed her eyes on her elderly business partner. "There's a lot riding on today, Rose."

Rose wiped at a spot on the counter with her finger and then redirected her attention to a sheet of paper beside the register. Even from her partially obstructed view, Tori could tell it was a to-do list. "There really isn't, Leona. We agreed we would try this inaugural crafting weekend and see how it goes. If it's successful, we'll hire this Miranda Greer to put together another one after the holidays. If it's a bust, we'll see if she has any other ideas we want to try."

"How many women are you expecting?" Tori asked.

Flipping over her to-do list, Rose pointed to a second list—this one made up of names rather than chores. "Counting Miranda and the bus driver, *seven*. But Miranda is confident that with more notice for future events, we can double, maybe even *triple* that number."

Margaret Louise wandered back to the table and

pointed at a jar in the center. "That looks like pickled shrimp. I love pickled shrimp!"

"That's for our guests!" Leona smacked her sister's hand away from the jar, turned it a half centimeter to the left, and then turned it back a half centimeter to the right. "There. That's centered now."

Tori looked from Rose's twitching lips to Margaret Louise's wounded face and then, finally, around the shop. "I love the way you made the sewing box display reflect the upcoming Thanksgiving holiday. Very classy."

Slowly, Leona stopped her incessant reorganization efforts and turned to face Tori. "Do you like the harvest-colored ribbons I tucked around the handles of the sewing box?"

She darted her eyes back to the display. Desperate to prove she was paying attention, Tori stepped closer to the display and ran a gentle hand down a nearby pilgrim-themed bolt of fabric. "Absolutely. And this . . . this makes me want to make a table runner for the big day."

"My intentions, exactly." Leona beamed with self-adoration just before she crossed to a shelf on the opposite wall. "And *this*? Isn't *this* genius, too, dear?"

She tried not to laugh at Rose's not so subtle eye roll, and instead, made herself focus on the series of familiar-looking items lining two different shelves. "Wait. Isn't that the porch pilgrim you made last year, Rose?"

"It is."

"And that fabric basket . . . isn't that *yours*, Margaret Louise?"

"Good eyes, Victoria!"

"They're examples of sewing projects customers can

do in time for Thanksgiving," Leona explained. "And do you see what's next to each one?"

Tori followed Leona's finger to the first in a series of small wooden boxes. Curious, she stepped closer and peered inside.

"Each one holds printed instructions on how to make that particular piece," Leona gushed. "With a detailed listing of the items needed in order to do so—items we just happen to have in stock, of course."

There was no denying the obvious. Leona was born to be a businesswoman.

"Wow-ee! If I didn't know any better—which I do—I might actually think my twin up and learned how to sew!"

Leona walked to the center of the room and extended her finger within inches of her sister's nose. "Not one word today about my sewing, Margaret Louise. Not one word, you understand?"

"Your *sewin'*?" Margaret Louise teased. "*What* sewin'?"

Leona's finger moved closer. "I swear, I'll—"

A quick but distinct jingle brought all four pairs of eyes toward the front of the shop and a clearly uncomfortable Debbie Calhoun.

"Did I interrupt something?" the bakery owner asked from around the stack of powder blue boxes in her hands.

Tori and Margaret Louise swarmed around the mother of two like bees to honey, lessening her load in record speed. "Nope. You didn't interrupt a thing."

"Unless, of course, you count Leona's usual threats." Margaret Louise carried the first pair of boxes over to the table and stopped. "Where do you want these, Twin?"

"I want the cookies taken out and put on the empty harvest plate. And I want the cupcakes arranged across the leaf-etched plate to its left." Then, turning back to Debbie, Leona sagged against the counter. "I was starting to think you'd forgotten."

"I didn't forget." Debbie flicked her dark blonde ponytail over her shoulder, took a quick but unmistakable inventory of the room, and then nodded approvingly first at Rose, and then Leona. "Inviting . . . motivating . . . cozy . . . well done, ladies, well done."

Rose lifted her finger into the air and then disappeared momentarily behind the counter. When she re-emerged, she had a whimsical holiday apron in her hand. "So what do you think?"

Tori put the last cupcake on the plate and handed the empty box to Margaret Louise. "Oh, Rose, I love it. It's fun and very timely!"

"It was between this and a door hanging, but I finally decided we should go with this."

"Finally decided at eleven o'clock last night." Leona plucked the empty boxes from Margaret Louise's hands and carried them back to the counter. "Nothing like waiting until the last minute."

Rose swapped the apron for one of the empty boxes now fanned out across the counter. With slow, arthritic moves, the elderly woman broke each of the boxes down for easier disposal and then handed them back to Leona to put in the trash can in the back room.

Leona, in turn, handed them to Margaret Louise. "Here. Get rid of these, will you?"

"Do I look like your maid, Twin?"

"No. My maid is taller, thinner, and far less bothersome." Then, before the quiet gasps to her left and right could built to a crescendo, Leona brought her lips to within inches of her sister's ear and said, in full voice, "There's an extra pickled shrimp in the kitchenette. If you throw those boxes away, it's all yours."

"Now you're talkin', Twin . . ."

In a flash, Margaret Louise was gone, and in her wake was a clock-peeking Leona. "The bus should be pulling up out front in less than fifteen minutes." Moving her gaze from Tori to Debbie and finally onto Rose, she added, "Are we ready?"

"I've never been more ready for anything in my life, Leona." Rose came out from around the counter with a rare burst of energy, powered, no doubt, by the breathtakingly beautiful smile spreading its way across the eightysomething's rapidly aging face. "Let's make their time here at SewTastic something they'll never, *ever* forget."

Chapter 2

Tori counted out the correct number of tags onto the counter and then gathered them into her hand, the mundane task bringing with it a much-needed chance to breathe. From the moment Miranda Greer had ushered the weekend crafters off the bus and into SewTastic, things had been nutty.

Sure, some of that nuttiness came with doing something new. But a big chunk came from the very real feeling that despite a ten-to-five ratio of helpers to crafters, they were grossly understaffed. To an outsider looking in, it made little to no sense. But to an insider who should have anticipated the driver's gender, and thus Leona's preoccupation with said driver, it made all the sense in the world.

Needless to say, Tori, along with Miranda, Rose, Debbie, Margaret Louise, the rest of the Sweet Briar

Ladies Society Sewing Circle members, and Charles, had spent the better part of the last hour on the move—answering the female crafters' endless questions, fetching all necessary supplies, troubleshooting any and all issues that arose, and keeping an eye on the store's regular customer traffic. Likewise, during that same hour, Leona hadn't budged from her spot beside Travis Beaker, the lone male in the visiting group.

If Travis had a question, Leona purred the answer into his ear. If Travis needed a refill of finger foods or dessert, Leona snapped her finger at whoever was standing around and then proudly set the plate—that was handed to her—at the man's spot. The fact that he wasn't one of the crafters who'd paid to be part of the event didn't seem to faze Leona.

"I don't get it," Charles whispered in Tori's ear as he skidded to a stop just outside the project room. Running a hand through his bright red spiky hair, the twenty-something jerked his head in Leona's direction. "Travis doesn't meet Leona's criteria."

"Leona's *criteria*?" Tori repeated.

"Yes." He loosened the knot on his accessory scarf and inhaled dramatically. "Leona prefers men in the twenty-to-forty range. Travis is pushing fifty-two, easy." Rocking back on his purple Keds, Charles peeked into the room, conducted a slow and thorough once-over of the man sitting beside Leona, and then turned back to Tori. "He also has a bit of a paunch—a major no-no in Leona's book."

Tori looked from Charles to Travis and back again. "You're overlooking one major factor."

Charles's perfectly arched left eyebrow shot upward. "What's that?"

"He's wearing a uniform."

"But it's a *bus driver's* uniform," Charles protested.

"It doesn't matter. A uniform is a uniform in Leona's book."

Charles's mouth gaped. "But I thought she meant pilots, or doctors, or cops . . ."

"Well, she has a preferred hierarchy, of course, but if there's only one uniform-wearing male in a room, he'll do." She swept her hand toward the object of Leona's current eyelash-batting affection and then dropped back against the wall. "Hence, the attention she is lavishing on one Mr. Travis Beaker. Though what I find most interesting is the fact that he seems unimpressed. Leona isn't used to that."

"Young man? Young man?" A woman's voice, shrill and commanding, wafted out the open door, taking with it all semblance of color from Charles's already pasty complexion. "Where *are* you?"

A rush of silent hand flapping was quickly followed by the warmth of Charles's breath against Tori's ear. "I swear, I'm going to strangle that woman if I have to hear one more of her complaints."

"I know she's a bit trying, but—"

"A *bit* trying?" Charles parroted. "Victoria, please. I realize you like to see the best in people whenever possible, but in this instance there's nothing to see. That woman is *impossible*—wait, no, she's *hell on wheels*—no . . . no, even better, she's a *menace* to the very image that is a southern woman!"

She nibbled back her laugh and, instead, made a face at her friend. "Now, Charles . . ."

"Don't *now Charles* me, sugar lips. Not one person

on that tour has even spoken with her since they got here. Not one word. Don't you think that says something? And if the lack of conversation with her fellow tour members isn't enough, have you seen the *looks* she's gotten from every single one of them except Saint Minnie?

"Not that I can blame them, of course," Charles added. "Because I can't and I don't. If I was faced with spending an entire weekend with her, I'd probably work on honing the art of flesh-melting glares, as well."

She felt her right eyebrow arch upward. "Flesh-melting glares?"

"Yes! Though, and I'm not sure why, I'd rather face those than have to deal with that raving lunatic one more time."

"Charles, please. You're sounding more and more like Leona every day. All drama, all the time."

He took a moment to preen at the perceived compliment and then leaned close to her ear once again. "If you take her this time, Tori, I promise I'll be on your doorstep tomorrow morning at the crack of dawn ready and willing to make you my famous chocolate chip pancakes."

"Did you say chocolate chip pancakes?" she asked over the sudden and rather loud answering grumble of her stomach.

Charles snapped his fingers in his favorite triangle formation and followed it up with a lip pop. "I did, indeed. And, honey, no one makes chocolate chip pancakes quite like yours truly."

"Young man!"

"Please, Tori. That woman scares me."

Laughing, Tori pushed off the wall and sidestepped her way into the project room so she could maintain eye contact with her overly dramatic friend. "I'll take my pancakes at nine o'clock. *Sharp.*"

"Nine o'clock. Got it," Charles echoed as he made a showy reach for Tori's hand. "Good luck, Tori. Godspeed."

Making a mental note to stop by Turner's on the way home for anything resembling an award she could present Charles for his stellar acting, Tori stopped, took a deep breath, and ventured in the direction of Opal Ann Goodwin, the single most negative person she'd ever met.

Granted, Dixie Dunn had held that distinction for the first twelve months Tori resided in Sweet Briar. But considering the woman had been ousted from her nearly lifelong job as head librarian of the Sweet Briar Public Library to make room for Tori, the daggered looks and woe-is-me attitude had made sense.

Opal, on the other hand, had gotten off the bus that morning wearing a maroon housecoat and the kind of scowl that had sent even the always-happy Margaret Louise scurrying off to help one of the other guests.

Looking back to the group's arrival, each of Tori's sewing circle sisters who were at the store that morning had seemed to instinctively latch on to the guest most like themselves.

Debbie had gravitated toward Lucinda Penning, no doubt because of the book-themed tote bag the woman carried. Sure enough, within a minute, maybe two, Debbie was sharing details of her husband Colby's best-selling novels and promising to give Lucinda a signed copy of his very first novel before the crafting weekend was over.

Georgina Hayes, Sweet Briar's long-standing mayor,

had teamed up with Dixie to look after Gracelyn Moses, a kindred spirit in everything from her age (probably somewhere between Georgina's early sixties and Dixie's mid-seventies) to her interest in current events. The trio had dissected modern-day society on so many levels already, it was hard to imagine there was anything left to say.

Margaret Louise and her daughter-in-law, Melissa, had sidled up to Samantha Williams in short order, as well. And while Samantha had a good twenty-five years on the energetic mother of eight, and didn't seem to share Margaret Louise's interest in cooking, they were unified on their love of detective shows. And when it was discovered that Samantha had once spent an entire year in England, Beatrice had temporarily broken away from Minnie Randolph, the sweetest crafter of them all, to share tidbits of her childhood and current work as a British nanny to a local family.

Rose and Miranda had flitted from guest to guest over the past hour, working tirelessly to make sure each and every guest was happy. But when Charles had found Rose poised and ready to wrap her arthritic hands around Opal's neck, he'd wisely sent her up front to tidy the food table and get a handle on her rapidly declining patience.

Opal Ann was, in a word, nasty. If there was something negative to say, she said it. And if there wasn't, she still said it. So far, the temperature in the store had been adjusted a half dozen times, her food plate emptied and refilled four times due to a "speck of dust" no one else could see, her thread spools swapped out twice although no one knew why, and her disinterest in the project expressed more times than anyone could count.

Tori deposited the tags on the table and then rested her hand on Opal Ann's shoulder. "Yes, Opal? What can I do for you?"

"What are those?" Opal groused, pointing at the tags.

"Those are in case you'd like to add a label to the inside of your completed project." Tori retrieved the example from the center of the table and turned it over to display Rose's personalized label. "Rose always embroiders her initials inside, but Dixie over there usually puts in her whole name. It's really up to you . . . if you even want to include a label at all."

"My work speaks for itself." Opal straightened in her chair, flicking her hand toward Rose's apron as she did. "Besides, if I was going to do a label, I wouldn't do something boring like a name. I'd do something distinctly my own."

"Your name *is* your own," Minnie said, glancing at Opal over her sewing machine.

Opal rolled her eyes at the elderly crafter with such disdain Tori, herself, gasped. "If you truly knew anything about sewing, you'd know what I'm talking about. A name is a name. I'm talking about an embroidered fingerprint that is uniquely your own."

Minnie removed her foot from the machine's pedal and leaned forward. "I'm not sure I could embroider my fingerprint . . ."

"It's not an *actual* fingerprint," Lucinda said, leaning around her own machine to address Minnie. "It's just—"

"Good heavens, you call yourself a seamstress?" Without giving Minnie a chance to answer, Opal snapped her fingers at Miranda. "You—with the freckles! Short of handing this woman a free pass to my upcoming exhibit on the elusive Lily Belle, surely *you* of all people can explain the concept of a signature to her, can't you? I've had more than my fill of ineptness for the day. And *you*"—Opal's eyes widened on Tori—"I called for the young man. Where is he?"

"Charles is attending to other things at the moment, Ms. Goodwin, but I'm happy to help with whatever you need."

"What things are more pressing than one's customers?" Opal spat. "I tell you, when I get back home, I will be writing a review of this awful little shop and its utterly useless staff!"

All chatter ceased as every eye in the room came to rest on Opal first and then, finally, Tori.

"If you'd just tell me what it is you need, Ms. Goodwin, I'll take care of it." She heard the pathetically pleading tone to her voice and hated herself for it. But, as she'd reminded herself many times already that morning when dealing with this particular guest, today was about Rose and the realization of a lifelong dream Tori had only recently come to know.

"You'll take care of it?" Opal sniped. "Okay, fine. I want a full refund for everything. And I do mean *everything*—this pathetic project, the cost of my meals for the weekend, my gas to and from my home to the tour's departure point, my hotel for tonight, and anything I might choose to purchase while I'm in this godforsaken town."

Tori felt herself draw back against the weight of the woman's unrealistic demands. But before she could formulate a response, Leona vacated her spot beside Travis and made her way around the center workstation Milo had helped erect in preparation for the event. "Ms. Goodwin, is there a problem?"

"And *you* are?" Opal inquired, widening her death glare to include an impeccably dressed Leona.

"I believe the question, Ms. Goodwin, is *who are you*?"

The eyes that had fixed themselves on Tori only moments earlier now collectively moved to the doorway, with Tori's following suit . . .

Rose.

With purpose to her shuffling feet, Rose flanked Leona, her bifocal-enlarged eyes dark with the kind of anger usually reserved for Leona, herself.

"Rose," Tori whispered. "I think maybe you should let Leona handle—"

"I repeat my question, Ms. Goodwin," Rose said through clenched teeth. "Who do you think you are?"

Clearly miffed by the sudden absence of the same kid gloves she'd been handled with all morning, Opal opened and closed her mouth a few times before pounding her fist atop the table. "Doesn't anyone know the meaning of customer service anymore? Why, in my day, the customer was always right and they were treated with dignity and the utmost respect—neither of which I have been shown by anyone connected to this—this *awful* little shop."

Leona reared back to answer but stopped as Rose put out a hand and maintained control. "It still *is* that way, Ms. Goodwin. That is why your every whim has been placated, your every complaint addressed, and your mind-blowing rudeness overlooked since the moment you shoved your way off the bus. But when your rudeness crosses into abusive, you no longer have my respect."

A trio of snaps just over Tori's shoulder was followed by Charles's distinctive voice. "You tell her, Rose Winters! Tell her good!"

"I'll have your job!" Opal shouted at Rose.

Rose's lips twitched with the faintest hint of a smile. "Considering the fact that I'm co-owner of this shop, I doubt you'll have much success."

"Then I want to talk to your partner!"

Leona eased Rose away from the table and then took her place front and center. "Yes? How can I help you?"

Opal's eyes narrowed to near slits. "*You're* her business partner?"

"That's right." Leona inhaled sharply and then took a moment to give a pleasant nod to each of the guests before turning her attention back to Opal. "My business partner and I have worked hard to make this event nice for everyone. And, from what I can see, the other members of your group are enjoying their project, the food, and the company of my friends. The only blight I can see is *you*, Ms. Goodwin—you and your refusal to be satisfied with anyone or anything. In fact, I suspect that's why you look as if you're frowning all the time."

"Oh, most definitely. The position of one's wrinkles can tell *a lot*," Charles interjected. "Happy people age happily. Unhappy people age unhappily."

Leona took her gaze off of Opal long enough to engage Charles. "The right makeup artist can always work wonders, though . . ."

"So-very-true," Charles snapped out. "You should see my neighbor—Arianna." He looked from side to side and lowered his voice. "Hmmm . . . how should I describe Arianna? She's . . . um . . . well . . ."

"Ugly?" Leona prompted.

Charles paused for a split second and then nodded. "But I have to tell you, Leona, when Bruce, my other neighbor, gets her in the chair and works his magic, she looks positively bea-u-ti-ful."

"Bruce is your friend who gave you that magical under-eye concealer?"

"No. That was my old roommate, Michael Anthony," Charles corrected. "Bruce is a true artist. He is to the human face, what Michelangelo was to the Sistine Chapel."

"We must meet." Leona air-kissed Charles's cheek and then turned back to a gaped-mouth Opal. "Anyway, you will not be getting a refund, nor will we be paying for your hotel, your meals, or any of the other ridiculous demands you made. We promised a project and food, and we delivered in both areas. So, unless you want to go back home tomorrow evening with nothing to show for your efforts, I suggest you get back to your sewing, Ms. Goodwin."

"Is the diva almost done?"

Tori looked up from the logbook Leona had created for the shop's special events and shrugged. "I'm not sure, Charles, but you could certainly check . . ."

"I don't want to know *that* bad, Victoria." Charles pranced his way to the front window and peered out onto Main Street. "I just know I've watched everyone else go into that room to retrieve their project at some point over the last thirty minutes, yet still no sign of . . . *her.*"

"That's because my twin shamed that woman into shuttin' her trap and finishin' what she started." Margaret Louise transferred the remaining cupcakes from the leaf-etched plate into a domed plastic container Debbie had found in her car. "And she had it comin', you know."

Dixie finished returning the unused inventory to its correct locations around the shop and then straightened, her hands firmly planted on her hips. "If *I* was running the show around here, Opal would have been shown the door. She didn't deserve the courtesy of being able to finish *a yawn* let alone a project she had nothing good to say about."

"And if you did, she'd find the closest computer and let everyone know how horrible your shop was," Leona countered as she closed the door behind Travis and made her way into the center of the room.

Rose emerged from behind the register, her sweater pulled tightly against her upper body despite the room's comfortable temperatures. "You say that like it's not something she's going to do anyway."

"She probably will, Rose. And you need to prepare yourself for that." Leona took a quick look at Tori's numbers and then focused on Rose once again. "But by allowing her to finish the project, we won't have to wonder if we could have done something different."

It made sense. It really did. Yet Tori couldn't really wrap her head around anything other than Rose's palpable sadness. SewTastic was supposed to be the thing that lifted the elderly woman's spirits and kept her feet moving. And, since the sewing shop's grand opening two weeks earlier, it had done exactly that. Suddenly, Rose's feet hadn't shuffled quite so much when she walked, and the often crippling pain from her arthritis seemed incapable of keeping her down. Instead of focusing on the end of her life, Rose was motivated by the experiences still to come . . .

"So what if Opal gives the shop a bad review?" Tori asked as she closed and put away the logbook once and for all. "There were four other crafters here for the same event, and every one of them seemed to have a good time. And I know that everyone who has walked through those doors since you opened two weeks ago has had nothing but good things to say . . ."

"I wanted *everyone* to love this place," Rose said between noticeable swallows.

Debbie finished helping Margaret Louise with the food cleanup and turned to face Rose. "I know from Colby's novels that one bad review against dozens of good reviews always stands out as suspect. It's either a wannabe writer jealous of his success, or someone who's a generally unhappy person. For people who make it a habit to read reviews, it's easy to pick those out and discard accordingly. The same will hold true with whatever Opal says. Especially when it's up against nothing but positive accounts of the same event."

"You really think so?" Rose asked, her gaze lingering on Debbie's for a moment before seeking Tori's for added confirmation.

"Debbie is right. One bad review is hardly front-page news." Tori came out from behind the front counter and slipped a reassuring arm around Rose's frail shoulders.

"Now, let's get this event done and over with, shall we? I promised Milo I'd be home at a reasonable time."

Charles stopped nibbling on a hangnail and looked up. "Hear! Hear!"

"Charles?" Tori asked, laughing. "Do *you* want the honor of looking in on Ms. Goodwin and telling her that Miranda and the rest of her group are sitting on the bus waiting for her to finish up?"

Leona's hand shot up. "No, no. I'll take this one. It'll be my pleasure . . ."

Sagging against the wall, Charles mouthed his love for his fellow fashionista and then followed it up with an air-kiss as she passed.

"Why don't you wrap things up for Opal the same way Daddy wrapped things up whenever somethin' was goin' on too long," Margaret Louise said as Leona reached the mouth of the hallway and stopped to take a breath. "Just tell her it's time to pee on the fire and call it a day."

A slow smile inched its way across Leona's mouth just before she disappeared from their collective sight.

"Leona was always Daddy's girl," Margaret Louise said, dropping onto a nearby chair. "Why, when she was not much higher 'n my knee is now, she used to—"

A bloodcurdling scream from the far end of the hallway extinguished the rest of Margaret Louise's memory and sent Tori racing for the project room.

Chapter 3

Tori looked down at the perfectly grilled slices of London broil and did her best to shove the afternoon's horror from her thoughts long enough to thank the man seated directly across the kitchen table. Her husband of just over six weeks, Milo Wentworth had a way of knowing when to step up to the plate, and for that and so many other things, she was beyond grateful.

"Thanks for pulling this together," she said in lieu of the smile he deserved. "I feel like I'm standing in the middle of a fog that just won't break, you know?"

Reaching across the table, he encased her hand with his. "I wish you would've called me when this first happened. I'd have been there in a heartbeat."

"In a clear-headed state, I know that, Milo. But in the moment, all I could really think about was Leona and whether she was okay. And then, when I realized she wasn't hurt and I really looked around the room, it took a few seconds to register what I was seeing."

He quieted the gathering emotion in her voice with a squeeze and then pulled his hand back beside his plate. "I can't get over the fact that someone strangled this poor woman with a power cord."

"From a sewing machine of all things," she mumbled. She closed her eyes against the image of Opal Goodwin slumped atop her sewing machine, the white power cord tasked with making it operate wound around the woman's neck. It was an image she suspected she'd revisit many times in the coming days. But as difficult as that sight was, it was the undaunted hum of Opal's machine as Leona's screams finally ceased that still chilled Tori to the core three hours later. "Milo, it was awful. I mean, I tried to save her, to unwind the cord as fast as I could, but it was too late. Opal was already gone.

"And then . . . when it hit me what had happened, I sent Margaret Louise to call the police chief, Charles to try and head Rose off at the pass, and everyone else to get Leona out of the room and to a place where she could sit down."

He met her eyes and gestured toward her plate. "You need to eat, Tori."

"I just don't know who could have done this. I mean, we were all in the store the whole time." It was, essentially, the same thing she'd said to Sweet Briar Police Chief Robert Dallas when he arrived on the scene with two of his officers in tow.

"How long was she in the project room alone?"

She picked up her knife and fork, cut off a few bite-sized pieces, and then simply stared down at her plate. "A half hour. Maybe forty-five minutes. Tops."

"And you never saw anyone go in the room?" Milo slipped a piece of steak into his mouth and chased it down with a sip of ice water.

"I know her fellow tour members all went into the room at some point or another to retrieve their projects, but, for the most part, they were checking out the main room, partaking in the remaining treats, and making mental notes of the various things Georgina insisted they do before heading out of Sweet Briar tomorrow night."

"And that was it for the people who went into that room during the time this woman was in there sewing?" Milo asked.

"Well, you know how Beatrice is—no matter how much tough love everyone else wanted to impart on Opal, Beatrice still felt the need to hand deliver a plate of pretzels at one point. And I know Charles even peeked in a time or two as well, but other than that, yes."

"Is there a chance someone came in through the back door when everyone was otherwise occupied?" He took another bite of meat and then switched to the creamed spinach he'd popped into the microwave during the last few minutes of grilling time. "Don't forget, there is an alley that runs behind all the shops on that side of the street."

"But this is *Sweet Briar*, Milo," she protested. "People don't lurk in alleys here waiting to strangle old women with sewing machine cords."

He pointed his empty fork in her direction and then lowered it to include her still-uneaten dinner. "Sweet Briar or not, someone killed that woman. And *you* still need to eat."

"The chief had one of the officers lift prints off the cord, but I can tell you right now that mine are going to be all over it." Stabbing a tiny morsel of meat with her fork, she brought it to her lips. "I guess we can hope my prints didn't block out the killer's."

"I don't think it works that way, but I guess we'll know for sure soon enough." He looked at her over the rim of his water glass, the amber flecks in his brown eyes muted by concern. "You *did* tell the chief that you touched the cord, right? I mean, he knows you were trying to save this woman, right?"

She heard the worry in his tone and did her best to smile it away. "If you're worried he's going to pin this on me, there are five witnesses who will swear they saw me take that cord off her neck and try to resuscitate her—Charles, Margaret Louise, Debbie, Beatrice, and Leona . . . assuming, of course, Leona can still remember her name, let alone what *I* was doing. Especially in light of the fact she was in the process of passing out when I ran into the room."

"Leona passed out?" Milo repeated. "Are you serious?"

"She did, but it was okay. Charles caught her before she hit the ground. Or at least that's what I heard Debbie telling the police." She stabbed a second piece of meat and popped it into her mouth. "I tell you, that boy can think awfully fast under pressure."

Milo ate some more spinach, obviously considering his next question as he chewed. When he was ready, he placed his fork on the edge of his plate and leaned back against his chair. "So where were these people from the tour when this all went down?"

"On the bus. Waiting for Opal. The plan was to head

over to that bed-and-breakfast on the edge of town and check in before dinner." She took a sip of water and then pushed her plate forward. As much as she loved when Milo grilled, she just didn't have the stomach for more than a bite or two at the moment. "That's why Leona went into the room. To tell Opal it was time to wrap things up and join her group on the tour bus."

A rhythmic knock at the front door brought Milo to his feet. "Try to take another bite or two and I'll see who that is."

"Milo, I can't eat. I'm sorry."

"Then I'll wrap it for you for later." He stopped, kissed her temple softly, and then ventured out into the living room and toward the front hallway beyond. Soon, the opening pop of the door was followed by a familiar voice and her own answering smile as it crept across her lips.

"Based on my nose—which never, *ever* leads me astray—I get the sense you're eating dinner," Charles said as he followed Milo into Tori's sight line. "And, I'd bet ten to one it's London broil . . . cooked on the grill . . . with a seasoning that incorporates some black pepper and"—he lifted his nose into the air and sniffed again—"a little garlic."

Shaking his head in awe, Milo gestured Charles into the kitchen and toward the empty chair next to Tori. "Take a seat. We've got plenty of food to go around, Charles, especially since my wife is *not eating*."

"Not eating?" Charles echoed as he dropped onto the seat and instantly rested a hand atop Tori's forehead. "You don't *feel* warm."

"Because I'm not sick." She looked down at her plate

once again, but still, she couldn't eat. "I guess everything that happened kind of squashed my appetite, you know?"

"Uh-oh. Not you, too, love . . ."

She looked up. "Me, too?"

He shoveled three strips of meat onto his plate and inhaled sharply. "Mmmm . . . Milo, this looks amazing." Then, pointing his still-empty fork at Tori, Charles addressed her question. "Leona had an ice pack on her head for close to an hour this evening."

"An ice pack? Why?" Milo lowered himself back down to his own chair and then shot his hands up in surrender. "Wait. Don't answer that."

"Seriously, Milo, I've never seen Leona so thrown by anything in her life," Tori said by way of agreement. "Although I find it highly doubtful an ice pack can help with that."

"It was off by the time I was getting ready to head over here. In fact, she was on the phone, walking someone through every detail of her trauma, when I left." Charles sliced off a piece and took a taste. "Mmmm, as good as it looks."

"A *male* someone, I take it?" Tori prodded.

Charles flashed a knowing smile. "She freshened her mascara before she made the call . . ."

"Mystery solved . . ." It felt good to laugh, even if the moment disappeared as fast as it came. "I wish Rose could rebound that fast. But I just don't see that happening. This shop means so much to her. I mean, from the moment she and Leona first made the announcement, Rose has been nonstop energy and smiles. It's like she's had a new purpose, something to fill her days. I just can't believe this has happened. At *her* store, no less."

"With all of us in the same building the entire time," Charles reminded before he moved on to his second slice. "Hard to fathom, for sure, but at least we have all of our suspects in a neat and tidy little bundle, à la Agatha Christie."

"Our suspects?"

"Of course. The ones on the bus tour with Opal. It has to be one of them." Charles accepted a roll from the bread bowl Milo passed him and quickly broke off a piece. "All we need now is a notebook and a pen."

"For what?" Tori countered.

"To list our suspects and the answers we need to unearth on each and every one." He chewed a moment in silence and then continued, his eyes wide with unrestrained excitement. "The only question now is whether we go this alone, or bring in Margaret Louise, who'll have our heads if we don't."

"Whoa, whoa, whoa." She scooted back her chair and stood, her focus shifting from Charles to Milo and back again. "Charles, I can't get involved with this. I mean, sure, I'm going to be there to get Rose through this, but I'm married now. I can't get wrapped up in another investigation."

Charles looked to Milo for help. "You don't mind, do you, Milo?"

"Tori, he's right." Milo stood and made his way over to Tori. "The sooner the person who did this is behind bars, the sooner Rose can get back to being happy again."

She tried his words on for size and then leaned against the wall. "She *did* make my wedding dress . . ."

"And helped put together your bridal shower at a time

I was able to come," Charles added, the hope in his voice unmistakable.

"You really don't mind, Milo?" she asked.

He pulled her in for a hug, his arms warm and welcoming. "Of course not. I love Rose, too. You know that."

"Then it's settled." Charles swiped another roll from the bread basket and rose to his feet. "Now, where can I find a notebook and pen?"

Milo kissed Tori's forehead and then pointed toward the far cabinet. "Top drawer for a pen and I'll be back with a notebook in a second."

"Wait a minute, Milo." She stopped her husband with a hand to his chest and narrowed her eyes on Charles. "You're leaving tomorrow morning. We can't possibly solve this before bedtime."

Charles floated over to the drawer, secured a pen, and air-traced his favorite triangle position, sans snaps. "I'm. Not. Leaving."

"Oh?"

"I can't. I've been ordered to stay."

"Ordered?" Tori asked. "By whom?"

"Chief Dallas, of course. In fact, everyone connected to what happened today has to stay. Which includes yours truly, *and* every member of Opal's tour group."

"He's making them stay?"

"He is, indeed."

Milo nodded at Charles. "It'll be good to have you around here a little longer. As for me, I'll go get that notebook right now."

"He is a doll, sugar lips," Charles declared as he watched Milo disappear into the living room. "You did a good job picking that one out, that's for sure. Then again, Mr. Milo did pretty well for himself, too, and don't you forget it."

There was no denying it. Tori was positively elated at the thought of having Charles in Sweet Briar for a few more days. He was, as Rose often said, a breath of fresh air. The fact that he also had a really good head on his shoulders and was one of the most observant people she had ever met only served as an added bonus under the current circumstances.

Seconds later, Milo was back with the notebook. "So who gets it?"

"I'll take it." Charles liberated the spiral-bound book from Milo's hand and carried it into the living room. "So we have four possible suspects—Lucinda Penning, Gracelyn Moses, Samantha Williams, and Minnie Randolph. Six, if you add in Miranda and Travis."

She watched him write each name on the top of a separate piece of paper, her limited bits of knowledge mentally filling in a tidbit or two for each person. But really, what did she know beyond inconsequential small talk? Being an avid reader didn't make one a murder suspect any more than a brief stint in England or a love of current events did. Which meant they really had nothing to go on, a point she shared with Charles.

He turned back to the first page—the one with Lucinda Penning's name scrawled across the top—and shrugged. "If it was *easy*, Victoria, it wouldn't be as much fun, now would it?"

Chapter 4

Tori had just finished brushing her teeth when Milo appeared in the doorway of the bathroom with her phone in his outstretched hand. "It's Rose."

Peeking around his shoulder, Tori noted the time on their bedside clock—10:05 p.m. "Is she okay?" she whispered.

When he didn't answer, she took the phone and stepped into the bedroom. "I'm here, Rose. Is everything okay?"

"I'm sorry I'm calling so late, Victoria, but . . ." The elderly woman's voice gave way to a deep cough that echoed between them. "I can't sleep."

"No, no, you did the right thing in calling. I'm here—twenty-four seven. You know that."

"But you're a newlywed now, Victoria."

"I am. But that doesn't mean our friendship has

changed. I'm still here, just like always." Tori turned back the sheets and climbed onto her side of the bed. "How are you holding up?"

A beat or two of silence was followed by an almost wail. "I don't have much time left, Victoria. I know this. But I wanted the time I have left to mean something."

The woman's despair was so raw, so powerful, Tori felt her own throat tightening. "I wish you wouldn't talk like that, Rose. *You* mean something—to me, to Milo, to Margaret Louise, to Charles, to Debbie, to everyone. Even Leona."

"Leona . . ." The despair morphed into something a lot like regret. "She didn't have to bring me in with her on that store. I have no money tied up in that business. She's taken it all on under the guise of owning another business. You and I both know, a sewing shop doesn't fit with that woman. She did that *for me*. To make amends she didn't have to make."

"That's debatable," Tori murmured.

"I love that shop, Victoria. I love the way it smells, the way it looks. I love arranging the threads and the fabrics. I love picking out just the right things to have on hand for our customers. I love it all." A second, louder cough ushered the despair back in. "And now it's gone."

She pulled the sheet up onto her lap and rested her head against the headboard, her eyes following Milo around the room as he locked the windows and turned off the bathroom light. "It's not gone, Rose. The shop is still there."

"I suppose it is. But it's like you said earlier, when I was worried about the impact of a bad review. You said a bad review wasn't front-page news, remember?"

"I remember."

"Well, *a bad review* might not be front-page news, but *a murder* certainly is."

Tori opened her mouth to speak, but closed it when she realized there was nothing to say. Rose was right. News of a murdered customer couldn't be good for business.

"It's over, Victoria."

Milo climbed into bed beside her and draped his arm across her shoulder, pulling her close as he did. And as was always the case whenever he was near, Tori breathed in his strength and let it enhance her own. "No, Rose, it's not. As soon as the building is cleared by police, you keep going. You keep making your displays pretty, and you keep smiling and chatting with customers. So you hold off on offering another tour until after the holidays—that's probably better, anyway. But in terms of regular, everyday business, you keep on going. You are not responsible for what happened to Opal Goodwin. The person who *killed* her is responsible."

When Rose didn't respond, Tori checked the connection and then returned the phone to her ear. "Rose? Are you still there?"

"I'm here. I'm just thinking is all."

"I'm right on this, Rose. I really am. To give up and roll over implies guilt. *You* didn't do this. *Someone else* did."

"I have to know what happened, Victoria."

She rested her head in the crook of Milo's arm and smiled up at her yawning husband. "And you will, Rose. You have my word on that."

Tori tiptoed out of the bedroom and made her way into the darkened living room. Even after six weeks

of living in Milo's house, it still took her a moment to
remember to turn left toward the couch instead of right.

If she had her druthers, she'd be sleeping as soundly
as Milo was at that moment. But try as she might, she
just couldn't fall asleep. Every time she closed her eyes,
she saw Opal slumped over the sewing machine, the
power cord wrapped around her wrinkly neck. And when
she found a way to push that image from her thoughts,
the faces of the other tour members took its place.

Sidestepping the couch, she flipped on the lamp and
squinted at the answering flood of light. What she hoped
to accomplish, she wasn't exactly sure, but maybe reading through the limited notes she and Charles had made
that evening would help her work off some of her ner-
vous energy. It was worth a shot, if nothing else. After
all, it wasn't like she'd be losing any sleep.

She sunk onto the couch and flipped the notebook
open to the first page, her gaze making short work of
its contents . . .

Lucinda Penning.

What we know: She appears to be an avid reader.

Questions to ask: Did she know Opal prior to sewing tour?

Was there any animosity between the two?

More background information.

Approximate age: forties?

Spent most time with Debbie—talk to her.

The second page was nearly identical, with the exception of the name on the suspect line, the estimated age, and the little bit of information they did know.

Gracelyn Moses.

What we know: very up on current events.

Questions to ask: Did she know Opal prior to sewing tour?

Was there any animosity between the two?

More background information.

Approximate age: sixties to seventies.

Spent most time with Georgina and Dixie—talk to them.

She grabbed the pen from its spot on the end table and added an offhand thought.

Did knowledge of current events cover the county as well as the country and the world?

For a long moment she studied her addition and then, finally, turned to the third page.

Samantha Williams.

What we know: loves detective shows. Lived in England for a year.

Questions to ask: Did she know Opal prior to sewing tour?

Was there any animosity between the pair?

More background information.

Approximate age: late fifties, early sixties.

Spent most time with Margaret Louise, Melissa, Beatrice—talk to them.

She reread Samantha's entry and then closed her eyes in an attempt to put herself back at SewTastic as each of the women arrived. Everyone seemed so happy, so eager to check out the new shop and learn the details of the project Rose had planned for them to do. Everyone seemed to get along with one another, with the lone exception of Opal Goodwin. At the time, she'd assumed the tension was because of Opal's demeanor. But now, in light of what happened, she had to consider the very real possibility that there was more going on. That maybe, just maybe, Opal was on edge about something, that her rude behavior was a symptom of worry . . .

Or maybe she was just reaching. Maybe Opal was simply a rude person who'd rubbed the wrong person the wrong way. But was rudeness a reason to kill?

Shaking her head, Tori flipped to the fourth page and a name that simply didn't fit.

Minnie Randolph.

What we know: sweet. Old. The perfect granny.

Questions to ask: Did she know Opal prior to sewing tour?

Was there any animosity between the two?

More background information.

*Approximate age: eighty-ish. Looks like Mrs. Claus
and laughs like her, too.*

Spent most time with everyone.

She smiled at the image of the elderly woman who'd
captured everyone's heart within moments of the group's
arrival, and flipped the page again . . .

Miranda Greer.

What we know: tour guide.

*Questions to ask: Did she know Opal prior to sewing
tour?*

Was there any animosity between the two?

More background information.

Approximate age: late thirties, early forties?

Spent most time with Rose—talk to her.

Sighing, Tori turned to the final suspect's page . . .

Travis Beaker.

*What we know: He drove the tour bus. He actually
participated, too.*

Questions to ask: Did he know Opal prior to sewing tour?

Was there any animosity between the pair?

More background information.

Approximate age: early fifties?

Spent most time with Leona, but seemed withdrawn even from her.

She uncapped the pen again and added two more lines:

How did Travis come to drive this group?

Does he remember anything re: Opal's arrival at the departure point?

Tapping the pen against her lips, Tori thought back over everything she'd learned about murder over the past several years. For the most part, people didn't kill for the sake of killing. There was always a reason. Sometimes the culprit was found before the reason, but more often than not, it was the reason that led to the culprit . . .

She took one last look at each page and then flipped to the first blank page after Travis's. In block writing, she added a new heading:

Motives for Murder

Then, with the help of the Internet on her phone, she filled in a few lines:

*Love/lust

*Revenge

*Hatred

*Greed/money/jealousy

*Obsession

Yet with each new line Tori wrote, she realized how little they knew about the victim beyond her reprehensible behavior. Had Opal been wealthy? Did Opal have a husband and children? How had she spent her days? All good questions that merited an eighth page:

Victim: Opal Goodwin.

What we know: nasty.

Things to find out: Where did she live? Was she wealthy? Family situation? Career?

Approximate Age: early to mid-seventies?

Spent most time with Charles, Rose, and me.

Leaning back against the sofa, Tori pushed past the memory of Opal's nastiness to the woman herself—the freshly pressed blouse, the expensive yet sensible shoes, the elegant necklace, the delicate gold watch, the propensity to snap her fingers when she wanted something . . .
Tori sat up tall.
Opal had money . . .
She looked back at the page devoted to the elderly

victim and circled the second question on the things-to-find-out line. No, she couldn't say with absolute certainty that Opal was wealthy, but all signs pointed to that being the case.

If she was right, the financial standing of each of the suspects certainly warranted closer examination . . .

Grabbing the pen, she added the question to each suspect's page.

Chapter 5

Tori was just turning off the front burner when she heard a familiar beat on the back door. Smiling, she tossed the dish towel onto the counter and turned in the direction of the sound, the face she saw peeking at her through the door's glass panel a perfect match of the one she'd expected to see.

"Margaret Louise, isn't this a nice surprise," she gushed as she opened the door and waved her friend inside.

"I come bearing donuts and more."

She took the powder blue bag from the woman's out-stretched hand. "And more? More what?"

"More friends." Margaret Louise hooked her thumb over her shoulder.

Tori peeked outside, shaking her head as she did. "I don't see anyone else."

"We're right here, love." Charles stepped around the back edge of the house, his arm gently guiding a bunny-holding Leona. "Just moving a little slow this morning."

Tori looked from the slow-moving pair to Margaret Louise and back again. "Is everything okay? Did you reinjure your hip, Leona?"

Leona waved off her inquiry with a dramatic hand and then shoved her way past Tori en route to the kitchen table. "My hip is fine, dear. I'm just suffering the ill effects of a disastrous night of sleep that has left my precious Paris every bit as fatigued as I am. Though, looking at you, Victoria, we're far better off than I realized."

"Twin!"

"Am I wrong?" Leona asked, hands on hips.

Margaret Louise averted her gaze to the floor and then plucked the donut bag back out of Tori's hands and carried it to the table. "Victoria just needs a little dose of sugary goodness, I reckon. After all, yesterday was a trying day for *all* of us, Twin, not just you."

"*I'm* the one who found that horrible old woman's body!"

"And Victoria is the one who touched her and tried to save her," Margaret Louise reminded while simultaneously removing a variety of donuts from the bag. "Victoria, I brought a chocolate-dipped one special for you. It should give you a nice boost."

"In light of the fact I'd been promised chocolate chip pancakes this morning and didn't get them, a chocolate-dipped donut is perfect, Margaret Louise."

Charles's face turned almost the same shade of red as the tips of his spiky hair. "I assumed I was released from pancake duty the moment the *reason* for the original deal was found with a cord wrapped around her neck."

"Nope. A deal is a deal, buster. Death doesn't change that." Tori returned to the stove and the still-hot kettle. "Anyway, I was just about to make myself some hot chocolate. Would anyone else like some?"

"Do you have whipped cream, sugar lips?"

She pointed Charles toward the refrigerator. "On the door, second shelf. Leona? Margaret Louise? How about you? Hot chocolate? Tea? Coffee?"

"Tea, please. And a carrot for Paris, of course." Leona sat in Milo's spot, settled Paris in her lap, and then looked around the small yet well-appointed kitchen. "So where is that handsome man of yours, dear?"

"Hidin' from you, Twin," Margaret Louise joked, earning herself a death glare in return.

"Actually, he's helping a friend paint his shed this morning," Tori said. "He'll be back after lunch."

"I just love the way your face goes all glow-y when you talk 'bout him, Victoria." Margaret Louise snatched a handful of napkins from a holder on the counter and placed one in front of each seat. Then, with careful thought, she doled out the donuts, placing the chocolate-dipped one on Tori's napkin as promised. "My Jake says Milo's face does the same thing every time *your* name comes up, too."

She couldn't help but smile as she set four mugs on the counter and filled two of them with hot chocolate mix and one with a tea bag. "Marrying him was definitely the smartest thing I've ever done." And it was true. Sure, she'd been happy when she was single. But she was even happier now.

Margaret Louise crushed the empty paper bag and carried it to the trash can in the corner of the room. On her way back to the table, she paused to look in the various mugs. "I have to say, a hot chocolate is sounding mighty tasty right 'bout now, assumin' the offer is still open, Victoria . . ."

"Of course it is. Whipped cream?"

"Is there any other way to serve it?" Margaret Louise asked, grinning.

"Touché."

Charles shook the can of whipped cream and brandished it over the freshly poured hot water. "Stand back, ladies."

"Victoria, dear . . . ," Leona stated over the spraying sound. "I have to ask. Why do you look so dreadful, dear? Did you and Milo have a fight?"

With Charles's help, Tori carried the mugs to the table, eyeing Leona as she did. "No, Leona, Milo and I didn't have a fight. I just didn't sleep much last night is all. Too much on my mind, I guess, with finding Opal the way we did and worrying about its effect on Rose."

Margaret Louise worked her donut into the side of her mouth long enough to speak. "Have you spoken to Rose this morning?"

"No. But she called last night, shortly after ten o'clock."

"What was that old goat doing up that late?" Leona asked.

Crossing to the refrigerator, Tori located a carrot for Paris and carried it back to the table. "She's upset about what happened with Opal, Leona. Very, *very* upset."

Waving the remaining half of her donut between them, Margaret Louise swallowed the contents in her mouth. "I called her place last night, 'bout seven o'clock, and she didn't answer."

"I don't know, Margaret Louise, maybe she wasn't home then or maybe she wasn't up to talking." Tori sat down and stared at her donut. "All I know is that Rose was almost borderline depressed when she called me. She really saw this shop as a new lease on life, so to speak, and she's afraid that's all gone now."

"And she's right," Leona mused across the top of her mug. "That dreadful Opal woman was killed in our shop. I don't know how we'll bounce back from that."

"Leona, please, you can't really believe that," Tori protested. "I mean, it's not like you or Rose had anything to do with what happened."

"It doesn't matter, dear. A body was found in our shop, regardless. Would *you* be anxious to visit a store where something like that happened?"

Leona was right. SewTastic was in trouble.

"Maybe things are different in Sweet Briar, but in the Big Apple, that's exactly the reason some people would be drawn to a store." Charles drummed his fingers atop the table and then returned them to his mug's handle. "Maybe we could entice people to the store on simple curiosity."

"What about offerin' a bargain of some kind?" Margaret Louise stuck her finger into her whipped cream and then popped it straight in her mouth. "A free spool of thread with every purchase, perhaps? Or buy three yards, get one free? Bargains have a way of ropin' people in."

Leona offered a noncommittal shrug. "Maybe."

"It could be worth a shot," Tori added.

"Between that and our investigation, I bet we can make all of this go away for Rose." Charles chugged his drink in one large gulp and then placed his empty mug on the table between them.

Margaret Louise stopped chewing and stared first at Charles, and then at Tori. "Investigation? What investigation?"

Uh-oh . . .

Charles jumped up from the table and disappeared into the living room, leaving Tori to fend for herself. Tori, in turn, picked at the remains of her own donut and slowly lifted her gaze to Margaret Louise's. "We really haven't done much. Just jotted some notes. You know, questions we might want to ask the folks who were part of the tour yesterday."

"And you jotted these notes without *me*?" Margaret Louise asked, her tone noticeably wounded. "I thought *I* was your go-to partner when it came to investigatin', Victoria."

She reached across the table and covered Margaret Louise's pudgy hand. "And you are. Charles just stopped by last night for a visit and he wanted to jot down what we know—which isn't much."

"I see you added some new things since last night, sugar lips." Charles rounded the corner with the open notebook in his hand. "Though I have to say, Opal having a page of her own is cringe-worthy."

"I couldn't sleep," Tori said by way of explanation. "So I opened the notebook and read what we had. Adding a page dedicated to possible motives and another one to Opal just makes sense. Now we just need to see what things Margaret Louise thinks we should add . . ."

A spark ignited behind the woman's warm brown eyes as she plucked the notebook from Charles's hand and began reading in earnest. Halfway through the third page, she looked up. "Samantha knew Opal, all right. As for animosity, I can't speak for Opal's feelin' 'bout Samantha, but I can 'bout Samantha's."

Tori and Charles leaned forward in unison. "You can?"

"She liked her 'bout as much as my grandbabies liked havin' chicken pox."

"And you know this because . . . ," Tori prodded.

"She told me so. Why, she pointed at Opal and said, 'If that one gets to Heaven, she'll be askin' to see the upstairs.' Made me think of my daddy." Margaret Louise licked the tip of her finger and quickly dabbed up any residual crumbs from her napkin. "You remember Daddy sayin' that 'bout ornery people, don't you, Twin."

"I don't remember him killing the person he was referring to." Leona took a slow, delicate sip of her tea.

"I'm not sayin' Samantha is the one who strangled Opal. All I'm doin' is answerin' this question Victoria wrote 'bout whether there was any animosity between Samantha and Opal."

Tori considered her friend's words and then segued into the next logical question. "Do you happen to know *why* there was animosity?"

With slow, deliberate motions, Margaret Louise rolled her napkin into a ball and stood. "No, but I reckon I could find out." She carried the napkin to the trash and then wandered back to the table, the notebook still open at her spot. "Assumin', of course, I'm part of the investigatin' the way I've always been b'fore."

"I'd be a fool not to include you, Margaret Louise," Tori said. "Your insight has been enormously helpful more times than I can count."

"Then I'm in? On the investigatin'?"

"You were never out." Tori stood, gathered the empty mugs, and carried them over to the sink. "We need a game plan, I think."

Charles snapped his fingers in a fast and furious triangle. "A. Game. Plan. Now you're talking."

"We could go over and see if the tour group has checked out of the bed-and-breakfast yet," Margaret Louise suggested.

"I can already tell you they haven't."

Margaret Louise and Leona turned to look at Charles, with Leona taking point on the question. "Oh? Why is that?"

"It's like I told Victoria last night. Chief Dallas wants everyone connected to Opal's murder staying put. That means I can't go back to New York, and the ladies from the tour can't return home, either." Charles wandered over to the ceramic cookie jar on the windowsill and popped the lid. "Um, Victoria? This jar is *empty*."

"I know. I haven't had a chance to do any baking the last few days."

"Oh." Charles slowly recapped the jar and stuffed his hands into the pockets of his burgundy jeans. "When you do, I like snickerdoodles best."

Chapter 6

Margaret Louise led the four-person parade around the side of Tori's house and toward the street, the promise of another investigation making it difficult for the rest of them to keep up. Halfway to Margaret Louise's car though, Tori slammed into Charles's back—hard.

"Whoa. Hey. I'm sorry. I didn't know you were stopping."

Charles peered over his shoulder at Tori, his face ashen. "Can you please drive, Victoria?"

"I can't drive Margaret Louise's car."

"You can drive your *own* car . . ."

Confused, she narrowed her gaze on Charles. "Is there a problem?"

"You know how she drives, Victoria," Charles whispered. "I—I'm not ready to die."

Tori adjusted her purse strap atop her shoulder and bit

back a laugh. "Wait a minute. You ride around in New York City cabs all the time, Charles. Surely you can handle Margaret Louise."

Sniffing indignantly, he turned his attention to the cause of his angst. "Margaret Louise? I'd be happy to drive. That way, um, you could, uh, sit in the back with Leona and, um . . . catch up. On . . . um . . . things." Charles stepped into the road, gesturing toward the powder blue station wagon as he did.

Margaret Louise swatted away his suggestion with her car keys. "Don't be silly, Charles. You've said yourself you've only driven a car once or twice in your life. If I let you behind the wheel, you could cause a month's worth of buryin's."

He opened his mouth to protest but closed it as Tori tapped him on the shoulder. "Sit in the back with Leona and fasten your seat belt. You should be fine."

"*Should be*?" he whispered back.

Tori shrugged. "Well, I can't be *sure* . . ."

"Now, now, dear. You're going to give our Big Apple friend indigestion if you don't stop." Leona stopped beside the rear passenger-side door long enough to transfer Paris from the crook of her left arm to the crook of her right arm. When the rabbit was safe and sound, she batted her false eyelashes at Charles. "Come. Sit with Paris and me. I have a gossip magazine in my bag we can look at."

"Which one?" Charles asked as he crept forward a step.

"*Society*."

His answering squeal perked Paris's ears up tall. "The latest issue? The one with that shrew Penelope Lawton on the cover?"

Leona bypassed a nod in favor of a wide-eyed lean. "Wait until you see the hairstyle she's sporting on the first page of the article—it brings new meaning to the word *hideous*."

And just like that, Charles opened the back door for Leona and Paris and then claimed the seat next to them, all worry over his safety a thing of the past.

"Looks like you're ridin' shotgun for the day's investigatin', Victoria!" Margaret Louise beamed at Tori across the top of the car and then disappeared from view momentarily as she took her place behind the wheel. "So where to first?"

Tori slid into the passenger seat and clicked her seat belt into place. "It doesn't really matter to—"

"I need you to drop me off at SewTastic."

Margaret Louise lifted in her seat just enough to afford a view of the backseat via the rearview mirror. "Will the chief let you inside?"

"We *are* talking about Robert, are we not?" Leona purred.

Rolling her eyes, Margaret Louise turned the key in the ignition and shifted the car into drive, her right foot instinctively finding and engaging the gas pedal. "I don't know what I was thinkin', Victoria. Seems even after all these years, I still forget the power of my twin's eye-battin'."

Leona touched her hand to the base of her neck and preened. "It's a gift few understand."

Margaret Louise turned left at the stop sign, right at the next block, and then left onto the rural two-lane road she favored when heading toward town. Pressing down on the gas, she rolled down her window and lifted her chin to the late-fall breeze. "Woo-eeee, it feels good to be movin', don't it?"

"It does." Tori peeked at Charles over her shoulder and noted his white-knuckled hold on the door as well as the rigidity of his upper torso. She tried not to laugh at his obvious terror, but she was grossly unsuccessful. "So is Penelope Lawton's hairstyle as bad as Leona said?"

When he didn't answer, Leona reached her bejeweled fingers across the space between them and gently patted his knee. He, in turn, tried his best to breathe, something he only seemed capable of doing if he closed his eyes to the rapidly passing scenery. "I—I . . ."

Shifting her focus back to the road in front of them, Tori pointed out their upcoming turn to Margaret Louise. "Okay . . . okay . . . we're here. You can slow things up a bit."

"Yes! Please!"

Margaret Louise studied her New York passenger in the rearview mirror. "Well I'll be, Charles. You look like you're not feelin' too well. I can drive you back to Leona's place as soon as I drop her at the store, if you'd like. And if you're really feelin' sick, I can get you there faster than an armadillo can get run over out on Route 150."

"No! No! I'm fine!" Charles snapped his head against the back of the seat and managed a smile for the woman peering back at him. "But, uh, maybe we could, uh, park the car and *walk* when we reach the shop?"

"Walk?" Margaret Louise echoed. "Clear out to the bed-and-breakfast? Good heavens, Charles, a walk that long would plumb tucker me out."

He looked at Tori, the mental pleading behind his

eyes impossible to miss. "But a walk like that would be good for you. It—it would be . . . exercise!"

"The only exercisin' I'd be interested in doin' would be makin' a second stop at Debbie's," Margaret Louise said as her focus returned to the road long enough to slam on the brakes to avoid a low-flying bird.

The pleading morphed into hope. "Then that is exactly what"—he snapped out a large triangle—"we . . . should . . . do."

"Go to Debbie's?" Margaret Louise clarified.

"Yes. We need sustenance for our investigation!"

Tori felt her left eyebrow lift involuntarily.

Sustenance?

Before Leona could even purse her lips in preparation for a response, Charles turned his pleading eyes in Tori's direction. "It's true! I read online once that the most successful detectives eat a lot!"

Like clockwork, the car noticeably slowed. "Would you listen to this, Twin?" Margaret Louise glanced back at Leona. "Why, I've been sayin' this kind of thing for years, haven't I?"

The car came to a stop in front of SewTastic, and Charles's breathing normalized. "So you see, Margaret Louise? Your idea about going back to Debbie's is brilliant. I mean, her donuts are good, but that's only the tip of the iceberg."

Margaret Louise slid the gearshift into Park. "Victoria? What's your take on this goin' to Debbie's stuff?"

"I . . ." She took a peek back at Charles and had to refrain from laughing as he mouthed the word *brilliant*. "I—I think it's a grand idea, actually. After all, it would give us a chance to visit with Debbie and find out what, if anything, she learned about Lucinda Penning that might be of use in our investigation."

Charles clapped his hands. "Yes! *See*? Brilliance—sheer brilliance, Margaret Louise."

Rolling her eyes, Leona tightened her hold on Paris and opened the back door. "It's getting a little crowded in here, so I will leave you to your brilliance. But just so we're clear, I'm taking the magazine."

They'd just settled themselves around the high-top table closest to the bakery's front window when Debbie came out from behind the counter with a dish towel in her hand. "Emma told me the three of you were out here. Were the donuts not good this morning?"

"They were fantastic as always." Tori patted the empty chair to her left. "Do you have a few minutes to sit with us?"

"I think I can manage that." Debbie slid onto the lattice-backed stool and pointed at the slice of black cherry pie on Margaret Louise's plate. "So? What do you think? Better than the original version?"

Margaret Louise forked up a piece of pie and held it up. "I was just thinkin' you'd done some tweakin' when you walked up." She paused, popped the flaky treat into her mouth, and closed her eyes. "This ain't just black cherry pie. There's somethin' different. Like a hint of chocolate and somethin' else."

Debbie nodded. "It's actually a Black Forest cherry pie with chocolate, marshmallow, cherry juice, whipped cream, cherries, and vanilla."

"Sold!" Charles leaned forward and stole a piece of pie off Margaret Louise's plate. The second the treat hit his tongue, the moans of pleasure started.

"Sounds like you created another winner," Tori mused.

Margaret Louise beat Charles's fork away from her plate. "There ain't no denyin' that, Victoria."

Debbie's cheeks flushed red from the praise even as her gaze came to rest on Tori. "Any word on what happened yesterday?"

"Nothing you don't already know. Except, perhaps, that Rose is taking all of this very, very hard." Tori looked down at the salted caramel cupcake she never should have ordered and then back up at Debbie. "She so wanted this craft event to be successful, you know?"

"Rose and just about every other shop owner in this town—including me." Leaning away from the table, Debbie wiped at a spot on its edge with the dishcloth. "New blood is good for everyone."

"Other shop owners?" Tori repeated.

Debbie moved on to another unnoticeable spot before finally tucking her dishcloth into her apron once and for all. "Think about it, Victoria. Yes, this tour group was small—just five people along with a bus driver and their organizer. But that's still seven new people trying out that recently opened coffee shop on the corner of Main and First, my bakery, Bud's Brew Shack, Shelby's Sweet Shoppe, Brady's Jewelry, Calamity Books, Turner's Gifts 'N More, and Leona's antique shop. If those seven like what they see, or find, or eat, then maybe they'll go home and tell their neighbors."

"It's like that old commercial, ain't it?" Margaret

Louise mused around her latest bite of pie. "They tell two friends, and so on, and so on, and so on."

"Then you see my point . . ."

Charles eyed Margaret Louise's now-empty plate with a hint of disappointment and then moved on to Tori's cupcake. "And if the promise of those folks was good for everyone's business, what happened to Opal stands to hurt everyone, too, yes?"

The jingle of bells announcing the arrival of a new customer halted Debbie's response until she was sure Emma was poised and ready at the front counter. When all was well, she turned back to Charles. "I suppose it could insofar as it might make people wary about coming here if they think a murderer is on the loose."

Using her index finger, Margaret Louise chased the last of the pie crumbs around her plate and deposited them into her mouth. "They won't be wary for long with the three of us"—she pointed her moist finger at Tori, Charles, and then herself—"investigatin'. Why, by the time we're done, the person who strangled Opal will be behind bars where they belong."

The left corner of Debbie's mouth twitched in amusement. "Investigating?" she echoed.

"That's right." Margaret Louise pushed her empty plate into the center of the table and then reached into the tote bag she'd slung across the back of her stool. As she brandished Tori's notebook above the table, the pace of Margaret Louise's words picked up drastically. "Charles and Victoria got things rollin' last night by makin' this here suspect notebook. They did a good job, but I had to do a little addin' this mornin'."

Tori felt the weight of Charles's eyes on the side of her

face and shook it off. If Margaret Louise wanted to count crossing things out and rewriting them as adding, that was perfectly all right. Whatever kept feelings from being hurt was worth a minor rewrite of reality on occasion.

"So who's on your list?" Debbie asked.

"I'll show you." Margaret Louise set the notebook on the table, flipped it open, and spun it around to make it easier for Debbie to read.

Debbie leaned forward, took in the name across the first page, and then pinned each of them with questioning eyes. "You think *Lucinda* could have killed Opal?"

"Because she was *there*, Debbie." Tori scooted her plate in front of Charles and watched as her cupcake disappeared once and for all.

"But so was I. And so were the three of you. That doesn't make us suspects, does it?"

Tori sat up tall. "No. But that's because we know one another, Debbie. All we know about Lucinda and the other women is that they like to sew. That's not enough to rule any of them out in Opal's murder."

"I know more about Lucinda than just her interest in sewing," Debbie protested as Margaret Louise retrieved a pen from her bag and leaned forward, preparing to write. "I know she loves to read and that she has an extensive collection of signed first editions. In fact, she showed me a picture of her most prized shelf, and I forwarded it on to Colby because I knew he'd be impressed.

"And when I offered to get her a signed first edition of Colby's very first blockbuster, she was beside herself with joy." Debbie snapped her finger. "Which reminds me . . . I still have to drop that off for her when I finish up here today."

"We could bring it by for you if you'd like," Tori offered. "We're heading out that way when we're done here."

Debbie's smile was back. "Oh, Victoria, that would be a lifesaver. I'd really like to get home to Colby and the kids sooner rather than later. And I know that if I deliver it myself, Lucinda and I will get to talking again, and an hour will go by without me realizing it."

"I'd be happy to."

Margaret Louise looked up. "Do you know if Lucinda has money?"

"Money?" Debbie parroted as her smile slipped away. "Why? What difference would that make?"

Tori rested a quiet hand atop Debbie's forearm and waited for the bakery owner's attention to swing back to her. When it did, she flashed what she hoped was an understanding smile. "It might not make any difference at all. Or, it could."

"In what way?"

Charles finished chewing and shifted on his stool. "Let's say Opal was very wealthy and Lucinda wasn't. Maybe she thought by killing her, she could get some for herself."

"I doubt sincerely that Opal was carrying enough money in her purse to justify her murder," Debbie argued.

"We're just contemplating *motives* for murder right now, Debbie. And seeing if any of them jive in relation to the suspects." Tori quickly showed her friend the other pages in the notebook and then brought it back to Lucinda's. "We're not saying Lucinda did anything wrong. We're just saying we can't be sure she didn't."

"I guess that makes sense."

Margaret Louise leaned forward, her pen poised and waiting above the notebook. "So what else can you tell us, seein' as how you spent the most time with Lucinda?"

Debbie pondered the question in silence before meeting Tori's gaze head-on. "I think money was tight for her."

Charles and Tori sat forward in tandem. "Oh? What makes you say that?"

"She said she was having to downsize to a studio apartment in her hometown because she could no longer afford the rent."

Margaret Louise jotted the information onto the page. When she was done, she gave voice to the question forming in Tori's thoughts. "Why doesn't she sell some of those special books?"

"I don't know. I didn't ask."

Tori considered Debbie's answer and then moved on. "Debbie? Do you know if Lucinda knew Opal prior to this tour?"

"I'm sorry, Victoria. I don't know that, either."

"Don't you worry none, 'bout that, Debbie," Margaret Louise interjected. "Your not knowin' just means more investigatin' for us."

Debbie nodded and then leaned against the back of her stool. "I really like Lucinda. She was interesting and funny and . . . *nice*. I—I don't want to find out I'm wrong about her."

"And neither do we." Tori tapped the notebook and then gestured toward the door. "Charles? Margaret Louise? Should we head out? I'd like to get back to Milo at a reasonable time, myself."

"I'm always ready for investigatin', Victoria. You know that." Margaret Louise scooted off the edge of her stool, closed the notebook, and placed it back in her tote bag along with the pen. "The new pie was delicious, Debbie."

"I'm glad. Now, if I can only decide whether to stay with the powder blue to-go bags or try something new . . ."

Charles gasped so loudly he drew the attention of a few customers on the other side of the dining area. "You wouldn't . . ."

"Bad idea?" Debbie asked.

"Powder blue is so *you*, Debbie."

Tori stepped in beside the now-standing Charles, nodding as she did. "I agree with Charles, Debbie. The color is as much a part of the Debbie's Bakery logo as the logo itself. Even little kids at the library who can't yet read know a Debbie's Bakery to-go cup by sight because of the color scheme. It's your signature, your—"

"Why, Debbie, in the words of the now-deceased Opal Goodwin, bless her heart, it's your *fingerprint*!" Margaret Louise said. "So don't you go changin' it, you hear?"

Chapter 7

Tori leaned against the station wagon and took a moment to study the Victorian-style home with its large front porch and gingerbread trim. There wasn't a chair in her line of vision that she didn't long to curl up in, book in hand. Then again, depending on the chair, maybe she'd prefer conversation or a quiet cuddle . . .

"Why, Victoria, you look like one of my grandbabies on Christmas mornin' right now."

"It's just so beautiful, isn't it?" she said, pointing at the home. "I remember the day I drove into Sweet Briar for the very first time. I nearly ran off the road looking at this place."

Charles pulled his mouth from the bag Debbie had thrust into his hand as they left the bakery, and slumped into place beside Tori, his breath slowly returning to its pre-car-ride cadence. "Is the inside as pretty as the outside?"

"In my imagination, yes. In reality, I don't know."

"You've never been inside?" Charles asked.

"I've never had a reason to."

"'Til now," Margaret Louise supplied. "And just wait 'til you do. It's magical in there, Victoria. Though, I declare, it'll be at its purtiest once Thanksgivin' is over and Nathan and Hannah start decoratin' for Christmas."

Charles refolded the bag for use during the drive home and stuck it in his fanny pack. "Who are Nathan and Hannah?"

"Nathan and Hannah Welch. They own this place." Margaret Louise hooked her thumb in the direction of Sweet Briar Bed-and-Breakfast. "I say we quit standin' out here yakkin' and get to our investigatin'."

Margaret Louise was right. The longer they stood in the parking lot talking, the longer it would be before she could bid her friends farewell for the remainder of the day and head home for a little alone time with Milo. So much of their time together since the wedding had been about getting the house organized. But now that everything was the way they wanted it, they could actually focus on each other again.

Pushing off the car, Tori followed Margaret Louise and Charles across the landscape-bordered walkway and onto the front porch she'd long admired, her gaze soaking in the kind of details she'd only been able to guess at from the road. To her left was a grouping of four chairs, their placement in relation to one another perfect for conversation among guests. Behind them by a few feet was a single chair angled in favor of the view of downtown Sweet Briar in the distance. To her right was a cushioned lounge chair perfect for an afternoon nap, and a porch swing that made her wish Milo was there, too.

"I reckon if you want to sit out here, Victoria, that would be okay." Margaret Louise paused her hand on the door knob and peered over her shoulder at Tori. "Charles and I can take care of gettin' Colby's book to Lucinda and followin' it up with any askin' we need to do."

She was tempted, no doubt, but really, she just wanted to get their task for the day done and get home. Sighing, she followed her friends into the inn's front hallway and then waited as Margaret Louise tapped the bell on the reception desk.

"Would you look at that purty paintin' on the wall. It looks like you could step right into it, don't it?"

Tori followed the path forged by Margaret Louise's index finger just as Charles sucked in his breath. "I think that's a Hans Marcus original!"

"You know art?" Tori took a step closer to the framed painting, her gaze riveted on the many details that made her feel as if she was standing on the beach with the painting's lone figure, staring out over the horizon.

"If it's a Hans Marcus original, I do." Charles reached out, stopping short of actually touching the painting. "He's known as the Painter of Life, and I'm sure you can see why."

"I feel as if I'm on that beach, too. Like I'm . . ." Not wanting to sound ridiculous, she let her sentence trail off.

But Charles continued right where she left off. "Like you're the person in the picture?"

She nodded.

"All of his paintings do that." Charles motioned toward the squiggled signature in the bottom-right corner. "He's so good at it, in fact, true fans don't even have to see his name to know it's his work. If you feel like you're the person depicted in the painting, it's a Hans Marcus original. "

"Kinda like my sweet potato pie is with me, I reckon." Margaret Louise pulled her hand from its resting place next to the bell and shifted her ample weight from her left leg to her right leg. "Why, if I put four different sweet potato pies next to each other on a table, there's not a person in this town who couldn't tell you which one was mine."

"That's because yours in the best," Tori mused.

"The moonshine is my signature ingredient. I'm the only one who uses it—"

"Mrs. Davis . . . and Miss Sinclair . . . isn't this a wonderful surprise!" Hannah Welch strode over to the desk, her warm smile a perfect accompaniment to the inn's pervasive aura. "And you brought a friend . . ."

"Victoria is Mrs. Sinclair-Wentworth now," Margaret Louise said with the kind of pride generally reserved for her son and his family. "Has been for 'bout six weeks. And this is Charles. He's from New York City."

Hannah Welch tucked a strand of gray-streaked hair behind her ear and then extended her hand to Charles. "Welcome, young man. Are you looking for a room?"

"I'm actually all set with a place to stay while I'm in town, but this place is"—Charles readied his snapping fingers—"To. Die. For."

"Charles stays with my twin when he's in town,"

Margaret Louise offered. "The two of them stay up all night gabbin' 'bout clothes and celebrities."

"Sounds like fun." Hannah stepped out from behind the desk and spread her arms wide. "So how can I help you, then?"

Tori transferred Colby's book from the crook of her arm to her opposite hand and held it up for Hannah to see. "We'd like to give this to one of your guests if she's in—Lucinda Penning?"

"I believe she is, but I'll need to check." Hannah led them into the parlor and waved them toward a small buffet-style table to the left of a massive stone fireplace. "Why don't the three of you enjoy a warm cookie and a glass of sweet tea while I ring Ms. Penning's room and see if she's available to come down."

"Thank you, Hannah." Tori waited until the woman had left the room, and then turned to face her cookie-eating cohorts. "How either one of you can even look at those cookies, let alone eat one is beyond me. That said, how are we going to do this?"

Charles licked a sliver of melted chocolate off his lower lip and reached for another cookie. "Do what?"

"Pump her for information without looking like we're pumping her for information." Tori waved off Margaret Louise's wordless offer for tea but gave in to the pull of the cookie plate. "The problem is, she really doesn't have to answer any of our questions if she doesn't want to."

Margaret Louise poured herself a glass of tea and then took a long sip, declaring it perfect by way of a brief but happy moan. "She'll want to."

"You sound awfully sure of that," Tori mused.

"Because I am. Who doesn't like to talk 'bout themselves?"

Charles lifted up the remaining half of his second cookie in toast-like fashion. "A murderer, perhaps?"

Margaret Louise nodded her acknowledgment of Charles's reasoning but held fast to her theory nonetheless. "If she quits talkin', we'll know we've got our killer."

"Maybe. Or maybe we've got someone who doesn't feel like answering questions from three strangers," Tori proposed.

"We ain't strangers, Victoria. Why, we spent four hours with this woman yesterday afternoon. And you've even got a present to give her."

"A present from *Deb*—"

"Victoria . . . Margaret Louise . . . Charles . . . is everything all right?"

The threesome turned as one toward the doorway with Charles stepping forward first to surrender an air-kiss. "Lucinda, darling, how are you? Did you sleep okay last night after—after everything that happened?"

Before Tori could speak, Lucinda squeezed Charles's hands and then glided over to the burgundy-colored sofa situated at a right angle with the fireplace. "I wish I could say I slept like a baby, but I didn't. I couldn't stop thinking about that dreadful woman."

Margaret Louise's head snapped up. "You mean Opal?"

Lowering herself to the sofa, Lucinda released a tired sigh. "Who else?"

Tori rounded the back side of the opposing sofa and sank onto the cushion directly across from Lucinda. "Finding her dead like that kept me awake most of the night, too."

"I just don't understand how a person can be so—so nasty, so hateful." Lucinda pushed at the air with her hands. "But that's for her to answer for now. The rest of us just need to put her out of our minds. After all, she can only ruin what we allow her to ruin. And I, for one, am determined to enjoy my final day here in Sweet Briar."

Charles stopped nibbling his thumb nail long enough to look up from his reclaimed spot by the cookie table. "The chief is letting you leave?"

Lucinda's eyebrows arched. "Chief? What chief?"

"Sweet Briar Police Chief Robert Dallas." Margaret Louise wiped her hands down the side of her polyester running suit and settled onto the couch beside Tori.

"What would he have to do with me leaving?" Lucinda asked in a voice etched with confusion.

Again, Charles stopped his nibbling. "He's going to want all of the suspects to stay, including me—although with me, it's really just in the interest of fairness."

"Suspects? Suspects in what?"

Margaret Louise started to answer, but stopped as Tori held up her hand. "So the chief hasn't been out here to speak with you yet today?" Tori asked.

"No. Why would he?" Then, like the flash of a summer storm, Lucinda's eyes widened in horror. "Good heavens, he can't think I had anything to do with that woman's death, can he? I—I hardly knew her!"

Tori pushed to a stand and then crossed the oval hook rug to sit beside Lucinda. "He has to question everyone involved with the store that day. It really doesn't mean anything."

Lucinda cocked her head back against the sofa and stared up at the ceiling. "I don't know what to say."

Sensing Charles gearing up to ask one of the handful of questions they'd set aside for Lucinda, Tori thrust Colby's book in the woman's direction. "Debbie is sorry she couldn't bring this out herself, but she's tied up at the bakery for a while longer and wanted to make sure you got this sooner rather than later."

After a moment or two of silence, Lucinda lowered her gaze back to Tori and, finally, Tori's hand. "Is this her husband's book? The one that was a blockbuster?"

"The *first* blockbuster," Margaret Louise corrected proudly. "He's got lots of 'em now. But that one right there is the first one that had people talkin' 'bout him outside of Sweet Briar."

With careful, almost reverent hands, Lucinda took the book and brought it to her nose in tandem with a deep inhale. "There's no better smell in the world than a new book . . ."

"You sound like I do 'bout that first sniff of a new grandbaby." Margaret Louise reached into her tote bag and pulled out her small leather album. "Victoria? Do you mind if we switch spots? I'd like to show Lucinda all of my grandbabies."

"How many do you have?" Lucinda asked.

"Eight. They belong to my son, Jake, and his sweet wife, Melissa." Rising to her feet, Margaret Louise snapped open the album and let a veritable accordion of pictures rain down to the floor. "There's Jake Junior, Julia, Tommy, Kate, Lulu, Sally, Molly, and the baby—Matthew. Aren't they just the cutest grandbabies you've ever seen?"

"*There* you are, Lucinda!" Miranda Greer stepped into the room, her forehead lined with worry. "I missed both you and Minnie at breakfast this morning and—oh,

I'm sorry, I didn't realize you were busy." Miranda pressed her clipboard to her chest as the identity of Lucinda's visitors clicked in her eyes. "Oh. Hello. You're Ms. Winters's friends . . . From the shop . . ."

"That's right. I'm Victoria, and this is Margaret Louise and—"

"Charles. Yes. I remember." Miranda spotted the pitcher of sweet tea on the table next to Charles and headed in that direction. "So what brings you by the inn?"

Lucinda lifted Colby's book off her lap and held it up for Miranda to see. "That author's wife I was telling you about last night? Debbie? She sent a signed copy of her husband's first blockbuster over with these wonderful people."

"That's awfully nice." Miranda poured herself a glass of tea but waited a moment to take a sip as her focus narrowed in on her tour member. "Are you all right, Lucinda? Were you not feeling well this morning?"

"I was fine. I never eat breakfast. I prefer to start my day with a good book."

"But I knocked on your door and you didn't answer."

"That's because I was outside." Lucinda took in the rest of Margaret Louise's pictures and then carefully folded them back into their pre-accordion state. "Last night, before I retired for the evening, Hannah told me about a lovely walking trail behind the inn. When I woke up, I headed in that direction, looking for a sunny clearing in which to read. Sure enough, I found one. Though, from what I'm hearing from these folks, I might end up wishing I hadn't read as many chapters as I did."

"Oh?" Miranda asked, setting her glass back down on the table. "Why is that?"

"Because if we're unable to leave this evening as originally scheduled, I'll need more to read."

"Colby's book'll keep you busy, ain't that right, Victoria?" Margaret Louise took back the album from Lucinda and looked down at it lovingly.

"I wouldn't think of reading a signed first edition," Lucinda protested. "I wouldn't want to crack the spine."

Margaret Louise's mouth gaped. "So you ain't gonna read it?"

"Oh, I'll read it. I'll just check my reading copy out of the library when I get home."

Charles took one last cookie and joined Tori on the couch. "Why wait until you get home? Victoria here is librarian of the Sweet Briar Public Library. She can fix you up with Colby's book and any others you might like to have, can't you, sugar lips?"

Miranda slumped against the wall. "So you know, then . . ."

"About having to stay a little longer than expected? Yes, I just learned of that little fact from Victoria and her friends."

"That's why I've been trying to find you and Minnie. To tell you what's going on." Propelling herself away from the wall with a fortifying inhale, Miranda straightened and made her way over to Lucinda. "But don't worry. It's really just a simple case of the police needing to dot their i's and cross their t's. We should be on our way by this time tomorrow, I imagine."

Margaret Louise's laughter echoed around them. "Spoken like someone who ain't from Sweet Briar, eh, Victoria?"

"I'm sorry, did I miss something?" Miranda asked

as she, once again, pulled her clipboard against her chest.

"You knowin' Chief Dallas."

At Miranda's obvious confusion, Tori took control of the conversation. "Things, um, can move a little slow around here sometimes."

"How slow is slow?" Miranda asked.

"S-L-O-W." Charles spelled out each letter with a snap, looping back to the top of his triangle with the fourth letter. "But that's why we're on the case."

Miranda looked from Charles to Tori and back again. "On the case?"

"Turns out the three of us are mighty good at investigatin'," Margaret Louise said proudly. "So don't you worry none, Miranda. We'll get you all back on your bus b'fore you know it."

Covering his mouth over a fake yawn, Charles lowered his voice so as to be heard by no one but Tori. "All but the murderer, that is . . ."

Chapter 8

Tori sank back against the door and slowly breathed in the calm that was her home with Milo. In just the short time she'd been there, the sight of his furnishings mixed with hers was like an oasis after a long day—an oasis topped only by the feel of his arms . . .

"Milo?"

She headed down the short front hallway and into the living room, her gaze skirting his couch, her plaid armchair, and the two-person lounge chair they'd picked out together the previous weekend.

No Milo.

Turning right, she headed through the dining room and into the kitchen. Still, there was no Milo to go with the car parked in their single-lane driveway . . .

"Milo? Are you here?"

A quick scraping sound from outside had her making her way toward the back door just as Milo appeared on the other side of its screened panel. "Hey there. I was hoping you'd get home soon." He held the door open for her and then pulled her in for the warm hug she'd been craving all day. For a few moments he simply held her, his breath warm against her hair. "So how's Rose doing today? Any better?"

"I haven't spoken to her yet today but I will. Later. Right now, I just need to unwind and spend a little much-needed time with you."

"Music to my ears." Encasing her hand with his own, he led her over to the Adirondack chairs he'd picked up for them shortly after their honeymoon. "I have a surprise that should help in the unwinding department."

Curling up in the cozy depths of the chair, she soaked up the sparkle in her husband's eyes, the joy in his smile, and the dimples in his cheeks. And, just like that, the day's nuttiness evaporated into thin air. "I already did."

"You already did what?"

"Unwind. Just now."

"By sitting in a chair?" he asked.

"Nope. By looking at you."

He leaned across the minimal divide between their two chairs and kissed her gently, the feel of his lips on hers as thrilling as ever. But just as things were starting to really heat up, he pulled back and grinned. "While I love where that was heading just now, I have to press pause so I can show you something."

"*Au contraire*. There is nothing you need to show me that was worth pausing *that*, mister."

"Oh?" Milo reached over the far side of his chair and hoisted a small white and red plastic bag onto his lap. "Not even pictures from our honeymoon?"

Her answering squeal disrupted a small bird from its meal on the hanging feeder and earned a teasing laugh from the man with the bag. "Hey, ho! Does that mean the usage of the aforementioned pause button was, indeed, a good move?"

"Milo!"

Pulling the bag just out of her reach, his grin took on a mischievous edge. "Well, does it?"

She rolled her eyes in the best Leona impression she could muster and then added a dose of the woman's infamous eye-batting. "Yes . . ."

"Okay, Leona," he joked back before stuffing his hand into the bag and removing the first of six picture sleeves from the local drug store's photo department. "*Anyyy-wayyy*, I know we'd been talking about getting these printed over the Thanksgiving break, but after yesterday, I figured you could use a dose of Smoky Mountain happiness."

"You mean, Milo-and-Tori-without-a-care-in-the-world happiness." At his emphatic nod, she dropped her feet back to the ground just long enough to scoot her chair up against his. "Wait. You haven't looked at these yet, have you?"

"I'd be lying if I said I wasn't tempted to check them out the second the clerk handed them to me, but I resisted." With a flick of his wrist, he flipped open the envelope and pulled out the first stack of photographs, the top picture eliciting a peaceful sigh from both of them. The snapshot, which had been taken by a fellow hiker, had Milo's left arm around her and his right thumb pointed upward, signaling their successful trek up the steep and winding mountain trail. They looked winded but proud, and oh so very happy and in love.

"Oh. Wow. That's a good one," Milo said, his voice husky with the same emotion that had Tori ducking the side of her head against his shoulder.

"It's perfect."

With a resistance that was palpable, he moved the picture to the bottom of the stack to reveal another snapshot. "Wow. I truly hit the lottery with you. You're smart, fun, sweet, and stunningly gorgeous. I mean, look at you. You're radiant."

She bit back the urge to self-deprecate and stared at her image. There was no denying it, she was positively beaming as she looked at the camera. "I can assure you, any radiance you see had everything to do with the handsome husband behind the camera."

"Okay, momentary un-pause." He kissed her again and then followed it up with a gentle tap of her nose. "Now let's keep looking. These are incredible so far . . ."

Picture by picture they made their way through the first stack—shots of Milo being silly, shots of Tori laughing, and the occasional shot together thanks to the kindness of a stranger. They were all different, yet each one captured a moment of their magical time together. "I was hoping we'd have a really good one or two to frame, but now I'm thinking a few framed collages might be in order," she said.

"Considering this is only the first envelope of pictures, I suspect you're right." Milo set the envelope beside him on the chair and reached into the bag for another.

"Which, by the way, is fine with me. The more reminders we have of that week, the better."

"We'll need to save some wall space for future trips . . ."

"So true. Which reminds me . . ." He stopped just shy of removing the second stack of pictures from their sleeve and smiled across at Tori. "What do you think of us maybe taking off for a few nights during my Christmas break? Think Nina could cover you at the library?"

"I don't know, but I can ask."

"Okay, cool. If she can, I'll look into making a reservation."

She rested her head on Milo once again and reveled in his nearness and his warmth. "Do you have a specific location in mind, or are you just plotting at this point?"

"I'm thinking it might be kind of cool to check out Lancaster County in the winter."

"Amish country?" she asked.

"Yes."

"Ooh, I'd love that." She straightened up as her thoughts veered momentarily in the direction of the day she really didn't want to resurrect in its entirety just yet. "Maybe we could find a quaint little bed-and-breakfast to stay in while we're there? Like maybe one that's in a really pretty Victorian with a wraparound porch."

His laugh warmed her even before he captured her hand in his. "If Nina can cover you, I'll do my best to find a place just like that. It sounds pretty special—although Pennsylvania in late December might not be conducive to porch sitting."

"That's okay. If we love the place, we can go back in the spring when it *is* porch-sitting weather."

He whispered a kiss across her temple. "You're on."

For the next half hour, they looked at each and every picture, recalling aloud the memories that went with them. There were snapshots of their honeymoon cabin, snapshots of their white-water rafting trip (they got drenched), snapshots of their dinners out and the private ones back at their cabin, too. All were special, yet their favorites were always the ones that showed them together. The happiness on their faces was contagious even now, six weeks later.

When they reached the very last picture of the very last envelope, Milo returned them all to the bag. "I think that was a pretty good unwinding pause, don't you?"

"The best." And it was. Something about losing herself in such a happy, uncomplicated time made the fog of the past twenty-four hours lift enough to let clarity rush in. "Oh, Milo, I want more than anything to put what happened in Rose's shop to bed for her, but I have a feeling it's not going to be easy."

"Why do you say that?"

"We just don't really know anything about the players beyond the fact they like to sew and maybe a few things gleaned from idle chitchat." She stood and made her way over to the edge of the patio. "That's *it*."

"Okay . . ."

Spinning around, she splayed her hands out to the side, the frustration she'd managed to shove to the side for a little while now back with a vengeance. "It's mighty hard to build a case against someone when you've got nothing to go on—no background information or current anything that might be able to lend itself to a motive."

"So you get to know them."

"We tried that today with Lucinda Penning—the first person in our notebook. We went out to the bed-and-breakfast where she and the others are staying."

"And?"

Tori wandered over to one of the planters Rose had gifted them, and tried to pick out any sign of life taking hold in the soil, but there was nothing. "We learned that she doesn't read any of the signed first-edition books she collects. Those are left untouched. She goes to her local library and checks out a second copy that she actually reads.

"Oh, and she got the complete rundown—with pictures, of course—of Melissa and Jake's crew."

Milo linked his hands behind his head and laughed. "So Margaret Louise was with you . . ."

"And Charles. Margaret Louise drove."

"Uh-oh. How did Charles do with that?"

Tori shrugged and headed toward the second of the two planters. Still, there was no sign of anything even remotely resembling a plant. "He was a little green around the gills when we first got to Debbie's, but she gave him a paper bag for the ride out to the inn, and that seemed to help."

"He got sick?"

"No. It kept him from hyperventilating."

"Ah. I see." He dropped his hands onto the arms of his chair and pushed himself onto his feet. With two long strides, he was looking over her shoulder into the planter. "What's so fascinating in there?"

"Absolutely nothing. My thumb is the antithesis of green." She turned to face Milo and stepped into his waiting arms, the feel of his chest against her cheek a welcome reprieve from the stress she felt building once again. "Lucinda is just one person on our list, Milo. If what we got from her is any indication of how it's going to go with everyone else, we'll still be trying to figure out who did it when I'm old and gray."

"Old and gray, huh?" He kissed the top of her head and let his lips linger there for a moment. "I can only imagine how cute you're going to be when we're old. I'm picturing a little bit of Rose and Margaret Louise all rolled into one."

"Margaret Louise doesn't necessarily qualify as old yet."

"But she's a doting grandma," Milo mused. "Which is exactly how I think you're going to be when the time comes—pictures and all."

She reveled in the surprisingly fun image and then shook it off. As much as she loved the notion of dreaming away the remainder of the day, Opal's murder was still an issue for Rose. "I only wish we had a better base with which to work. Like maybe some inside knowledge of each of these women's lives."

"So get some."

Cocking her head back, she peered up at her husband. "That's what we tried to do today, but there's only so much you can get in one conversation."

"In the lobby of a bed-and-breakfast, maybe. But here, maybe not."

"Here?" she echoed.

"Yes."

"You lost me, Milo."

"You're having a sewing circle meeting here tomorrow night, aren't you?"

"Yes . . ."

"These women like to sew, don't they?"

"Yes . . ."

"And they're kind of trapped here until Chief Dallas has whatever he needs, right?"

She bypassed the verbal response and simply went with a nod.

"Well, it seems to me that maybe you should invite them to your sewing circle meeting."

"Invite them to our—" She stopped, bookended Milo's face with her palms, and rose up on her tiptoes to kiss his forehead. "Milo Wentworth, you are a genius, do you know that?"

He bobbled his head in a show of drama-filled humility and then tapped her on the nose. "About *this*? Not really. About *marrying you*? Genius doesn't come close to cutting it."

"I love you, you crazy, crazy man."

"Crazy about you, yes." He captured her hands with his and held them to his lips for the briefest of moments before releasing them and pointing to the grill. "You want me to cook tonight?"

"No way. After the honeymoon pictures and your idea just now, I think it's more than fair I repay you by making your favorite dinner."

His eyebrows shot upward. "Lasagna?"

"With garlic bread." She pivoted on the balls of her feet and headed back across the stone patio. At the back door, she glanced over her shoulder and winked. "After that, maybe we can get back to dessert."

Chapter 9

Tori silently counted the rings in her ear, her anxiety over Rose's state of mind ratcheting up a notch as the sixth ring came and went.

"No answer?" Milo lowered the stack of math papers to his lap. "We can drive over there and check on her if you—"

She waved away the rest of his sentence as Rose's voice filled her ear. "Hello? Who's calling?"

"It's me, Rose. Victoria." Oh how she'd tried to convince the elderly woman to make the transition from a landline to a cell phone for safety reasons, but Rose wasn't having it. What was good enough for her ten years ago was good enough for her now.

"Don't you have a husband to be heading to bed with instead of checking in on me every night?"

Tori smiled at the woman's daily dose of grousing

while shaking off any lingering worry from Milo. "I do, but that doesn't mean our nightly calls stop."

"I'm not going to drop dead just because the sun's gone down. And if I do, I'm quite sure my body will still be warm when you send out the search party."

It was a sentiment she'd heard many times from her friend, but one that never quite made the leap into being funny. Not for Tori, anyway. "Would you please stop? I call you because I like to say good night."

"You *call*, so you can check on me." Rose's sigh served as the nightly transition from agitated to grateful. "You're a special young woman, Victoria Sinclair-Wentworth. Your great-grandmother is surely smiling down at you with love and pride."

She switched the phone to her opposite ear and then swiveled her feet up onto the couch. "Thank you, Rose. So how are you this evening?"

"Don't you mean how am I after one of my customers was murdered in my shop?"

"No . . . but if you happen to want to answer that particular question, I'm certainly happy to listen." She felt Milo studying her and flashed him a smile while she waited for Rose's sudden coughing fit to subside.

"I had a long talk with Miranda on the phone today. She made me feel better."

"Oh?"

"Like you, she thinks this is something the shop can move beyond, provided we handle it right. In fact, she's going to meet with me at the shop tomorrow to start the brainstorming process—for free."

She made a mental note to thank Miranda the next time they crossed paths. "Will Leona be at that meeting?"

"Leona is really leaving the day-to-day of SewTastic to me. If she wants to sit in on the meeting, that's fine. If not, we won't have to waste time waiting for her to stop primping or go through the ridiculousness of waiting to see if Paris has an opinion about everything."

"*Paris?*"

"She's our silent partner, didn't you know that?" Rose asked, her voice tinged with sarcasm. "Anyway, enough of that. Have you heard anything about Opal Goodwin's death?"

She considered a slew of possible answers ranging from a simple no to some song and dance about the police surely working hard behind the scenes, but she opted to go with the truth, instead. Besides, Rose had a knack for knowing when she was holding back. "Nothing from anyone official, no. But Margaret Louise, Charles, and I went out to the inn where they're all staying."

"Why?"

"Just to check things out."

"Who drove?" Rose asked.

Unsure of where the woman's questions were leading, Tori sat up. "Margaret Louise. Why?"

"You're investigating, aren't you?"

She closed her eyes and took a deep breath, biding her time until she could find just the right way to frame her answer. Before she was even finished exhaling though, Rose's voice was back in her ear. "I don't need a response, Victoria. The only reason that young man would knowingly get in a car driven by Margaret Louise is if he was getting to play Sherlock Holmes with the two of you."

To argue would be futile. "We're trying to help, that's

all, Rose. The longer this whole thing drags on, the harder it will be for SewTastic to rebound."

"We *do* have a police department, Victoria."

"We do. They have a very nice building behind town hall, don't they? Oh, and let's not forget their spiffy uniforms."

Rose's laugh, peppered by an occasional cough, caught Tori off guard and had her wishing for a way to record the sound. As much as she hated to acknowledge reality, Rose was aging. Fast. SewTastic needed to rebound in order to slow that process down.

"I see your point, Victoria. So, did you learn anything that could be of use in figuring out who strangled that nasty woman?"

"No. Not yet. We only really had a chance to talk to Lucinda, and there was only so much we could talk about in the brief window we had."

"No Minnie?"

"Nope, didn't see Minnie. In fact, while we were there, Miranda came in looking for both Lucinda and Minnie. Apparently both of them had skipped breakfast this morning and she was worried about them."

"Did she find Minnie?" Rose asked.

"I don't know. We left shortly thereafter. Why?"

A brief hesitation on Rose's end of the conversation gave way to a funny noise Tori couldn't quite identify. "Rose?"

"If I answer that, I'm afraid you're going to think I've gone crazy."

"No I won't," Tori insisted. "Tell me."

"Last night, after we were done talking on the phone,

I tried to remember who went in and out of the project room while Opal was in there working. At first my mind was a jumbled mess and I was unable to recall anything. But, after a while, bits and pieces of that time frame came back to me, and I realized that I *did* remember something odd."

"You did? What?"

"I'm not sure what made me look up when I did— maybe a funny observation from Margaret Louise or Leona's unrequited flirting with the bus driver, but whatever it was, I noticed Minnie heading down the hallway toward the project room. I assumed she was getting her holiday apron, of course. The next thing I knew, ten minutes or so had gone by and I realized she hadn't come back. I started to worry that maybe she'd fallen or something, but just as I'd made the decision to check on her, she showed up beside the dessert table looking unsettled."

"What do you mean she was looking *unsettled*?"

"She was pale and shaky, as if something was bothering her," Rose explained, her voice so hushed Tori had to strain to pick out every word. "At the time, I assumed she was in need of a little sugar and that's why she was over by the table. But now, looking back, I can't help but wonder if she looked like that for an entirely different reason."

"And you're talking about *Minnie*? As in *Saint Minnie*?"

"Yes. I didn't approach her about it because I know, firsthand, how tiresome it is always being asked how you are—like everyone is just waiting for you to keel over at any moment. And when her spirits seemed to perk after her treat, I simply assumed I'd been right about the sugar."

Tori did everything to keep her disbelief in check, but it was hard. The notion was preposterous. "And there's no reason to think you weren't. I mean, *Minnie*? It's—it's . . . crazy."

"I knew you'd say that," Rose whispered.

"I don't mean *you're* crazy, Rose. Just this notion that Minnie up and strangled someone!"

"Strangled *Opal*," Rose corrected. "A woman who seemed to take great pride in making Minnie look foolish at every turn, if you'll remember."

"She took great pride in making *everyone* look foolish, Rose. Including me and you."

"Well *someone* had to kill her."

"Which is why Margaret Louise, Charles, and I sought Lucinda out this afternoon." Tori pulled the closest throw pillow onto her lap and traced its simple design with her fingertip. "Unfortunately, it's hard to pump a virtual stranger for information without raising too many flags."

Silence filled the space between them before Rose finally spoke. "I'm grateful you tried, Victoria. It means more than you can ever know."

"I didn't say I was done, or that I'm giving up," Tori said in an attempt to head off any backward slide in Rose's mood department. "I just said it's a little awkward to get information when you don't really know where to start. But that's why Milo's idea is perfect. Especially if we're all on our toes and listening to every word they say from the moment they arrive until the moment they leave."

"What are you talking about, Victoria?"

"Well, since the tour group members have to stay in Sweet Briar longer than expected and they're all avid sewing enthusiasts, Milo thought that maybe, just this once, we'd open up our weekly sewing circle meeting to a few special guests. After all, we're always uncovering new things about one another while we're sewing, aren't we?"

Chapter 10

Tori checked in the last book from the depository slot and added it to the closest of three stacks. "Well, those are done. And not a late fee among them."

Nina Morgan grabbed the stack at her elbow and headed toward the aisle devoted to self-help. "I heard about what happened at Miss Rose's store over the weekend. She doing okay?"

"I won't lie. It's thrown her for quite a loop, as you can imagine." Tori scooped up the second stack and followed her assistant, veering off at the last minute to shelve a book in the ever growing do-it-yourself section. "But I'm hoping that a swift resolution will lessen any negative impact on SewTastic."

"Were you still there when it happened?" Nina put the top book in its spot and then looped around to the aisle devoted to large-print mysteries.

Tori glanced at the cover of the how-to manual on kitchen makeovers and did her best to blot out the image now claiming her mind's eye. "I tried to revive the victim but it was no use."

"*You* found her?"

"No. Leona found her." She squeezed her eyes closed until the image was gone. When it was, she squatted in line with the second-to-bottom shelf and slid the book into its waiting spot. "Now tell me about your weekend. Did you do anything fun?"

"Duwayne and I took Lyndon to a puppet show in Tom's Creek on Saturday. And then Duwayne's mom watched Lyndon that night so we could have a date."

"Ooooh . . . a date. Very nice." Tori sorted through the next two books in her stack and headed toward the mystery section as well. "What did you guys do? Where did you go?"

"We went for a walk around the Green and then stopped at Bud's Brew Shack for dinner."

The last three books had her dividing her time between government and local interest while Nina finished her stack and returned to the information desk for the third and final one. "I'm glad. I know how much you and Duwayne treasure your time with Lyndon, but it's good to have a little couple time once in a while, too."

Nina met Tori in the local interest aisle and popped the top book in her latest stack into place. "It is. But I have to tell you, we spent almost the entire evening talking about him."

"Seriously?"

"Just you wait, Victoria, just you wait. You and Milo will be the exact same way once you two have a baby."

Tori wandered over to the information desk and plopped onto the stool. "I think about that sometimes, you know? Especially since Milo will be such a great daddy."

"And you, my friend, are going to be an amazing momma . . . with a pack of babysitters you'll have to fend off with a stick."

"What are you talking about?" Tori asked as she settled her back against the counter and watched Nina slide the last two books into place.

"Miss Rose . . . Miss Margaret Louise . . . Milo's mom . . . Miss Dixie . . . Miss Leona. They're all going to want to babysit your child."

Her answering laugh earned a raised brow from Nina. "You think I'm wrong?"

"About the Leona part? Most definitely. Leona despises anything that wears a diaper. She thinks they smell bad, cry too much, and mess up a person's clothes with spit-up and other sorts of mishaps." Tori surveyed the bank of computers and various reading chairs in her line of vision, yet still lowered her voice despite the absence of any patrons. "But if or when we have a little *boy*, I'm going to trick her into changing her mind."

Nina's dark eyes sparkled with intrigue. "How?"

A blast of sunlight stole her answer and sent her focus toward the library's main door and the trio of two-year-olds marching in front of their mother. "Good morning." Tori slid off the stool and stepped out from behind the counter. "Miss Nina, look who we have for this morning's story time! We have Silas, Sam, and Suri. Hi, friends!"

A chorus of sweetness answered back with a hi, a few hand waves, and even a quick dance.

Nina checked the clock on the far wall and then held her hand out for whichever triplet wanted to latch on. "We have a few minutes before story time starts, but let's head into the children's room and get your carpet squares all ready, what do you say?"

Suri took Nina's hand and directed her mother and her brothers to follow, and the fivesome disappeared down the hallway and into the room Tori had transformed into a special place for kids. Even remaining where she was, she knew that Nina was already helping the little ones secure a carpet square from the pile while their mother wandered the aisles looking for new bedtime books for her children.

A buzz from the vicinity of the computer broke through Tori's mental field trip and she reached for her phone. "Hey there, Charles. I'm on the floor right now, so can I call you back when I take my lunch break?"

"Actually, sugar lips, when you're eating your lunch, I'm going to be sprawled out on a leather-wrapped table with cucumbers on my eyes and a revitalizing mask on my face."

She volleyed her gaze between the hallway and the front door and then pulled the phone closer to her cheek. "You're what?"

"Leona is taking me to her day spa for a little pampering. You should ask Nina to cover you and come with us—wait, Leona is saying something, hold on." A string of mutterings in the background gave way to Charles's voice once again. "She says if you went, you wouldn't be in with us anyway because we're doing the rejuvenation package."

"And I couldn't do that one?"

Charles hemmed and hawed for a minute before Leona took the phone. "You'd be better suited to the complete overhaul package, dear. It's more expensive, of course, but considering everything they'd have to do to bring you up to speed, it would be a price worth paying."

Tori rolled her eyes toward the ceiling, noting the presence of a previously unnoticed water stain in the area above the study corner in the process.

Great . . .

"Victoria, dear? Are you still there? Don't be frightened of the price factor. I'd be happy to cover the cost if you decide it's time to finally address the issues with your face."

She considered a slew of possible responses but opted to hold her tongue. Besides, it wasn't like Leona would listen, anyway. "Moving on . . . Are you coming tonight?"

"I stopped at Calamity Books and picked up the latest issue of *Travel the World* just this morning, so yes, I'll be there."

"And Charles?"

A funny sound in her ear morphed into Charles's voice. "Hey there, gorgeous. What's up?"

"I just wanted to make sure you're coming tonight."

"*Tonight*? Whatever could be going on tonight?"

She covered her laughter with her palm and then pulled it away when she remembered the only occupants of the library so far were in a completely different room. "Hmmm . . . I don't know. Maybe I'm wrong. Maybe there's nothing going on. After all, it is a *Monday* night—in Sweet Briar, South Carolina."

"I wouldn't miss it for the world, sugar lips."

And then he was gone, the timer on her phone's

screen indicating the end to the call. Chuckling to herself, Tori slipped the device into the drawer beneath the computer and turned her face toward the morning's second blast of sunlight. "Good morning, welcome to Sweet Briar Public Library."

"Good mornin' to you, too, Victoria." Margaret Louise deposited her second-youngest grandchild on the floor beside the counter and gestured toward the hallway. "Nina doin' story time?"

"She is." Tori squatted down beside Molly and tucked a strand of strawberry blonde hair behind the little girl's ear. "Hi, sweetie. I think you're really going to love the books Miss Nina has picked out to read to you today. There's puppies, and kitties, and sea lions, too!"

Molly's bright blue eyes ricocheted up to her grandmother. "Mee Maw! Mee Maw! Puppies!"

"Ain't that excitin', Molly Sue!" Margaret Louise scooped the little girl's hand into her own. "Let's get you settled in so you don't miss a single page."

Three minutes later, Margaret Louise was back, her smile reaching clear to her eyes. "She didn't even notice me leavin' the room she was so excited 'bout Nina's books."

"We aim to please around here," Tori joked. "So how are you this morning, Margaret Louise?"

"I've been figurin' most of the mornin'."

Tori snapped her fingers and then grabbed the plain notepad she left on the counter beside the main computer. "That's right, I need to balance the library's checkbook this afternoon before I head home. Thank you for that reminder."

"I wasn't talkin' 'bout that kind of figurin', Victoria."

Margaret Louise waited for Tori to finish making the addition to her day's to-do list and then continued. "I was talkin' 'bout our investigatin'. Too much time is a-passin' and it's got me worryin'."

"Too much time? What are you talking about?"

Margaret Louise pointed at the stool behind the counter and, at Tori's nod, hoisted herself onto the cushioned seat and let out a sigh. "Woo-wee it feels good to be sittin' for a minute. Been goin' since my eyelids opened this mornin'." Looking around the library, the woman shrugged. "Nobody lookin' at books this mornin'?"

"Not yet. But that'll change. It always does." Tori looked again at the list and then set it off to the side so she could focus on her friend. "So what's with this 'too much time' stuff?"

"It's already Monday mornin' and we haven't added a thing to our suspect notebook. Not one blessed thing. And now you're workin', and I'm helpin' Melissa with Molly Sue, and Charles is God knows where . . ."

"He's preparing to have cucumbers placed on his eyes." Tori straightened the stack of paper squares she kept within reach of the patrons and then moved on to the cup of eraserless pencils.

Any hint of surprise born on her words disappeared as Margaret Louise shook her head. "I'm tellin' you, Victoria, I think we're losin' Charles to my sister and her ways."

"He'll never be so far gone you can't entice him back with one of your dinners," she quipped.

"From your mouth, Victoria . . . from your mouth." Margaret Louise parted the opening of her shoulder-mounted tote bag with her hand, reached inside, and pulled out their suspect notebook. "We've got a lot of people to be investigatin' b'fore Chief Dallas lets 'em leave."

"I agree. So how's tonight sound?"

Margaret Louise's head snapped up. "How does tonight sound for what?"

"Investigating."

"Aren't you forgettin' somethin', Victoria? You're s'posed to be hostin' our meetin' tonight. In fact, that's one of the things I was doin' first thing this mornin'— bakin' cookies and tryin' to figure out which project I need to start workin' on next. I'm thinkin' maybe I could do some sewin' on Sally's little scout vest while Melissa works on Jake Junior's."

"Oh, I haven't forgotten." She knew she was being intentionally evasive, but it was fun. "I'm going to start that skirt I've been planning to make for Milo's mom for Christmas. Rose brought in the exact shade of emerald green fabric that I was looking for, so I'm finally ready to go."

"Do you *know* you're not makin' any sense right now, Victoria? Or is this that newlywed fog head I've been sayin' is a thing since Jake and Melissa got married?"

Tori laughed so hard she actually snorted. When she recovered enough to speak, she gave Margaret Louise just a little bit more. "I'm thinking we can investigate and sew all at the same time."

"Investigate and . . ." Margaret Louise's words petered off as reality dawned on her round face. "Wait a minute. Are you sayin' what I think you're sayin'?"

"That depends. What do you think I'm saying?"

"You're thinkin' of invitin' the tour group to tonight's meetin'?"

"Nope. It's already been done," Tori said, grinning. "Rose called over to the inn and spoke to Miranda about it first thing this morning."

Margaret Louise leaned forward so far she actually grabbed hold of the counter to keep herself from falling off the stool. "And?"

"And they're coming. Travis is going to bring them over on the bus."

Throwing her free hand into the air, Margaret Louise let out a library-friendly squeal. "Why Victoria, every time I think you're as smart as can be, you just get smarter."

"Well . . ." In a near-perfect mimic of Leona, Tori pursed her lips, struck a pose, and then relaxed. "I'd love to take credit, but I can't. It was Milo's idea."

Margaret Louise repositioned her weight more evenly across the stool. Then, with a flick of her hand, she ripped a piece of paper from the back of their notebook and began jotting a list of ingredients. "Looks like I just added another bakin' session to my day."

"Why? We always have enough dessert left over after a meeting to feed a small nation. I'm sure the cookies you made this morning, along with everyone else's treats, will be more than enough, Margaret Louise."

When her list was done, Margaret Louise folded the slip of paper and thrust it into the pocket of her polyester jacket. "I'm not worried 'bout havin' *enough* dessert, Victoria, I'm worried 'bout havin' the *right* dessert."

Tori eyed her friend closely. "You lost me."

"You ever eaten somethin' so sinful you feel as if your brain quits workin'?" Margaret Louise returned the notebook to her tote bag and vacated the stool.

"With you and Debbie as my friends? Many times."

"Well that's what I'm aimin' to do—to make somethin' so good our guests can't help but start runnin' off at the mouth 'bout this, that, and the other. 'Cause maybe, one of them others might be just what we're lookin' for to figure out which one of 'em strangled Opal Goodwin in Rose's project room."

Tori fell into step with Margaret Louise as the woman made her way back toward the hallway to sit in on the last ten minutes of story time. "You really think a dessert can do that?"

At the mouth of the hallway, Margaret Louise stopped and turned to face Tori. "I'm bettin', based on that question, that I've never made my Truth Serum Brownies for you, have I?"

"Truth Serum Brownies?" she repeated.

"That's what I said."

"But—"

Margaret Louise's brown eyes slid left to the front door and then right toward the children's room, her voice morphing into a rare whisper. "How do you think I know the things I know in this town, Victoria?"

She drew back. "I—I don't know . . ."

"Well, you do now."

Chapter 11

Tori maneuvered the vacuum cleaner across the final section of living room carpet, mentally moving the chore into the done category of her brain as she did. As much as she loved sewing circle Mondays, hosting one after a full day of work certainly upped the fatigue factor. Still, the prospect of having her friends all together, in the same place and at the same time, had a way of making up for the added workload.

Each one of her sewing sisters brought something special to her life . . .

Rose brought wisdom, love, and a poignant reminder that true friendships were blind to things like health and age. When Rose found herself in the hospital for an infusion treatment tied to her arthritis, Tori was by her side, telling her stories, keeping her spirits high, and holding her hand. When the pain in Tori's heart over the loss of her great-grandmother came to the surface as it was prone to do, Rose was always there with tissues, a comforting hug, and an understanding ear.

Margaret Louise brought joy—plain and simple. The sixty-year-old's zest for life and unshakable loyalty had provided Tori with a road map of sorts for her own life. In fact, through Margaret Louise, she'd come to realize how something as seemingly inconsequential as a chocolate chip cookie and a glass of milk could mean a world of difference to someone needing a boost. Just knowing that Margaret Louise was always willing and able to roll up her polyester sleeves and help anyone anytime was both inspiring and humbling.

Leona, while prickly and downright rude, had taken Tori under her wing. And though there were times when Leona's life coaching came unprompted and unsolicited, it was never without a measure of genuine affection.

Dixie served as an ever-present reminder to never give up on oneself or others. It was a lesson that hadn't come easy thanks to Dixie's once intense hatred for Tori, but with time, the seventysomething had come to realize that her forced retirement at the hands of the library board hadn't been Tori's doing. Slowly, through their shared love of books and their shared affection for the patrons of the Sweet Briar Public Library, they'd forged a patch of common ground big enough to coexist until true friendship had taken root.

Debbie set the bar for Tori in terms of the kind of life she wanted with Milo—a life guided by love, respect, and hard work. Watching Debbie with her husband Colby and their two kids had helped Tori shed any residual fear over the notion of getting married while simultaneously teaching her to trust herself and her own heart. It was an aspect of their friendship Tori would always hold dear, even if the woman's baking prowess was to blame for Tori's need to increase her workout routine from three times a week to four.

Georgina Hayes, the town's mayor, was a true believer in the notion that one could never have too many friends. A native of Sweet Briar with a plethora of friends she'd known since childhood, Georgina had still made it a point to welcome Tori to Sweet Briar, even going so far as to invite her to a sewing circle meeting. The rest, of course, was history, but it was because of that history that she'd be forever in Georgina's debt.

Melissa Davis was simply the kind of mom Tori hoped to be one day. Endlessly patient with each one of her eight children, the thirty-six-year-old had a smile and a word of encouragement for anyone and everyone. The fact that her children had such giving hearts by the time they could walk was a testament to the woman's belief system.

Beatrice Tharrington, although still young, had taught Tori so much about the power of listening. When you listened, you learned. And when you learned, you grew . . .

Looking down at the patch of carpet she'd vacuumed at least a half dozen times in the past few minutes, Tori turned the handle perpendicular with the floor and shut off the machine.

"I was wondering when you were going to finally declare that corner clean."

Startled, she glanced over her shoulder to find Milo's amber-flecked eyes watching her with amusement. "Oh. Wow. I didn't hear you come in."

"I'm not sure you'd have heard me if I'd been an elephant." He grabbed hold of her waist and turned her around, pulling her close as he did. "So where were you just now?"

She inhaled his scent and felt the smile it ignited across her face in response. "Thinking, I guess."

"Thinking about what?"

"The crew." Slowly, reluctantly, she unlatched her hands from the back of her husband's neck and stepped back. "Each and every one of them has been a blessing to me."

"And to me." He bent down, kissed her full on the mouth, and then motioned toward a wrapped package on the couch. "I stopped at the store on the way home from school and picked up a little something for us."

"For us?"

"You'll understand when you open it."

"Oooh, I'm intrigued." She pulled the plug from the wall socket and instantly found herself back in Rose's project room with a very different cord in her hand . . .

"Tori? You okay, hon?"

Blinking away the memory, she finished looping the cord into place on the back of the vacuum and returned to a stand. "Yes, yes, I'm fine. So, can you give a gal a hint?"

He followed her gaze to the package. "Nope."

"Gee, thanks." She sidestepped her way around Milo and sat down next to the package, any lingering stress over the memory of Opal taking a backseat to anticipation. With careful fingers, she worked the wrapping off at the tape spots until she could finally reach inside and pull out the gift.

As she did, she found herself looking at a framed

collage of some of her favorite honeymoon pictures. In the center of the mix was the one taken on the top of the mountain. "Oh, Milo," she whispered. "It's perfect. Absolutely perfect. But when did you do this?"

"On the way home from school just like I said. Once I had the frame and the reprints, I went back to my classroom, put it together, and wrapped it." He took the frame from her hands and carried it over to the fireplace. "So do we want to hang it here—above the fireplace—or do we want to put it in the dining room?"

With just a simple upward motion of her hand, he moved the frame up a half an inch from where he'd placed it. "Yes. There."

He pulled a pencil from his back pocket, made a mark on the wall, and then rested the frame on the mantel while he secured a hammer and nail from his toolbox. Three strikes of the hammer later, the picture was in place and his arm was around her shoulders. "It looks awfully good hanging there, doesn't it?"

"It looks amazing." She took a moment to absorb each and every picture one more time, focusing in on the happiness they both wore like a second pair of clothes. "Promise me we'll carve out special time like this throughout our marriage . . ."

"I promise." He squeezed her to him, lingering his lips on her temple as he did. "Hey, did you happen to ask Nina about that week between Christmas and New Year's? Can she cover the library for two or three days?"

She hated that she had to say no, but she couldn't lie, either. "I'm sorry, Milo. I'd intended to ask her about that after story time, but Margaret Louise was around and it slipped my mind. Then, when I thought of it again later, Nina was on her lunch break."

He released his hold on her and returned the hammer to its spot in his toolbox. "Why didn't you just ask her after her lunch break?"

"I was distracted."

"By . . . ?"

She waited for him to close the box and then led him back to the couch. Once the wrapping paper was balled up and thrown away, she joined him on the cushion. "One of the women from the tour group came into the library to borrow a book for however long the chief says they need to stay."

He nodded to show he was listening but remained silent as she continued. "I guess I was so shaken up by the book she checked out, all thoughts of a post-Christmas getaway slipped my mind completely."

"I don't understand."

"Of the five ladies in the group on Saturday, Minnie Randolph was, hands down, my favorite. She's this tiny little thing who looks just like Mrs. Claus and laughs like her, too." Tori rested her head against Milo's outstretched arm and examined the image in her head for more details to share. "I'd put her at about Rose's age, though not quite as frail and just a wee bit absentminded, but in a very endearing way.

"She seemed to love the *act* of sewing, even if she wasn't necessarily versed in the *art* of sewing, if that makes sense. But we all took to her right away. Heck, even Margaret Louise, who is the very epitome of a grand-mother, said Minnie was the kind of granny everyone wanted. Sweet. Happy. Endearing. You know, the whole package."

"Go on. I'm listening."

Tori took a deep breath in and let it slowly work its way back through her parted lips while she readied the next part of her tale. "Okay, so Minnie walks into the library at around two o'clock this afternoon with the same smile and sweetness she had on Saturday. I told her I was happy to have her at the library and even showed her around a little. She'd heard Margaret Louise mention the children's room at some point during the event on Saturday and so I showed her that, too. When we were done, I walked her back up to the counter and asked her if there was anything else I could do for her."

"And that's when she asked for some sort of book that upset you?"

Tori pivoted her body so as to afford the best view of Milo's face while she filled in the remaining part of the story. "She asked for a book called *Getting Away with Murder.*"

"*Is* there such a book?" Milo asked.

"Dozens, actually. Some fiction. Some nonfiction." She looked down at the half inch of cushion between them, then back up at Milo. "She didn't seem to know that there were multiple books with that title, which gave me a chance to get my shock under control."

"Wait. Shock, why?"

"Think about it, Milo. By her very presence on Saturday, she's on the suspect list. But until that moment, she was merely on it to be fair. I didn't think she actually could have *killed* that woman."

"And you think so now?"

"Why else would an eighty-year-old woman want to read a book with that title?"

He drew back. "You think she was looking for tips?"

"I don't know what to think. I just know that the very title of that book has to raise *some* suspicion, don't you think?" She stopped, brought her breathing under control, and moved on to the other troubling piece in the puzzle. "Couple that with Rose's recollection of Minnie spending a rather lengthy period of time in the project room with Opal and then coming out looking a little *unsettled*."

He took everything in and then grabbed hold of Tori's hands. "Okay, so maybe she's the one."

"But she can't be. She's old . . . and sweet."

"Did she and Opal get along?"

"Opal was horrid to her," Tori mused. "She was constantly putting Minnie down and treating her like some sort of brainless child."

"Then you may have to accept the possibility that old and sweet may have finally snapped."

"I'm sorry, Milo, but I just can't believe Minnie would do something like—"

"Hello? Is anyone home?"

Pulling her hands free, Tori rose to her feet and turned toward the kitchen just as Charles, Leona, and, Rose came around the corner.

"I told them we should have knocked harder, but I was outnumbered." With trembling hands, Rose lifted her foil-wrapped plate in line with her chest while motioning toward the dining room table with her chin. "Should I put my lemon bars on the table?"

"I'll take them." Tori crossed into the dining room and took the plate from Rose's hand. "How'd your meeting with Miranda go today? Did you come up with any good ideas?"

"We came up with one before we adjourned for the day." Rose pointed at the still-wrapped plate. "I made those from a favorite recipe of my mother's."

Tori peeled back the foil and peeked inside. "Mmmm, Rose, these look and smell delicious."

Leona snapped her fingers in the direction of the kitchen and waited as Charles relocated the plate of store-bought cookies from the wrong table to the right table. "I hear my sister is bringing the big guns this evening."

"Margaret Louise is bringing *guns*?" Tori repeated as Milo joined them long enough to kiss both Rose and an eye-batting Leona before excusing himself to the bedroom for the remainder of the evening. "Don't you think that's a little excessive? I mean, if we figure out who did it, we'll call the chief."

A loud, boisterous laugh from the kitchen yielded Margaret Louise and her own foil-wrapped plate. "She's referrin' to my Truth Serum Brownies, ain't you, Twin?"

Tori welcomed the new addition with a hug and then lifted the wrap just high enough to reveal the mound of carefully cut brownies inside. "They look like normal brownies to me . . ."

"Looks can be deceivin'." Margaret Louise balled the foil inside her free hand and placed the brownies in the center of the table. "But once a person bites into one, they just start talkin'. Been that way since the very first batch I made 'bout fifty years ago. Why, Leona, don't you remember Lucy Mae eatin' one and then spendin' the next thirty minutes tellin' us 'bout the way her older brother was sweet on you?"

Leona's eyes narrowed. "*Fifty* years ago, I wasn't even *alive*, Margaret Louise."

Rose and Tori each took a step back, with Tori palming Charles's shoulder and pulling him to safety, too.

"Fifty years ago, I was almost thirteen, and considerin' you and me were born a minute apart, I'm quite sure you were thirteen then, too."

Dead silence descended across the room as Tori, Rose, and Charles braced for the fallout of Margaret Louise's words, but Leona simply turned and faced them. "Remember when word got out that Mac Saunders wasn't going to run for a councilman spot before he was ready to announce it?"

Tori and Rose nodded in unison.

"That was my brownies!" Margaret Louise announced.

Leona kept going. "And remember when the truth came out about Van Morgan's wife and Mary Sue's husband?"

Again Tori and Rose nodded.

"That was my brownies, too!" Margaret Louise waved her hand over the plate of chocolate squares and then rocked back on the heels of her Keds as Leona took the floor again.

"And that time when we were trying to find out what Georgina wanted for her birthday but she was playing coy and wouldn't tell anyone?"

Tori stared at Margaret Louise. "That was your brownies?"

"That was my brownies."

"And that's only the tip of the iceberg, dear. There are many, *many* more examples of their power."

"They really work *that* well?" Tori asked as she looked from Margaret Louise to Leona and back again.

Charles rose up on the balls of his feet, pointed out the front window to the approaching bus, and then clapped his hands like a sugared-up cheerleader. "It looks like we're about to find that out right now."

Chapter 12

There was no denying the oddity of looking across the living room and finding four veritable strangers sewing. And based on the occasional glances she fielded from just about every member of the Sweet Briar Ladies Society Sewing Circle at some point during the first twenty minutes or so, Tori wasn't the only one who felt that way.

Still, she couldn't have been prouder of the way Lucinda, Gracelyn, Samantha, and Minnie had been welcomed into the tight-knit fold from the moment Travis and Miranda dropped them off at the curb.

As expected, Debbie had gravitated toward Lucinda, patting her far away from Paris and over to the pair of Adirondack chairs Milo had pulled inside for the evening. Based on the snatches of conversation Tori could make out between the pair, books were still the favorite topic.

Gracelyn was bookended on the couch by Dixie and

Georgina, all talk of current affairs tabled for the time being by a new commonality—hems. Who was going to win their passionate debate over the best technique to use when hemming a knee-length skirt though, remained to be seen.

"I still can't believe I'm here. Me—Charles. At a Sweet Briar Ladies Society Sewing Circle meeting," Charles whispered out of the corner of his mouth. "Pinch. Me. Now."

Tori shifted her focus from Gracelyn to her spiky-haired friend and pointed her needle at his right hand. "I didn't know it was possible to snap while holding a needle."

"It's not, unless you're a"—he readied himself for a triangle encore—"snapmaster. Like. Me."

"A snapmaster, huh?"

"You know it, sugar lips." With a quick stick of his needle into the side seam of his jeans, Charles brought his hand to his mouth and pretended to yawn. "I've been dreaming of this moment since I first saw you ladies on *Taped with Melly and Kenneth* last spring."

She guided his focus back down to his leg. "I'd be happy to give you one of my pincushions, you know."

"Why? My jeans work fine."

Why indeed . . .

"Suit yourself." She cut a piece of emerald green thread from its spool and guided it through her own needle. "As for this meeting, are you forgetting the one you came to just before my wedding?"

"That wasn't a real sewing circle meeting, Victoria. That was just a bridal shower disguised as one." He turned his wide eyes on her as horror dawned across his face. "Not that the bridal shower wasn't fabulous—because it was. Minus, of course, the whole ring announcement Leona made that got everyone even angrier at her." He stopped, took a breath, and continued on, his recollection of events impressive. "The fur was really flying there at the end, wasn't it, sugar lips? There was a moment when I actually thought Dixie was going to throw a punch. And if she had, Leona's plastic surgeon would have been fit to be tied, that's for sure."

She felt her mouth go slack a half second before Charles's skin blanched beneath his spray tan. "You're hallucinating, Victoria. You did *not* just hear that."

Leona's plastic surgeon?

"I—I . . ." Tori's stammering fell off as she glanced toward the dining room and the always stylish, always perfect Leona. On Leona's lap was her precious Paris. In her hands was the latest travel magazine.

"Please, Victoria," Charles whisper-pleaded. "I'm begging you. You did not hear that."

"I—I mean I always . . . *wondered*. Everyone does. But—"

Charles pitched his upper body over his knees, pulled a familiar powder blue bag from his satchel, and brought it to his mouth.

"Charles? What are you doing?"

"I need air," he said between dramatic gasps.

She grabbed the bag from his hand and thrust it onto the cushion between them. "What? Do you think I have some sort of death wish?"

For what seemed like an eternity, he merely stared at her as if searching for something. When his breathing was finally normalized enough to speak, he did. "Are you sure?"

"Yes, I'm sure. Your secret is safe with me."

"*Leona's* secret," he corrected.

"Leona's secret."

Clasping the base of his neck, he slumped back against the couch and shuddered. "I can't believe I said that. I'm a locked vault of secrets."

"No worries—wait!" She pointed at the empty plate on the closest end table and studied her friend. "Did you happen to eat one of Margaret Louise's brownies?"

He bolted upright. "That's it! It was the Truth Serum Brownies!"

"Shhhh . . ." She took in the plate of brownies on the dining room table and then swung her gaze back to Charles. "So they really work?"

"I just blabbed Leona's biggest secret, didn't I?"

It was Tori's turn to flounce against the back of the couch, her threaded needle still untouched on her lap. "Wow. Just wow."

"I know Samantha took one when we were over at the table together," he whispered.

Tori fixed her attention on the redhead bent over one end of Jake Junior's scout uniform while Margaret Louise worked on the other. "What's your take on her?" she asked. "Besides being in her late fifties or early sixties?"

"She knows forensics, that's for sure."

"Forensics?"

He nodded and reached for his last bite of Rose's lemon square. "When I was over at the table, she was poking holes in that new crime show *Cause of Death*."

"What kind of holes?"

"The kinds of things the quote un-quote accomplished killer left behind in the first episode that tied him to the crime. She said an accomplished killer would know to wipe their fingerprints off the murder weapon. The fact that he didn't cheapened the whole show in her eyes."

"Anything else of note?"

"You mean other than the way she followed up her hole poking with ways an accomplished killer might actually opt to murder someone? No. That's it."

"Huh."

When the lemon square was gone, he elongated his neck to afford a view of Samantha and Margaret Louise's corner of the living room and then tapped the face of Tori's watch. "Unless the brownie on that plate between them is Margaret Louise's—which I doubt because it's still there and she knows its effects—it appears as if Samantha has another bite or two to go. I'm putting the time between when I finished my brownie and the padlock on my lips malfunctioning at about ten minutes. So, assuming there's no variation in effects based on age or gender, I think I'm going to trade my needle for a pen and another lemon square for our notebook of suspects . . ."

She registered most of what Charles was saying, but some of it she was pretty sure she missed as her gaze shifted from Samantha and Margaret Louise to Minnie and Rose. Two days earlier, she'd been drawn to the eighty-year-old woman by many of the same things that drew her to Rose. But now, as she considered Minnie's hands and the fact they didn't shake as much as Rose's, she couldn't help but wonder about their strength.

Were they strong enough to kill another person? Especially if that person was only five or six years younger than Minnie?

"I don't know about the rest of you, but I really didn't like that Opal Goodwin."

Charles's elbow hit just below Tori's rib cage and brought her attention back to Samantha Williams. "Oh, oh, oh, here we go. Lights. Camera. Action."

One by one, hands stopped threading needles, and fingers stopped moving them in and out of fabric. Samantha looked at each and every person before scooting Jake Junior's uniform off her lap. "She was mean and nasty for the sake of being mean and nasty, and she's been that way for as long as I've known her."

Margaret Louise turned a knowing eye in Tori's direction and winked.

Leona turned a knowing eye in Tori's direction and smiled smugly.

Charles merely flipped open the notebook, uncapped his pen, and waited.

"You knew Opal before this tour?" Tori asked.

"Did I ever." Samantha held up Jake Junior's ziplining patch and sighed. "I did this for the first time just this past summer. While on vacation in Virginia. I felt like I was flying . . ."

On the page devoted to Samantha, Charles wrote:

Ziplines.

"Inconsequential," she whispered.

"You don't know that. Zipliners are proficient with ropes, are they not?"

He had a point . . .

Margaret Louise took the patch from Samantha's

outstretched hand and added it back on top of the pile still to be sewn onto her eldest grandchild's vest. "How did you know Opal?"

"God, I love that woman," Charles mused as he held his pen at the ready. "Well, maybe not her driving, per se."

"*Maybe*?"

"Shhhh . . . Samantha is gearing up to answer."

Tori turned her head just as Samantha rose to her feet and wandered back to the dining room table. "A few years ago, I approached our town council about doing one of those citizen police academy programs in conjunction with our local police department. If you're unfamiliar with them, it's a chance to get a taste of what police officers do on a daily basis. You go out on calls, do simulations of real life and death scenarios, et cetera. It was something I'd always wanted to do, but didn't necessarily want to incur the costs of a hotel in some other town in order to do it."

Samantha inventoried the various remaining desserts on the table and then helped herself to a second round of Margaret Louise's brownies.

"I don't know if you should be eatin' two of those," Margaret Louise said, jumping up.

"Why on earth not? One can never have too much chocolate." Samantha made her way around the room, stopping to inspect what each and every person was working on. When she saw the shirt Debbie was making for her preteen daughter, she made a few appreciative noises and then popped a piece of the brownie into her mouth. "Mmmm . . . these are absolutely delicious."

Clearly torn between worry and pride, Margaret

Louise settled on pride. "I make them from a secret recipe I invented myself."

Desperate to get the loose-lipped woman back on topic, Charles leaned forward with rapt interest. "So did they do it? Did your town host one of those academies?"

"No. Thanks to Opal."

Tori, Charles, and Margaret Louise exchanged looks.

"Oh?" Leona chimed in. "Why is that?"

"Because Opal, who apparently attends every town council meeting for the express purpose of keeping everyone in line, pitched such a fit over the prospect of local tax money being used in that way, they dismissed my request completely." Samantha crossed back to the table, plucked a carrot from the vegetable plate Debbie had brought along with a host of sinful desserts, and carried it over to Paris. "If I could have gotten away with it, I'd have leaned across the seat I was sitting on and strangled that woman with my bare hands right then and there. Fortunately for me, I had the presence of mind to realize the chief of police and two of his deputies would have seen the whole thing."

Keeping her finger low to the couch, Tori pointed at Samantha's page and waited for Charles to stop gawking and start writing. A quiet snap eventually did the trick.

Wanted citizen police academy. Opal nixed idea.
Wanted to strangle Opal.

"Good?" Charles mumbled.

"Good." She looked up again as Leona, clearly touched by Samantha's gesture toward Paris, patted the vacant chair to her right. Samantha accepted.

"I take it there were others in the room that disliked your suggestion?" Tori asked loud enough for Samantha to hear.

Samantha gave Paris a gentle scratch between the ears and then shook her head so emphatically, Tori was actually concerned it would fall off her neck. "Quite the contrary, actually. Several residents, upon hearing my idea during the open forum, expressed interest in participating in such a thing. One gentleman even went so far as to say it could benefit the police department to have more citizens properly trained in dealing with emergencies."

Something about Samantha's story wasn't adding up. But before Tori could craft the best question to uncover the issue, Margaret Louise beat her to the punch.

"I don't know 'bout your town, Samantha, but here in Sweet Briar, Georgina—she's our mayor and a member of our sewin' circle who ain't here tonight—wouldn't put the rantin' of one over the feelin' of many."

"She would if that one was Opal Goodwin."

"Why?" Tori asked, intrigued.

"Opal Goodwin is the old money in our town. Old money has deep connections and loyal followers, if you know what I mean."

When no one spoke, Samantha continued. "In our town, it's not Springdale Elementary. It's Goodwin Elementary. And the new teen center that just opened in September? That's called the Opal Goodwin Center for Teens."

"So Opal was a *philanthropist*? Wow. Didn't see that one coming . . ."

The laugh Samantha hurled in Charles's direction was

anything but joy filled. "Hmmm, let's check that, shall we?" Samantha searched around for her purse, located it next to the couch she'd inhabited with Margaret Louise, and pulled out her phone. A flick of her wrist and a few taps of her finger later, she began to read. "The definition of a philanthropist is one who seeks to promote the welfare of others, especially by the generous donation of money to good causes."

"And that wasn't Opal?"

"No, Charles, that wasn't Opal. Opal wasn't seeking to promote the welfare of anyone other than herself. She liked control in all settings and she knew how to ensure she always had that control."

"Meaning?" Tori prodded.

"She bullied people into doing what she wanted by way of her money. IF she didn't want a citizens' academy, she merely had to voice her displeasure. If she wanted to keep a particular company from leasing a vacant building in town, she opened a museum dedicated to sewing in that very space."

Gracelyn's snort earned a raised eyebrow from Charles, but before Tori could turn a question in her direction, Samantha continued. "If Opal wanted to remind people just how critical she was to our town, she opened a teen center and made sure her efforts got the attention of every television news station in the state." Samantha returned her phone to her purse and sat down beside Margaret Louise, yawning loudly as she did. "In fact, until Saturday, I'm not sure Opal had ever been told no before—not without serious repercussions for the person who did, anyway."

Leona retrieved her travel magazine from its temporary

holding spot beside her chair and snapped it open to her desired page. "I will not be bullied. By anyone."

Samantha's head lolled back against the couch, her eyes drooping heavily. "My . . . sentiments . . . exactly . . ."

Chapter 13

"Now you've seen it with your own two eyes, Victoria." Margaret Louise released her hold on the living room curtain, taking with it the sight of the tour group's minibus as it made a left at the end of the road and headed toward Sweet Briar Bed-and-Breakfast. "My Truth Serum Brownies get people talkin', don't they?"

Leona took a sip of her favorite nighttime tea and then ran a hand down Paris's back. "That's why, aside from the calories and potential for skin blemishes, you'll never see me eating one, dear."

You don't have to. We have Charles . . .

A jab just under her rib cage snapped her eyes to the right.

"You promised," Charles reminded via a hissed whisper.

"I know, I know." Tori stepped back from the window

and surveyed the room. Other than a handful of extra chairs and the plate of leftover desserts Rose had compiled for Milo, there was little evidence that a dozen women had been present less than ten minutes earlier.

"I was sorry Georgina and Beatrice couldn't make it." Debbie pulled the drawstring on the bag of trash she'd collected and carried it into the kitchen. "But I know Georgina had a meeting she couldn't get out of, and Beatrice wanted to help Luke finish his science project for school."

"That's why Melissa didn't make it, neither. Sally wanted to practice her presentation on her momma." Margaret Louise dropped onto Tori's plaid armchair and hoisted her feet onto the brown leather ottoman. "Can you imagine little ones pretendin' they're talkin' to the folks at NASA?"

Rose reentered the room from the kitchen and began to wipe down the dining room table, her movements slow but methodical. At the midway point of the table, she looked up at Margaret Louise. "Should we be worried about that woman falling asleep the way she did?"

"No, ma'am. That's just what happens if you eat two of them brownies. The first one gets your jaws a-flappin' and the second one gets your eyes a-droopin'. But it don't really matter none, we got what we wanted—a real honest-to-goodness suspect with means and motive."

"Do you think we have enough?" Rose asked as her bifocal-enlarged eyes settled on Tori. "Can we really put what happened to Opal behind us and get SewTastic back on track?"

More than anything, Tori wanted to confirm Rose's hope, but to do so would be premature. "I-I'm not sure yet, Rose. I think we need to do a little more investigating. There were *three* other potential suspects in the room today that we didn't really vet."

"Oooh, *vet* . . . that sounds so—so *official*."

Margaret Louise nodded knowingly at Charles and then moved on to Tori. "Now, Victoria, I was raised knowin' that just 'cause a chicken has wings don't mean it can fly, but after the revealin' my brownies did tonight, I'm pretty sure this chicken is flyin'."

"I agree." Spying a previously unseen napkin on a chair next to the fireplace, Debbie crossed the room, retrieved the crumbled item, and carried it back to the kitchen. "Besides, I stand by my conviction that people who love books as much as Lucinda does aren't the type to strangle old ladies with sewing machine cords. It simply doesn't add up."

Dixie finished packing her sewing box and turned to face the bakery owner, hands on hips. "As much as I'd love to agree with you, Debbie, I must point out that criminals on death row are often avid readers. It's well-informed people—like Gracelyn—that don't strike me as the type to take a life."

"I was hopin' that one would take a brownie, too," Margaret Louise said between yawns. "But I wasn't countin' on anyone bein' gluten-free. Seems maybe I need to start experimentin' with a version for them folks, too."

Tori meandered over to the fireplace and pointed at the photo collage. "Milo surprised me with this today . . ."

"I was lookin' at that earlier, Victoria. Your smile in those pictures is nothin' short of dazzlin'."

Charles bounced up on the balls of his feet and gave a little clap. "My favorite is the selfie you took on the mini-golf course. You look positively divine in emerald green, Victoria."

"You should see *me* in emerald green." Leona pinned Charles with a stare atop her stylish glasses. "If you did, you might feel differently about using the word *divine*."

Debbie muttered something unintelligible under her breath and then joined Tori in front of the collage, her pale blue eyes studying each and every picture with rapt interest. "You can just feel how much the two of you love each other."

"It was such an amazing honeymoon, it really was."

"Victoria?"

Tori turned to find Leona's twin studying her. "Yes, Margaret Louise?"

"Not more 'n a few minutes ago you said there were *three* other potential suspects in the room. I know we can't quite rule out Lucinda or Gracelyn just yet, but you can't possibly be thinkin' *Minnie* is responsible for what happened to Opal, can you?"

"Of course she doesn't, Margaret Louise," Charles said as he sashayed across the room to the bag of chips Rose had just clipped closed. Removing the clip from the top, he helped himself to a handful. "The only reason Minnie has a page in our notebook is because she was there that day, that's all. No one in their right mind could ever seriously think Sweet Minnie has a mean bone in her entire five-foot, one-inch body."

"Gee, thanks." Tori took one last look at her pictures with Milo and then sat down on the edge of the hearth.

Charles pulled a chip out of his mouth and grabbed for the corner of the table with his free hand. "You can't be serious, love . . ."

"I wish I wasn't. But I am."

"H-how?" Debbie sputtered.

Clearing her throat, Tori searched for the best way to make her friends understand her fears. "Think back to Saturday. Opal was testy with all of us at one point or another, but with Minnie she was downright mean-spirited. If Minnie praised something, Opal came behind and bashed it. If one of us said something encouraging to Minnie about her project, Opal picked it apart. If Minnie made an observation about life, Opal called it stupid. It was ongoing and ceaseless, remember?"

"I remember. But that was Opal's doin', not Minnie's."

She hated to be the bearer of bad news, but ignoring the truth wasn't in her friends' best interest, either. "You're right. But that ongoing humiliation could be a motive."

"And what I shared with you on the phone last night could be the means."

All eyes trained in on Rose, with Margaret Louise breaking through the blanket of silence that had enveloped the room. "You, *too*, Rose?"

"I'm the one who put the thought in Victoria's head, Margaret Louise." Rose shoved the dishcloth in Charles's non-chip-holding hand, and took up residency in the center of the living room. "Minnie was in that room with Opal for a good twenty minutes or so toward the end of the day. When she came out, she looked visibly unsettled."

"Probably because she'd been on the receiving end of another series of insults," Debbie countered. "I can't imagine *not* being unsettled by someone so malicious."

The top of Charles's triangle got two snaps as he rocked back on his heels. "No. Way. No. How."

"Sweet people can snap, too," Tori said, borrowing her husband's earlier statement. "It happens all the time."

"But Minnie is over eighty years old!"

Rose's shoulders hunched forward with a cough and stayed that way as she began to speak. "*I'm* over eighty, Debbie, and emotions can make me capable of things I might not otherwise be able to do any longer."

Charles gave a single snap. "Wait! When did Minnie go into the room? Maybe it was before I did . . . in which case Opal was alive and just as nasty as ever."

"I'm not sure. I—"

Tori silenced the rest of Rose's sentence with a hand. "Minnie came into the library today to inquire about a book."

"That doesn't mean anything," Dixie snapped.

"But the title of the book might." All eyes in the room rebounded back to Tori with Dixie's raised eyebrow serving as the question Tori hated to answer. But she had no choice. "*Getting Away with Murder.*"

Milo was waiting for her in the bed when she emerged from the bathroom with her teeth brushed and her face scrubbed clean. Somehow, just seeing him there, smiling at her from the pillow next to hers, made everything feel a little less hopeless.

"So while you were having your meeting this evening, I did a little research on the computer."

She sat on the edge of the bed and slid her feet from her slippers. "Research on what?"

"Amish country."

"Milo, I still need to check with Nina first, remember?"

"I remember. I was just looking is all." He bolted upright, wrapped his arms around her torso, and pulled her onto the bed next to him. "Now, that's better . . ."

She rested her head on his chest and sighed. "I agree. So, did you find anything exciting?"

"Other than the perfect bed-and-breakfast, you mean?"

Rising up on her elbow, she smiled down at him. "You found one?"

"I did. It's in Heavenly, Pennsylvania—a quaint little town right in the heart of Amish country. The pictures of this inn are incredible, and the sample dinner menus posted on its website made me hungry."

"And that's different because . . . ," she teased.

"Ha. Ha. Seriously though, if Nina can cover you, I'm confident you're going to love this place."

"Does this bed-and-breakfast have a name?"

"Sleep Heavenly."

"Sleep Heavenly," she repeated, her lips inching upward with a smile. "Sounds perfect."

"Doesn't it though?" He guided her head back down to his chest and kissed the top of her forehead. "Anyway, I don't want to get too excited in case this doesn't pan out, you know?"

"Even if it doesn't, we can go a different time, can't we?"

"We can."

She took a moment to trace her index finger along his

ab muscles and then flopped onto her back and stared up at the ceiling. "Ugh. Ugh. Ugh! I so don't like the way the meeting ended tonight."

"So what did they say when you told them about the book Minnie checked out?"

"Charles covered his ears, Dixie went all turbo on me, Debbie tried to say in a slightly nicer way than Dixie had that I must have misunderstood Minnie's request, and Leona just kept petting Paris."

"What about Margaret Louise?"

She fiddled with the button on her pajamas as her eyes remained glued straight ahead. "You know, my great-grandpa used to paint the ceilings in his home every five years or so. Maybe I should do that in here. You know, brighten it up a little . . . And while I'm at it, I can put a fresh coat on this entire room."

Milo's hand closed over her finger and guided it back down to his chest. "The ceiling and the walls are fine, Tori."

She lowered her gaze to his. "Margaret Louise is the only one who seemed a tiny bit swayed by the title of the book Minnie requested."

"What did she say?"

"Nothing. But she didn't argue with me like Dixie and Debbie did, and she didn't stare at me like I'd grown a second head the way that Charles did. She just sat there for a few moments in utter silence and then fished the notebook and pen out of Charles's bag."

"And?"

"I don't know. She wrote something down— presumably on Minnie's page."

"Okay, see? That's a good sign. Maybe Margaret Louise, at least, is willing to consider the possibility that Minnie might be responsible for Opal's death . . ."

"But what happens if I'm still not sure *I'm* willing to consider the possibility that Minnie did this?"

Releasing her hand, Milo rolled onto his side and gently tapped her nose. "That's all it is, Tori. A possibility. One you can't ignore. But choosing to explore it doesn't mean you're ready to snap the cuffs into place and cart this woman off to jail. Give the others time to absorb what you told them tonight. It's really not much different than how you felt last night when Rose called her out as a suspect. You didn't want to believe it, either."

"I still don't."

"I know you don't. And I'm hoping that this whole book thing is simply some sort of really strange coincidence. But until you know for sure, you can't ignore it. Not if you're truly committed to figuring out what happened on Saturday."

She, too, rolled onto her side, the sight of her husband looking at her with such love and tenderness making it difficult to speak. "I—I am. For Rose."

"Then you have to look at all of the facts. Even if that means you have to look at ones you don't like or that make you the unpopular kid in the room for a little while."

"The unpopular kid in the room," she repeated. "Yup, that pretty much sums up what I was by the time everyone took their empty plates and sewing stuff and headed out the back door."

"They all love you, Tori, you know that. Just give them a little time to step back, that's all."

Everything Milo was saying made perfect sense. The key was getting her heart to catch up with what her head knew to be true.

"At least I've got Rose in my corner."

Milo pulled her close. "Rose and me," he corrected.

Chapter 14

Tori counted the number of people in line at the counter and, with the help of a little mental math, stepped inside Debbie's Bakery. Assuming all but maybe one or two of the patrons knew what they wanted before they approached the register, she'd be able to sit down with her order and still make it to the library on time.

Taking advantage of her wait, she scanned the tables to her right. She recognized a town council member (reading a paper and sipping a coffee), Lana Turner, owner of Turner's Gifts 'N More (feverishly working on a crossword puzzle), and a man she was almost certain lived in Milo's neighborhood (laughing softly into a cell phone).

"Victoria, right?"

At the sound of her name, she turned to find a vaguely

familiar man studying her as he, too, waited in line. She tried to place him, but other than knowing he was out of context in the bakery, she was at a loss.

A friend of Milo's from his men's group, maybe?

He thrust out his hand. "Travis—Travis Beaker. I met you the other day at—".

"Oh yes, I'm so sorry," she said as her hand briefly disappeared inside his. "I knew you looked familiar . . ."

Pointing down at his navy collared shirt, he made a face. "When I took this gig, I wasn't expecting to be hanging around for more than a night. Fortunately, the fella who owns the bed-and-breakfast where we're staying is the same size as me."

Ahhh, yes, the reason I couldn't place him at first . . .

"Anyway, any chance I might see that friend of yours here?"

"Friend?"

"You know, the young, attentive one." He pointed to the moving line and waited as she scooted up a spot. "Frosted hair, long eyelashes, has some sort of pet rabbit . . ."

"Oh, you mean Leona."

"That's it! Leona."

She contemplated correcting him on both the young and frosted part, but, in the end, she let it go. Besides, without his uniform, Travis was off Leona's radar, anyway.

"Leona is a busy woman. Between running two businesses, caring for Paris, and entertaining a dear friend who is in town for a few days, I doubt she'll be making an appearance here this morning."

They stepped forward in unison as yet another

customer paid for their order and exited the line. "Oh. Okay. Any chance you have her phone number?"

"I'm sorry, I can't give that out without her permission, but I'll be sure to let her know you were asking about her the next time we cross paths."

Disappointment pulled at his stature as they stepped still closer to the counter. "Oh. Right. Yeah, I'm sorry, I guess I shouldn't have put you in that position just now. But could you do me a favor? If you see her, could you tell her thank you for her kindness the other day? If I came across as unfriendly, it wasn't her."

"I'm sure she didn't think that, but I'll let her know." With just three people to go until she could place her order, Tori pointed at the chalkboard sign on the back wall. "While everything is pretty much mind-blowing in this place, I highly recommend the blueberry scone. They're to die for."

To die for . . .

Blinking away the image of Opal's face as it had looked in death, Tori cast about for something else to say before it was her turn to order. She considered (and discarded) Leona and the weather from her list of possibilities before settling on the only one that made any sense.

"So, um, how's it going?" Then, aware of her own vagueness, she stepped it up a notch. "You know, with having to remain in Sweet Briar to be questioned by police?"

He raked a hand through his graying hair, shrugging as he did. "Obviously, if I had my druthers, I'd rather be home. But considering nothing is really there, either, I guess I shouldn't complain."

"I suppose it's safe to assume you didn't know the victim before Saturday's event?"

"Actually, I did. Though that wasn't necessarily a good thing."

She felt her head jerk back a hairbreadth before she reined in her shock. "I'm sorry, I guess I don't understand."

"Yeah you do. You saw Opal on Saturday. She was like that all the time—to every person she came in contact with. If you passed too closely to her on the sidewalk, she'd glare. If you turned to offer her the sign of peace at church and she deemed you to be unworthy, she'd merely offer a finger wave in response and then roll her eyes as she turned away. And if you happened to see her out and about in a place just like this, she didn't take kindly to waiting her turn. So she didn't. But the part I hate most was her money's pull in Jasper Falls. It came ahead of everything—safety, common sense, life."

Tori took advantage of the line's forward motion to ponder her next question. On one hand it was good Margaret Louise had taken possession of the notebook after the previous night's sewing circle gathering, but on the other hand, she could have jotted down what Travis had said while he was placing his order . . .

"So you and Samantha knew her before," she mused aloud, as much for her own ears as his.

His dark eyes swung back to Tori. "I'm pretty sure we all did, except maybe Miranda. Jasper Falls isn't much bigger than Sweet Briar, you know? The biggest difference of course is the fact that we've got two bars— one on each end of town, a standard run-of-the-mill roadside motel, a teahouse for the rich and famous, and a sewing museum instead of a shop."

"A teahouse for the rich and famous?" Tori moved up as the person in front of her gave their order.

"According to my Ginny, the women who go there all wear skirts and dresses and, I imagine, drink their tea with their pinkies extended. Unlike this place"—he hooked his thumb toward the line of people behind them—"where it's just normal people looking for a cup of coffee and a decent muffin while they read the local paper."

"Is Ginny your wife?"

His eyes shifted to the floor in lieu of an answer just as Emma's voice filled the sudden silence. "Hey there, Tori. Hot chocolate and a blueberry scone to go?"

Unsure of what to make of the change in the man's demeanor, she turned and smiled at Debbie's employee. "Hi, Emma. Actually, I'll take the scone on a plate today, but let's stick with the to-go cup for the coffee."

"*Coffee*?" At Tori's answering nod, Emma grinned and reached for a small powder blue cup. "I take it your sewing circle ran later than normal last night, eh?"

"Something like that, I guess." She reached into her purse and pulled out her wallet while Emma busied herself with Tori's order. When the blueberry scone was plated and the coffee poured, Tori handed the girl a twenty and gestured over her shoulder. "I've got his order, too."

Emma took the bill, counted back the change, and handed it back. "He left while you were placing your order, Tori."

*   *   *

She tossed her keys onto her desk and stared out over the library grounds, the hundred-year-old moss-draped trees dappling the morning sunlight across the grass. As was usually the case at that time of the day, Mr. Downing was seated on the bench to the right of the front walkway, his ankle balanced atop his right knee while he chuckled to himself over whatever comic strip had caught his fancy at that exact moment.

More often than not, when she stood there at the window looking out over the very same scene each day, she imagined herself enjoying a leisurely start to her day—relishing the sun on her face, waving to friends, and immersing herself in the local news.

"That's it!"

"What's it, Victoria?"

Tori spun around so fast she bumped into the back of her chair and sent it hurling into the edge of her desk. "Margaret Louise! How did you get in here?"

"You left the back door unlocked and so I just came walkin' right in." Margaret Louise waddled into the room, took note of the open-topped to-go cup on Tori's desk, and then slowly lowered herself onto the closest folding chair. "I tried wavin' from the grass but you were lookin' somewhere else."

"I guess I was zoning more than I realized."

"I was figurin' you were still mad at me."

She backed the chair up enough to sit down and tried to focus on her sweat-suit-wearing friend. "Why would I be mad at you?"

"For not standin' by you last night when you were pointin' your sleuthin' finger in Saint Minnie's direction."

Tori opened her mouth to protest, but closed it as Margaret Louise held up her hand. "Now b'fore you start explainin', I've got some explainin' of my own to do first. I wasn't expectin' to hear that stuff 'bout Minnie. But if I've learned anythin' in all our investigatin', it's that ignorin' things helps nothin'. And ignorin' two plus two ain't smart, neither."

"Two plus two?"

"Minnie's disappearin' into the project room on Saturday plus her wantin' a book 'bout gettin' away with murder."

She set her elbows on the desk and lowered her chin onto her hands. "I don't want to look at Minnie for this any more than anyone else does, Margaret Louise. That woman is completely and utterly adorable. But that said, if she took a person's life—even a person as nasty as Opal Goodwin—I'm not going to look the other way. That's not who I am."

"I know that, Victoria. I just needed to do a little digestin' is all."

"And now?"

"I'm done digestin'."

"So you're willing to consider Minnie even if it's not what you want to do?" she asked.

"If you can, I can." Margaret Louise pulled Tori's to-go cup close enough to peek inside. "*Coffee*, Victoria?"

"Stressful night," she said by way of explanation.

Leaning over, Margaret Louise grabbed hold of her tote bag and hoisted it onto her lap. Then, reaching inside, she rummaged around until she found their notebook of suspects and opened it to Minnie's page. "We were so busy waitin' for my brownies to get Samantha's gums flappin' we forgot to really find out whether any of them knew Opal before Saturday. Course now we know Samantha did, but we don't know 'bout the others."

"Yes we do."

Margaret Louise's eyes narrowed. "We do?"

She dropped her hands to the desk and leaned back against her chair. "They all did, except Miranda."

"Have you been investigatin' without me, Victoria?"

"Nope. Just getting coffee." She grabbed her cup, took a sip, and then handed the rest to her friend.

Margaret Louise downed the rest of the now luke-warm liquid and tossed the empty cup into the trash. "What does gettin' coffee at Debbie's have to do with investigatin'?"

"Travis was there. And it was in chatting with him that I found out they're all from Jasper Falls."

"I've been to the sewin' museum in Jasper Falls!"

"I'm guessing that's why everyone was from Jasper Falls—because Rose and Miranda probably figured a town with that much interest in sewing would take note of a few flyers advertising a sewing weekend."

"Makes sense to me." Margaret Louise jotted something on each suspect's page and then turned back to Minnie's. "So what were you gushin' 'bout when I came in just now?"

"I don't remember—wait! That's right. I forgot." Tori swiveled her chair to the left and powered on her office computer, her mind already skipping ahead to the time she'd need to complete the task—time she didn't necessarily have during her workday. "How busy are you today?" she asked, stealing a quick glance in Margaret Louise's direction."

"I'm here, ain't I?"

She punched in her library password and waited as her start-up screen sprang to life. "It may be an exercise in futility, but I'm thinking it might be a good idea to go through the Jasper Falls newspaper archives over the past few months and see what we can find on Opal, specifically in relation to any of the tour members. Maybe Samantha isn't the only one who had an issue with the woman."

"Surely you don't have those papers here, do you? Jasper Falls is almost two hours away."

"Not in hard-copy form, we don't. But as a library in the state of South Carolina, we have access to the catalogues of every other library in the state. That means we can see what's on each other's shelves, as well as access each other's local newspapers." She pulled up the correct site and plugged in Jasper Falls. Seconds later, she found the name of the town's paper—the *Jasper Falls Courier*—and was directed to their main site with no restrictions on content. "Okay, cool. See this search bar right here in the upper right-hand corner? That's where you're going to plug in Opal Goodwin's name. If she's as important in that town as both Samantha and Travis indicated, a whole slew of articles about her should pop up on the screen. Read as many of them as you can and see what you can learn about Opal. With any luck, one of the other names from our notebook will show up a time or two and hand us a motive for murder."

"Victoria? Have I told you b'fore how smart you are?"

"Yes, you have, although I suspect you're rather biased

at this point." Tori moved the cursor into the search bar, typed in Opal's name, and hit enter. Forty hits dating back over the past twelve months popped up on the screen. "Whoa. Samantha and Travis weren't kidding when they said Opal was a presence in Jasper Falls . . ."

The folding chair creaked as Margaret Louise pushed herself up and onto her feet. "Now, Victoria, it's two minutes to nine and you've got a library to open."

Reluctantly, Tori pushed her chair away from the computer and stood, her eyes still riveted on the screen. "Just make a note of what you do and don't read so I can get the rest either on my lunch break or when my workday is over, okay?"

"That's a ten-four, Victoria." Margaret Louise shoved her way past Tori and into the desk chair, the woman's excitement over the task ahead impossible to miss. "Now get to work and leave me to my investigatin', will you?"

Chapter 15

Tori pulled her ham and cheese sandwich from the brown paper lunch sack and extended half of it across the picnic table. "So, did you find anything that could help us?"

"I can't take your lunch, Victoria."

"Yes, you can," she insisted. "You've been reading through news archives for me all morning long. You've got to be hungry."

"I ain't sayin' I'm not hungry. I'm just sayin' I can't take your lunch."

"And I'm just sayin' you can . . . or I won't eat, either."

Margaret Louise's brown eyes danced. "You're startin' to sound like me, Victoria, you know that?"

Resting the woman's half of the sandwich on a napkin, Tori moved on to the small bag of pretzels she'd packed along with her sandwich earlier that morning. "There's enough of these for us to share, too."

"I really shouldn't," Margaret Louise said as she reached into the center of the table and helped herself to three pretzels. "Librarians need their sustenance."

"And so do Mee Maws of eight grandchildren who also happen to be helping one of those librarians solve a murder case."

"Touché!"

Tori took a bite of her half and waited for her friend to answer the original question. When nothing transpired other than a few happy eating noises, she tried again. "Okay, Margaret Louise, the suspense is killing me. Did you find anything we can use? Anything at all?"

Margaret Louise matched Tori's bite with a larger one while gesturing around the library grounds with her free hand. "When the board first mentioned puttin' a few of these picnic tables 'round the library, I thought it was silly. All I kept thinkin' was libraries are for readin', not eatin'. But I can't tell you how many times I've used one since they put them out—for readin' with Lulu when she just couldn't wait to get home with whatever book she checked out, for a post-story-time snack with Molly Sue, and sometimes for just some plain old sittin' and watchin'."

"I couldn't agree more." Tori shook a pretzel between them in mock frustration. "I also know you're stalling and that I only have about twenty-five minutes left of my lunch break."

"Anyone ever tell you you're an impatient little thing, sometimes?" Margaret Louise plucked the pretzel from

Tori's outstretched fingers and popped it in her mouth with a mischievous grin.

"Anyone ever tell you you're a pill—albeit a loveable one—sometimes?"

Margaret Louise's grin morphed into a belly laugh and a nod of surrender. "Many times, Victoria, many times."

She returned to her own sandwich but kept her attention firmly on the woman seated on the other side of the table. "So tell me, what do we or don't we have?"

"Oh, we got somethin' all right, Victoria." Margaret Louise collected her sandwich crumbs into her hand, brushed them into the empty bag, and then moved the notebook from its holding spot on the bench to a prominent position on the table. With a flick of her thick wrist, she opened the notebook and flipped to the final third of its pages. "In the beginnin' I was plannin' on addin' anything I found to the correct suspect's page, but then I thought it made more sense just to put it all in one place and divvy it up later."

"Okay . . ."

Keenly aware of the information she possessed, Margaret Louise took a slow, deep breath and shifted her weight forward against the edge of the table. "Gracelyn Moses had a run-in with Opal, too—the last one bein' one so silly Nina caught me mutterin' under my breath when she came into the office to fetch her lunch."

Tori sat up tall, her last two remaining bites of sandwich forgotten. "Last one? You mean there was more than one run-in between them?"

"The articles I found didn't make mention of Gracelyn's feelin' 'bout things, but as a mama I can imagine how much her buttons must've been poppin'."

"Tell me."

"Well, it seems Gracelyn's children like ownin' their own businesses like my Jake. And 'bout a year ago, her son tried to open a motorcycle shop. Opal, from what the article said, wasn't havin' that in Jasper Falls. Said a shop like that would bring in the kind of people their town didn't need or want. The council tabled the request, and Opal bought that buildin' space right out from under Gracelyn's son."

Tori plucked a pretzel from the napkin in the center of the table and nibbled off a few pieces of salt. "Interesting . . . what did *she* put in that space?"

"That, right there, Victoria, is why we do such good investigatin' together. We think alike." Margaret Louise tapped the tip of her index finger to her temple. "I read that story and thought the same thing. So I did a little research on the address of that particular space, and guess what?"

"What?"

"It's vacant. Neat and tidy, yes, but empty."

With no more salt left to nibble off, Tori popped the bite-sized pretzel into her mouth. "And the other incident between Gracelyn and Opal?"

"Well, 'bout a month ago, Gracelyn's daughter approached the board 'bout openin' a clothin' shop for teens. Seems Gracelyn's daughter is quite a seamstress and has always wanted to stock a shop with her own creations."

"And?"

"Seems Opal didn't want that shop, either."

She stopped chewing and stared at the woman on the other side of the table. "Why on earth not?"

"Gracelyn's daughter brought a few of her creations to the meetin' to show, and Opal took objection to some of the skirts bein' too short and the shirts bein' too revealin'." Margaret Louise consulted her notes for a moment and then slowly lifted her gaze back to Tori's. "Opal said she wasn't goin' to support the further downgradin' of today's young people in Jasper Falls. So she bought that buildin', too."

"Wow."

"I know. Don't that just jar your preserves, Victoria?"

"Something like that, I guess." Tori scooped up the napkin that had housed her sandwich and crumpled it into a ball. "Can you imagine actually having the kind of money that would enable you to buy a building and use it for nothing just so you can dictate what kind of businesses do or don't come into your town?"

"No, I can't. Nor can I imagine dashin' people's dreams like that. Opal should be ashamed of herself."

"Opal's dead." Tori stuffed the crumpled napkin into the lunch sack and then swiveled her left leg over the back side of the bench. "I've still got about fifteen minutes. Should we walk around the grounds a few times?"

"Sounds good to me. My twin is always gettin' after me 'bout exercisin'."

They crossed the grass to the sidewalk and followed it east across the front edge of the property, the afternoon sun warming the tops of their heads between open breaks in the tree coverage. "I would imagine Gracelyn wasn't a big fan of Opal's after that whole thing with her kids, but was it a motive for murder?"

"If my Jake had his heart set on openin' a business, and someone came along and stepped all over his idea for no reason than bein' mean, I'd be as mad as a bear with a sore butt."

"I would be, too," Tori said. "But would that be enough to make you *kill* someone?"

"Put a hurtin' on 'em? Sure. But killin' 'em? No. But then again, wantin' a citizens' police academy and havin' the idea get shot down by Opal ain't a reason to kill, either."

Margaret Louise had a point. Yes, Samantha and Gracelyn both had reasons to despise the very ground Opal walked on. But there was a big gap between disliking someone and being able to wrap a cord around their neck and pull.

"I'm afraid you're right, Margaret Louise." Tori released a sigh as they reached the southeast corner of the library grounds and turned left, the chance to stretch her legs proving to be more and more invigorating with each passing step. "I really should do this every day. It's nice to get a little fresh air after being cooped up all morning."

"I prefer my fresh air sittin' on the front porch blowin' bubbles with one of my grandbabies."

"Until I have my own children, I'll have to settle for walking, I guess." Tori lifted her chin to the sun and smiled. "Milo wants to take me to Amish country over the holidays. He found a bed-and-breakfast there that he's all excited about."

"Sleep Heavenly?" Margaret Louise asked between labored breaths.

Tori stopped. "You've been there?"

"Once. 'Bout eight years ago while Jake's daddy was still alive, God rest his soul. There was a wonderful woman runnin' that place all by herself. Put my cookin' to shame each and every night we were there."

"I find that hard to believe. You are the most amazing cook I've ever met." And she meant it. Margaret Louise's talent in the kitchen was practically legendary throughout Sweet Briar.

"Then you ain't never met Diane Weatherly—Sleep Heavenly's innkeeper extraordinaire. If you had, you'd be singin' her praises, too, Victoria."

"Wow. You and Milo sure know how to paint an irresistible picture, don't you?"

"I ain't speakin' nothin' but the truth, Victoria." Margaret Louise touched her stomach and gave it a jiggle. "See that? A good ten pounds of that came from that woman's cookin'. I thought I'd died and gone to Heaven."

"But that was eight years ago," Tori reminded.

"I reckon that's true. But that woman's cookin' is why I *put on* that ten. My eatin' is why I've *kept on* that ten."

"Good afternoon, ladies. Beautiful weather we're having on this fine November day."

Tori looked up to find Mr. Downing caning his way across the grounds. Under his left arm was a folded newspaper with the crossword puzzle he'd opted not to finish that morning. She knew this with absolute certainty because the elderly man's day followed a very specific routine—half the puzzle in the morning while sitting on the bench to the east of the library, half the puzzle in the late afternoon on the bench turned to face the western side. "Indeed it is, Mr. Downing. So how are you? Did you have a nice walk over to the fire station?"

"I did. And, for what it's worth, I beat Chief Granderson at a game of checkers. And when I was done, I beat

Chief Dallas at a game, too." The elderly man slowed to a stop with the assistance of his cane. Once his balance was established, he pulled out the paper from its holding spot between his elbow and his side and waved it between Tori and Margaret Louise. "Most people in Rose Winters's position would probably close down their shop and give up. But not her—no siree. I like that in a woman."

"You like *what* in a woman, Mr. Downing?"

"Spunk." He unfolded the newspaper to reveal a sale flyer wedged inside. "I just hope it pays off."

Confused, Tori followed the man's attention down to the brightly colored paper, its notification of a sale registering a split second before the SewTastic logo. "Oh. Wow. So Rose is really doing it—good for her."

"You know somethin', Victoria? I've been wantin' to make some new placemats for Thanksgivin' Day. Somethin' festive and fun—like maybe Pilgrims and Indians. Wanna come with me to pick out just the right fabric when you get off work?"

At Tori's nod, Mr. Downing tucked the flyer back inside his paper and tightened his hold on his cane in preparation for his trek across the grounds to his favorite afternoon bench. "Now you ladies be sure to tell Rose I was asking about her, will you?"

Chapter 16

Tori was so busy absorbing the latest holiday touches in SewTastic's front window, she was unprepared for Margaret Louise's sudden stop just inside the doorway.

"Whoa. Sorry about that, Margaret Louise," she said, disengaging herself from the woman's back. "I didn't know you were stopping."

"I—I—I . . ."

"Margaret Louise? Are you okay?"

Once again, Margaret Louise tried to speak, but as was the case the first time, nothing of any consequence came out.

Confused, Tori followed her friend's wide eyes across the shop to the woman standing behind the counter.

Tori did a double take.

Leona?

"I—I didn't know her forehead was capable of scrunchin' like that," Margaret Louise whispered. "I thought Dr. Silverman's magic needle kept that from happenin'."

"Am I the only one in this town who didn't know Leona has started consulting a plastic surgeon?"

Margaret Louise's brown eyes turned on Tori. "Started? How 'bout she's had Dr. Silverman on speed dial for 'bout ten years now."

"How come I didn't know about this?"

"She wants people to believe she's been blessed with some sort of internal fountain of youth."

"Then how come Charles knew?" Tori asked, her tone indignant even to her own ears.

"I'm not the one you should be askin' that question—"

Leona's chin whipped upward with a hint of boredom and disdain. "I should ask the two of you to stop clogging up the entryway, but since we haven't had a customer all day, you may as well just keep standing there babbling incessantly."

"No one's come in?" Tori made her way around Margaret Louise and over to the counter. "At all?"

"Actually, that's not true. Manny from Bud's Brew Shack brought over the chef's salad I ordered at lunch . . . a handful of teenage boys came in on a dare . . . and Miranda is in the back office with Rose as we speak. Other than that, all interest shown toward SewTastic came from the sidewalk via pointed fingers and not-so-hushed voices."

"What were they sayin'?" Margaret Louise ambled past Tori and leaned against the counter.

Leona pushed the store's ledger off to the side and

removed her glasses long enough to break her personal mantra regarding eye rubbing. "I believe the first group— those insufferable women from the town's springtime beautification committee—said they wouldn't be caught dead in this store. Of course the tall, gangly one with the gap in her teeth took the opportunity to make some sort of snide comment I chose to ignore." Leona ventured out from behind the counter to flop down on the chair Rose had insisted they have for customers who needed to take a break from shopping. "Then, about an hour later, there was a woman clearly on her way into the shop when someone from the sidewalk pulled her aside and quite obviously filled her in on what happened over the weekend. Needless to say, she turned and walked away. I must say I hope she found herself a shoe store to stop in because the ones she was wearing were beyond hideous."

Tori didn't know what to say, so she said nothing. Even Margaret Louise remained silent.

"Oh, and then there was the group who pulled out some sort of stick from one of their bags and used it to take a picture of themselves in front of the SewTastic sign. One picture was of them all smiling, one was of them looking shocked, and the other was of them pretending to choke one another with their bare hands."

"Maybe they take crazy pictures everywhere they go and they just decided to take this one in front of the shop because of how pretty it looks."

Leona cast a tired glare in Tori's direction. "And if you believe that, Victoria, I have the recipe for a perfect man I can sell you."

"Victoria already has that, Twin."

Clearly too tired to spar with her sister, Leona took off her glasses again and rested the back of her head against the chair. "SewTastic has become the tourist stop Rose and I wanted it to be—only it's for a reason that has nothing whatsoever to do with making sewing-related purchases and everything to do with Opal being strangled to death in our project room."

"Was Rose around to see these people taking pictures of the shop and pointing at it all day?" Tori asked.

"Yes. She's the one who noticed it first." Leona fiddled with her glasses for a moment but left them on her lap. "I just wish she could recognize the writing on the wall for what it is, rather than seeing it as some sort of indication we need to try something else—like this sale she insisted we have that hasn't even brought one single person through those doors today."

"It brought in me and Victoria, didn't it?" Margaret Louise wandered over to the fabric containers and rifled through the one dedicated to the upcoming holiday season. "I'm wantin' to make placemats for our Thanksgivin' dinner this year, so I'm gonna be needin' a lot of fabric."

Placing her glasses across the bridge of her nose, Leona stood and made her way over to the cutting table, the click of her heels against the tiled floor echoing around them. "I know what you're trying to do, Margaret Louise, and it is appreciated, but you can't make enough placemats to singlehandedly keep this place open."

"Now Twin, we've all seen sicker dogs that got well."

Tori looked from Leona to Margaret Louise and back again. "Dogs? When did we start talking about dogs?"

Positioning her hands on her slender yet still shapely

hips, Leona narrowed her eyes on her sister. "Name one, Margaret Louise."

"Brady's Jewelry."

"Hello?" Tori jiggled her hands between her friends but neither acknowledged the gesture. "Can one of you take a breath long enough to get me back up to speed?"

"That doesn't count!" Leona protested.

"Course it counts, Twin. If that shop can recover from a scandal *and* a murder, SewTastic can come bouncin' back after this thing with Opal. Ain't that right, Victoria?"

"This *thing*?" Leona snapped. "You mean this *murder*?"

Still unsure of how dogs tied in to the subject at hand, Tori finally managed to get the gist of the conversation volleying around her head. "You know something, Leona? Margaret Louise is right. Brady's Jewelry rebounded from way worse. If *they* can, so can you and Rose."

Leona pointed to the fabric that had thus far garnered the most attention from Margaret Louise and, at her sister's nod of agreement, began to unravel it from its base. For a moment, Tori simply watched, the sight of uncut fabric one she'd loved since she was a little girl. She supposed some of that was the promise it held—of a new shirt or skirt, a placemat or a curtain. Some of it was also the knowledge that with a new project came time with dear friends like Rose.

Rose . . .

"So where is Rose again?" she asked, looking around.

Leona waited for Margaret Louise's approval on the amount she'd unraveled thus far and then prepared to cut. "She's in the office with Miranda. Brainstorming."

"I thought that was on yesterday's agenda."

"It was. This is, apparently, part two," Leona drawled.

"May I check in with them?" she asked, hooking her thumb over her shoulder.

"Of course. And when you do, can you let Rose know I'll be closing up in about ten minutes? Charles and I have plans this evening, and I want to go home and freshen up a bit first."

"What are you two plannin' on doin'?"

If Leona answered, Tori didn't hear the details. Instead, she headed down the hallway toward the surprisingly animated voices coming from the partially open doorway at its end. She couldn't make out what was being said, but she could tell, by her elderly friend's tone, that pessimism was giving way to something that sounded a bit like hope.

Tori stopped just outside the open door. "Rose?"

"Oh, Victoria . . . come in, come in." Rose started to rise from her rocking chair, but stopped as Tori motioned for her to remain seated. "Miranda, you remember my special friend, Victoria, don't you?"

"Of course." The business consultant stood and extended her hand to Tori. "I want you to know that it was lovely of you to bring that signed book all the way over to the inn for Lucinda on Sunday. It really lifted her spirits."

"The book was from Debbie Calhoun, actually, but it was my pleasure to bring it by." Tori waited for Miranda to reclaim her folding chair and then took possession of an empty one on the other side of Rose. "How is everyone doing? I imagine being forced to stay longer than anticipated must be rather upsetting for everyone."

Brushing a renegade brown curl from her field of

vision, Miranda tsked softly under her breath. "For Samantha and Gracelyn, it's tiresome. From what I gather, Samantha is a real go-getter and doesn't like to sit idly by for any stretch of time. And Gracelyn is getting antsy because her kids are coming to visit her next weekend and she wants to be home, rolling out the red carpet and cooking all their favorite meals. So for them, yes, it's upsetting. But for Minnie and Lucinda, they're starting to see this as a sort of impromptu mini-vacation."

At the mention of Minnie, Tori and Rose exchanged glances. If Miranda noticed though, she didn't let on. Instead, the woman Tori estimated to be somewhere between five and ten years her senior, continued. "I've talked to all of them as a group over breakfast at the inn, and individually in the parlor, and none of them seem to be equating this whole mess to SewTastic itself, so that's good. If they don't see it that way, they won't portray it that way. Unfortunately, that doesn't mean others won't."

"I think the sale was a good step."

Rose's shoulders hunched forward ever so slightly. "A good step that netted nothing in return."

"Margaret Louise is buying some fabric right now," Tori offered.

"We need other people, Victoria."

She knew Rose was right. But she wasn't ready to accept defeat yet. "The sale just started, Rose. Give it a little time."

"And we will, of course, but what happened here over the weekend is going to require use of a complete reset button." Miranda tapped her finger atop the clipboard in her lap. "And this time, we need to work even harder to generate the kind of buzz that will overpower any lingering negativity."

"That makes sense. But how do you propose doing that? I mean, I'm sure you can host more tours, but don't you think a little distance between this one and a new one might be a good way to go?" Tori asked.

"We'll definitely do more tours," Miranda replied. "But yes, we'll wait a few months before trying to fill a new one. And when we do, maybe we can get a few of the other businesses in town involved and bill it as a complete weekend away for the sewing enthusiast."

"So then what kind of reset button are you talking about in terms of the immediate future?" Spying a bowl of pretzels atop Rose's makeshift desk, Tori helped herself to one and then held the bowl out for Miranda and Rose.

"We need to come up with a media campaign—radio, print, Internet, TV. But in order to do that, we need to hand deliver some aspect of this shop that will appeal to people. Like Rose's history as a seamstress, or maybe something about two unlikely forces uniting in a common endeavor, something like that."

Tori set the bowl back on the desk. "And you think that could work?"

"I do. If we hit it hard and don't let up."

She looked at Rose, the rapt interest on her friend's face setting off the faintest of warning bells in Tori's head. "This sounds all well and good, but I would imagine this would require a lot of time and attention on your part, Miranda—time and attention that will undoubtedly carry a hefty bill. Are you sure Leona is going to want to sink even more money into this place on what is, essentially, a gamble at this point?"

Miranda hugged her clipboard to her chest and shared a knowing smile with Rose. "Normally, yes, services like this would be billable. But I've agreed to do the work, free of charge, in exchange for a testimonial from Rose and Leona. Like them, I'm trying to get my business up off the ground, and positive word of mouth is the best form of advertisement there is."

"And Miranda knows the TV side of things really well. She even thinks we could wrangle a story on one of the local morning shows!"

There was no denying the unrestrained hope in Rose's voice—hope that had been sorely missing in every telephone conversation they'd had since Opal's murder. Even better though, was the sweet smile helping to ignite a rare light in her bifocal-enhanced eyes.

"Miranda, I don't know how to thank you," Tori said, scooting forward on her chair. "I've been so focused on trying to help figure out who did this, I haven't had any time to really brainstorm ways to help keep the shop afloat."

"Leave the business-saving part to me and Rose. I'm confident we can turn things around before there's any lasting damage to the shop's reputation." Miranda stood in unison with Tori but remained in front of her chair, all outward signs of enthusiasm temporarily fading. "I know you're going to think I'm crazy, and I probably am, but if you're serious about trying to figure out who killed Opal, I think you have to look at everyone— including Minnie."

Rose's head snapped up. "Did you say Minnie?"

Miranda shifted nervously from foot to foot, her gaze taking in all aspects of Rose's office except Rose and Tori. "I wish I could say I didn't, but I can't."

"Did you hear what she said, Victoria?" Rose asked. "She's thinking it might be Minnie, too."

She nodded at Rose but kept her focus squarely on Miranda. "Are you saying that because of something you saw or heard?"

"More like something I *didn't* hear."

Again, Tori and Rose exchanged looks.

"I'm not sure I understand what you mean," Tori said.

Miranda fidgeted with the corner of her clipboard for a few moments, her discomfort at both the question and the subject matter palpable. "It was just after I boarded the bus and found everyone sitting in their seat, waiting for Ms. Goodwin to finish her project."

"Go on . . ."

"Minnie was sitting in the front row just as she had on the trip from Jasper Falls that morning. She was listening to everyone's thoughts on the day to that point, chiming in with a little positive note each time—the food was great, the extra helpers were great, the shop was great, the inventory was great, the instructions were great. That sort of thing. But when one of them—I believe it was Gracelyn—made mention of Ms. Goodwin's atrocious behavior toward everyone connected with the event, Samantha and Lucinda vehemently agreed. Minnie, however, said absolutely nothing. She simply turned her attention out the window and let the conversation go on around her as if she wasn't there."

"Maybe she didn't have anything to add," Tori suggested. But even as she posed the possibility, she knew it didn't hold water. Opal had treated everyone poorly that day, but none worse than Minnie.

Miranda stopped fidgeting and ran her fingers through her wavy brown locks. "I don't know how she *couldn't*. What you saw in the shop was only part of the picture. The bus ride to the shop was another."

"Maybe Minnie is just the kind of person that doesn't like to speak ill of people," Tori suggested, although, even to her own ears, it didn't really fit. Minnie was probably one of the sweetest people Tori had ever met, but even the sweetest people had feelings and breaking points.

"She didn't react *at all*, Victoria. Not an eye roll, not a grunt, not a mumble—nothing."

Miranda had a point. Even if Minnie was the type who didn't like to say mean things, wouldn't the treatment she'd received at the hands of Opal have warranted some sort of reaction in that situation?

Not if Minnie was trying to fly under the radar . . .

Tori shivered away the unsettling thought and willed herself to focus on the positive for the moment. "Miranda, what you're planning to do for Rose with this media campaign is really pretty awesome. Thank you."

"It's my pleasure. Rose took a chance on me and my idea, and it's time I return the favor."

"Is there anything I can do to help?"

Miranda started to decline Tori's offer but stopped herself mid-swipe. "Just keep talking up the shop to everyone you know—friends, neighbors, loved ones, et cetera. Between that and giving the police a person to focus on for this crime, we should be on the way to disassociating SewTastic from Opal's murder once and for all."

"Even though it still happened here?" Tori challenged.

"Right now, people associate what happened to Ms. Goodwin with the store because there is nothing else to chew on at this particular time." Miranda checked her wristwatch and then slowly made her way to the door. "Once the police have someone to point to as a killer, that person will push to the front of people's thoughts in terms of this particular crime. Might they remember it happened at a store? Maybe. Heck, they might even remember it happening in a sewing store simply because of the way in which Ms. Goodwin was killed. But outside of those living in Sweet Briar at the present time, it will be a rare few that remember the name SewTastic in relation to Opal Goodwin's murder."

Chapter 17

As much as Tori loved her job and her friends, there was no denying the utter peace she felt when she and Milo were alone together. It didn't matter if they were refinishing a piece of furniture, weeding the front landscape, or taking a post-dinner walk around the neighborhood; as long as they were in each other's immediate vicinity, all was well.

It was as if his very presence made the tough parts of life less daunting and the bright spots all the more brilliant. How he did that, she wasn't entirely sure. But if she had to call out a few reasons, she'd choose his listening ability, his kind heart, and the same dimple-accompanied smile that was trained on her face at that very moment.

"So your day was good, I take it?" Milo handed her a glass of ice water and then took his place next to her on the couch.

She rested her cheek on his shoulder and basked in the warmth of his skin through his shirtsleeve. "What makes you say that?"

"That smile you were just giving me, for one . . ."

"Oh. No, that was just because I was marveling at my good fortune in landing you for my husband."

He pressed his lips to the side of her forehead and held them there for a moment. "Trust me, baby, the feeling is mutual."

"I'm glad." She popped up her head long enough to take a sip of her water, the vast change in pace from the rest of her day a welcome respite. "So how was school today? Kids good?"

"I think I'm beginning to see the early signs of holiday-itis. The conversation of choice during our opening time in the morning is all things Thanksgiving. By the time I wrap it up so we can start our lessons, my stomach is grumbling and I have an insatiable desire for turkey with all the trimmings. Well, all except cranberry sauce."

She returned her glass to the table and studied her husband closely. "Since when don't you like cranberry sauce?"

"Haven't you heard?" he asked, wide-eyed. "Cranberry sauce is the new gross."

It felt good to laugh and even better to hear Milo match it with his own. This was the part of her day she loved the most—the time spent getting caught up with Milo. He had a way of making her feel as if she'd been in the classroom with him instead of on the other side of town.

"So I guess I'll be taking cranberry sauce off the menu this year?" she teased.

"Don't you dare, Victoria Sinclair-Wentworth."

Victoria Sinclair-Wentworth . . .

Releasing a tired yet happy sigh, Tori brought her cheek back down onto Milo's shoulder. "I love the way that sounds, you know. Especially when it comes out of your mouth."

"I love saying it." He wrapped his arm around her shoulders and slowly guided her down until she was looking up at him from the center of his lap. Then, with a gentle hand, he smoothed her hair away from the sides of her face. "So how did things go for you today? Anything new on the whole Opal Goodwin front?"

She gazed up at the amber flecks in his eyes and weighed her options. She could answer him and risk ruining the mood she wasn't ready to lose just yet, or she could divert him back to his own day.

"Tori?"

Realizing he was waiting for her to say something, she worked to keep her smile in place even though she felt it losing its genuineness. "Your day sounds so much more appealing to me, though . . ."

"There's not much else to share. There was a mid-morning assembly with the fire department, followed immediately thereafter by lunch and recess. So other than giving you a blow by blow of the papers I graded during recess, and the paint Joey accidentally got in Chloe's hair during art, there's not much else to report."

"Please, please, please? Can't you find *something* else to tell me?"

He crossed his arms and shook his head.

"Nothing?" she prodded.

Again, he shook his head, only this time the smile

he was trying to hide behind a pretend pout won out, eliciting a laugh from her in the process.

"You're such a stinker." She reached above her head, wrapped her fingers around the edge of a throw pillow, and smacked it into his chest. "My day was so not laugh-worthy."

"Let me be the judge of that."

"Suit yourself." She pulled the pillow down onto her own chest and hugged it close. "I ran into Travis at Debbie's Bakery early this morning. He was in line behind me at the counter. Or, at least he was until I placed my order. Then he just sort of disappeared. Without getting anything to eat."

"Who's Travis?"

"The guy who drove the bus for Rose's tour."

"Oh. Okay. And?"

"Seems everyone knew Opal before Saturday—knew and *despised* Opal, I should say."

Milo captured her hand atop the pillow and interlaced his fingers with hers. "Anything specific as to *why* they all despised her so much?"

"From Travis, no. I get the sense that his issue with Opal stemmed from her attitude toward him and people like him."

"People like him? What does that mean?"

She revisited her conversation with Travis in her head and then did her best to convey the part that mattered to Milo. "People with less money, fewer connections."

"What kind of money did this woman have?" Milo asked, his tone of voice confirming the intrigue she saw crackling in his warm brown eyes.

"From what Margaret Louise was able to learn this morning, I'm guessing a lot."

"Margaret Louise was with you at Debbie's?"

"No. She showed up in my office about three minutes after I got there. She was determined to move our investigation along, so I set her up on the computer and let her do her thing while I did what I needed to do in the library." Swinging her feet onto the rug, Tori sat up and reached for her water glass. Two long sips later, she gestured toward the clock on the mantel. "I probably should start thinking about dinner. Can we move this into the kitchen so I can start pulling something together for us?"

"Sure." He followed her across the dining room and into the kitchen, his next question a testament to his ability to remain focused. "So what was Margaret Louise doing on the computer?"

"Looking through archives of the *Jasper Falls Courier* for anything that could tie Opal to any of the other tour members."

"Was that your idea?"

Tori opened the refrigerator, removed a covered baking dish from the middle rack, and carried it to the counter. Peeling back the cover, she inhaled the aroma of the teriyaki marinade she'd added to the pair of uncooked chicken breasts prior to leaving for work that morning. "I think it was something Travis said at Debbie's that made me think of the newspaper angle. So when Margaret Louise was itching to do something, it seemed a good way to get information without taking time away from my real job."

"Did she find anything?" Milo asked as he gathered his favorite grilling tools from the drawer.

"Remember how I told you that Opal put the kibosh on the citizens' police academy Samantha Williams wanted to get off the ground in Jasper Falls?" At Milo's nod, she continued. "Well, it seems Samantha wasn't the only one who had something she wanted squashed by Opal. Gracelyn Moses's kids each tried to get a business up and running in Jasper Falls over the past year. One— Gracelyn's son—wanted a motorcycle shop, and the other—her daughter—wanted to open a teen clothing shop. Opal kept both from happening."

Milo tucked the tongs and spatula under his left elbow and retrieved the baking dish with his right hand. "How?"

"By buying the building each was trying to lease."

Stopping halfway to the back door, Milo turned and stared at Tori. "Are you serious?"

"That's not even the best part." She opened the cabinet above the stove, pulled out a container of uncooked rice, and then readied a pot with water. "Opal didn't buy those buildings because she was trying to open a business. She bought them simply to keep Gracelyn's kids from doing so. Seems Opal didn't want the kind of clientele she feared would come with a motorcycle shop, and she wasn't terribly fond of the clothes Gracelyn's daughter was planning on selling in her store."

"So she bought the space out from under them?"

"Crazy, isn't it?"

"Wow." He finished his trek to the door but stopped short of actually stepping out onto the deck. "I can't even fathom someone doing that. Then again, I can't fathom someone killing because of that, either."

"I agree, but at least it paints a picture of Opal."

"An unattractive one, yes." He hooked the tongs over his shoulder in the direction of the deck. "I'll get the chicken going on the grill and then I'll be back in to help with the salad."

"I'll take care of that while I wait for the rice to cook. Should we eat out—"

The ring of her phone from its holding spot on the window ledge cut her question short and had her scrambling to check the Caller ID screen.

Rose.

"Milo, it's Rose. I'll keep it short, okay?"

"You're fine."

She smiled and brought the phone to her ear. "Hi, Rose."

"I don't want to keep you, Victoria. I've been doing far too much intruding on your time with Milo these past few days, but I wanted to say thank you before it slipped my mind."

"First, you're never an intrusion, okay?" She checked the status of the water in the pot and then headed back toward the refrigerator for the lettuce and assorted salad fixings. "And second, I'm not sure what you're thanking me for."

"For checking in on me all the time, for supporting me with this shop, and for trying to figure out what happened to that nasty old woman so it doesn't affect SewTastic any more than necessary . . ."

"It's nothing you wouldn't do for me in the same circumstance." With the phone balanced between her ear and her shoulder, Tori carried the salad fixings over to the counter. "Have you eaten yet? I could wrap a plate and bring it over in about an hour."

"I already ate. With Miranda. And before she left, she showed me how to fix that stitch in my kitchen curtain I've redone a half dozen times." Tori waited as Rose's sudden cough multiplied tenfold. When the woman finally returned to the line, her voice sounded tired. "I don't know if it helps or not, but Miranda mentioned trying to encourage the group to get out and about tomorrow. Seems they're getting a little short-tempered and she thinks a change of scenery might be good."

"It's worth a shot, I guess." Tori wedged the phone between her shoulder and her ear again and began to cut the cucumber she'd salvaged from the refrigerator. "Anyway, tomorrow is my day off. If you need anything, call my cell, okay?"

"Thank you, Victoria. For everything."

Chapter 18

"Tell me I'm not seeing you sitting at that desk tapping away on that computer."

"No, it's me." Tori peeked around the edge of the monitor and smiled sheepishly at her assistant. "I wish it wasn't, but it is."

Nina took a few steps forward and then stopped. "It's your day off. That means you can do anything you want. So why are you here?"

Why indeed . . .

To Nina, she simply shrugged and gave voice to the same explanation she'd been giving herself for the past hour. "I wanted to do a little more research on Rose's tour group members, and I don't have access to the *Jasper Falls Courier* at home."

"So do it tomorrow when you're working again."

It was the same argument she'd had with herself

when she abandoned her original plan for the day and, instead, got in the car and headed for the library. "But then another day has gone by. Don't you see, the sooner I figure out what happened, the sooner I can put this whole thing aside and truly focus on Thanksgiving and everything else I'd rather be thinking about."

Nina opened her mouth to protest but closed it along with a defeated shake of her head. "I feel like I should try to convince you to go home, but I know better. I'll leave you alone now."

"Thanks, Nina."

"You're not welcome." Nina gave a rare roll of her eyes and then headed back out into the hallway.

She knew Nina was right, knew she should be home making her shopping list for their Thanksgiving dinner, or putting the honeymoon pictures into the album she'd purchased, but knowing and doing were two very different things. Still, maybe if she focused really hard for the next hour, she could still manage to enjoy some of her day off . . .

Forcing her attention back on the screen, she continued scrolling down the list of articles in which Opal's name had appeared over the last year. Some of the links she clicked on netted a brief mention—a town council meeting on which she'd given a quote, a generous donation she'd made to a local charity, and on and on it went. Some links procured far more details, including a handful of feature stories about Opal Goodwin herself.

In each and every story, Tori was struck by the same thing—Opal had money and she liked people to know it. But despite all the posturing and boasting, Tori found herself seizing on the fact that Opal was more about doing rather than having. When Jasper Falls Elementary School needed a new playground, Opal donated the equipment and the manpower needed to get it up and running. When Jasper Falls Public Library needed to upgrade the patron computers, Opal replaced them with the latest technology. When the Jasper Falls Volunteer Fire Department needed new uniforms, Opal got them the best of the best.

Yes, everyone in Jasper Falls knew Opal was behind each and every one of those donations, but when all was said and done, the fact that the school had a new playground, the library had new computers, and the fire department had new uniforms was what mattered most. And Opal had made those things happen while also being the single driving force behind the construction and running of the Jasper Falls Sewing Museum.

Tori exited out of the article about the museum's ribbon-cutting ceremony two months earlier and quickly counted the remaining links pertaining to Opal Goodwin. "Seven more to go," she mumbled. Stretching her arms above her head, she swiveled her chair around until she was looking out over the library grounds, the mid-morning sun putting up a valiant fight against the first chilly day of the season. She scanned the benches and sidewalk to her left, the sight of Mr. Downing and his morning crossword puzzle bringing an instant smile to her lips. Turning her head to the right, her eyes found and followed a stout woman in her late sixties down the sidewalk and toward the library's front steps, her shoulders curved forward from a weight Tori could sense but not see. Grateful for the distraction, Tori leaned forward in an effort to put a name to the rosy-cheeked face, the thick eyebrows, the—

Gracelyn Moses . . .

Spinning around in her chair, Tori minimized the page of Opal-related links and stood, her self-made promise to avoid the library's main room no longer applicable. After all, information gleaned on the Internet lacked two key components in any investigation— body language and facial expressions.

She left her office and headed up the hallway to the library's main room. A quick inventory of her surroundings netted an elderly man using one of the public computers, an elderly woman—probably his wife—searching the mystery fiction aisle with a contented smile on her face, a young mother and her preschool-age child looking at the schedule of upcoming events, and Gracelyn making her way toward the front desk.

Nina was just opening her mouth to greet Gracelyn when the young mom diverted her attention onto the schedule. "Excuse me. Is the toddler-age story time mentioned on here a once-a-week activity?"

Tori moved in behind Nina and quietly tapped her on the shoulder. "You take this one and I'll take care of the new visitor."

"But you're not supposed to be here, remember?"

"It doesn't matter. I've got this." She turned as the new visitor approached the counter, a smile of recognition lighting the woman's otherwise tired eyes. "Good morning, Gracelyn. Welcome to our library."

"Victoria, hello. I was hoping you'd be here. I want to thank you for including us in your sewing circle meeting the other night. It was a bright spot in what has been an otherwise not-so-great week, let me tell you."

"Are you not enjoying your stay here in Sweet Briar?" Tori asked, lowering her voice.

"When it was just a visit, yes, I was enjoying it very much. But I was ready to go home two days ago."

Tori motioned Gracelyn to follow her to a small reading corner just beyond the bank of computers and invited her to sit. When the woman was settled in a chair, Tori pulled one of the opposing chairs closer. "I'm sorry you're going through this, Gracelyn. I'm sure you know that Rose and Leona never wanted anything like that to happen to anyone, much less inside their store."

"I know that, Victoria. I really do. I even know this pull of mine to go home makes no sense. In the grand scheme of things, there's nothing there for me anymore, anyway." Sadness played across Gracelyn's features only to be pushed aside by something much closer to a controlled rage. "But making that so wasn't enough for her, was it? No, now she's going to affect my life from the grave, too."

She tried to stop the gasp before it made it past her lips, but it was too late. All she could do now was hope that the man peeking at them around the computer monitor would go back to whatever it was he'd been doing before Tori claimed his attention. "Are you talking about Opal Goodwin?" she asked quietly.

Gracelyn's tone remained angry. "Who else?"

"Sh-she's affecting your life from the grave?"

"I'm being forced to stay in this town because of her, aren't I?" Gracelyn hiked her purse onto her lap and reached inside for a tissue. Balling it up against her nose, she blew. "And she's *dead*."

"I don't understand."

"I don't, either," Gracelyn said, her anger showing signs of fatigue. "I've always believed that the afterlife would be a time for people to fix the mean things they did on earth. Sadly, it appears as if I was wrong. Now, instead of just exiling my kids, she's found a way to get me out of Jasper Falls, too."

She contemplated playing dumb and doing whatever it took to get Gracelyn to bring her up to speed on everything Tori already knew thanks to Margaret Louise's legwork, but time was of the essence. The sooner she figured out what happened to Opal and why, the sooner Rose and Leona could get back to growing SewTastic's customer base and Tori could get back to basking in her newlywed status with Milo. "I read about what happened with your kids' business ideas. I'm sorry they didn't get to run with them the way they'd hoped."

"They should have, you know. They were both brilliant and well thought out." Gracelyn dropped her face into her palms and let out a long yet surprisingly quiet groan. "I thought for sure they'd get approved. Heck, I was the one who pushed my son, Marcus, to consider Jasper Falls for his motorcycle shop in the first place. I thought it would be a good fit for him, and I saw it as a way to keep him there where I could be a part of my grandchildren's lives whenever he and Sherry—that's his wife—get around to making some babies.

"And Alison's clothing shop for teenage girls? Clothes like that are usually found in the big cities—like New York and Chicago, not Jasper Falls, South Carolina. The high school girls would have swooned over Alison's designs, and I could have had my little girl home with me every night instead of smiling at me from my computer screen once a week."

"Your daughter *moved away*?" Tori asked as the pieces of the puzzle finally clicked into place.

"They both did—Alison *and* Marcus. They had dreams but, because of Opal Goodwin, they had to leave the only home they've ever known in order to make them come true."

"Where did they go?"

"Alison went to California, and Marcus went to Texas," Gracelyn said, her voice heavy with emotion.

"Wow. That had to be hard."

Gracelyn's eyes drifted to a point somewhere beyond Tori, the rage that had ruled them earlier now muted by pain. "I have no one now—no one to eat with, no one to sit on my front porch with, no one to fuss over, and no one to spoil with special treats. My children have made new homes without me."

She sat perfectly still, afraid to speak, afraid to make a sound. Less than twenty-four hours earlier, she'd been convinced Opal's power move against Gracelyn's children wasn't a strong enough motive for murder. Yet now, after everything she'd just heard, she couldn't help but feel as if the who and why had just been handed to her with a great big sparkly bow on top.

"I—I don't know what to say."

And it was true, she didn't. Not to Gracelyn, anyway . . .

Lifting her hands up, Gracelyn pushed at the air as if she were shifting an invisible weight off her shoulders. "I'm sorry, Victoria. I didn't come here to unload my trials and tribulations on you."

"No, no, it's okay." Tori scooted forward on her chair until her knees were almost touching Gracelyn's. "I can't imagine how difficult it's been for you since your kids left."

"They're coming back this weekend. For a visit." Gracelyn clasped her hands together with wide-eyed hope. "And maybe now, with Opal out of the way, they can give some thought to moving back and opening those businesses after all."

With Opal out of the way . . .

It took everything she had not to jump to her feet, run for her phone, and speed-dial either Margaret Louise or Charles. But just as she was contemplating a host of polite ways to extricate herself from the conversation without raising suspicion, Gracelyn reached back into her purse and pulled out a familiar white book with red lettering.

"When I mentioned to Minnie that I was heading into town this morning, she asked if I'd drop off this book for her." Gracelyn rested the book, *Getting Away with Murder*, atop Tori's legs and stood. "My daddy always used to say it was the quiet ones you had to look out for in this world."

"The quiet ones?" Tori echoed.

"That's right. He used to say they were more dangerous than the loudmouths because no one ever pointed in their direction. Out of sight, out of mind, I guess." Gracelyn looked from Tori to the book and back again. "You won't tell anyone she checked this out, will you? I mean, Minnie is old, you know . . . And it's not like she didn't do something everyone else thought of at some point that day."

"Wait. You think Minnie had something to do with Opal's death?"

"Of course. We all do."

Tori drew back, shock sending a shiver down her spine. "Because she's quiet?"

"No. Because she's had little to nothing to do with the rest of us since that woman was found dead. She won't look anyone in the eye, won't engage in idle chitchat, and I've heard her crying off and on since we checked into the inn."

"I don't think that means she killed Opal," Tori protested.

You, on the other hand—

"On its own, you'd probably be right. But considering I've heard her cry out for Opal's forgiveness at least a half dozen times since Saturday night, I'm inclined to believe there's something there . . ."

If it wasn't for the changing of the guard on her favorite radio station, another ten minutes might have passed before Tori finally pulled her keys from the ignition and tossed them into her purse. But now that she had, the next logical step was to actually get out of the car and engage the porch's lone figure in conversation.

The concept was easy enough—grab purse, open door, step out of car, take steps onto porch, and say hello. Really, it was common courtesy when you drove across town for the sole purpose of spending time with someone.

Yet no matter how many times she tried to psych herself up to do just that, the second-guessing started.

There's no way Minnie did this . . .

Minnie is far too sweet . . .

What kind of person am I to even think such thoughts about someone like Minnie?

Sure, she tried to counter each incident of mental browbeating with an equally strong counterpoint, but every time she did, she came back to the same fact: Minnie looked just like Mrs. Claus.

"Forget about Mrs. Claus, dummy," she admonished herself. "This is about helping Rose."

Sighing, she grabbed her purse, opened the driver's side door, and stepped out onto the gravel lot. Minnie's head slowly turned in her direction, followed by a moment of recognition and an emphatic wave.

"Hi, Minnie!" Tori crossed the grass onto the stone walkway tasked with leading her onto the porch. When she reached the top of the steps, she veered left toward the swing and its neighboring set of rocking chairs.

"I was just starting to wonder if I should alert Nathan and Hannah to the fact that someone was sitting in their driveway . . ." Minnie toed the swing to a stop and then patted the empty spot created by her sudden shift to the left. "There's room for you on here, Victoria."

"No, it's okay. I'll take this rocker right here." Slowly, Tori lowered herself to her chosen chair and rested her purse at her feet. "I'm sorry if my sitting in the car so long like that worried you, Minnie. I guess I got a little wrapped up in my imagination."

It was true, of course. She had gotten wrapped up in her imagination. Minnie just didn't need to know that included an image of Mrs. Claus in shackles . . .

"I do that, sometimes." Minnie slowly resumed the lazy pace of her swing. "Only my imagination takes me to a time when I was young. You already *are* young, Victoria."

She searched her thoughts for something to say that would address the elderly woman and ease her own twisting conscience. "My husband wants to take me to a bed-and-breakfast in Amish country next month. I'm not sure if we're going to be able to make it happen, but if it's as picturesque as this place is, we're going to have to find a way."

Minnie's answering smile had Tori bracing for a *ho-ho-ho*. "Yes, do find a way. If I've learned one thing in my eighty-three years, it's that life zips by when you're busy doing things that don't matter. It's inevitable."

"Rose says the same thing."

"Of course she does, Victoria. Wisdom comes with age. That's why you'll hear us old farts imparting such tidbits on the young. Because we want you to learn these things before it's too late for you, too." Minnie ran her weathered hand along the swing's armrest. "Can't you just see yourself sitting in a swing like this, with your husband's arm around you, neither of you caring about anything but each other for a little while?"

Scooting her body all the way onto the rocker, Tori gave in to its rhythmic motion and instantly felt the stress of the day begin to to slip away. "That's the way it was on our honeymoon last month. It was just the two of us with no papers to grade for him and no board business to attend to for me. There was nothing to really decide besides whether we wanted to eat dinner in our cabin or go out to a restaurant."

"*Those* are the memories you'll carry in your heart forever, not the ones related to jobs and to-do lists."

There was something about Minnie that made Tori want to remain in her rocking chair for hours, soaking up every word the woman uttered. It was the way she felt whenever she was around Rose. And it was the part she missed most about her late great-grandmother.

Ask her about Opal . . .

Bumping her head against the back of the rocker, she stared up at the ceiling. More than anything, she wanted to ignore the voice in her head and keep on with the ruse that was her visit thus far. But to do so wouldn't do anyone any good.

"Victoria? Are you okay? You seem troubled all of a sudden."

She cast about for something to say only to land on her only choice—the truth. "I guess I'm just worried about Rose. When she hurts, I hurt."

Minnie stilled the swing once again. "Did she fall?"

"No. No. I'm talking about her shop. In just the two weeks or so it's been open, it's given her spirit a lift. It's as if having that gave her a purpose she didn't feel she had before." Tori looked down at her hands and then back up at Minnie. "But now, after everything that happened there on Saturday with Opal, all of that is poised to be ripped from her hands if I don't get to the bottom of what really happened."

There was no mistaking Minnie's reaction to the mention of Opal. Surprise turned to discomfort before Tori had even finished talking. The million-dollar question though was why . . .

Minnie cleared her throat and then hoisted herself off the swing and onto her feet. "There's something about this time of day that always makes me sleepy. So while it's been lovely chatting with you, Victoria, I think it's time I head up to my room for a wee nap."

Tori stood, too, her vantage point no longer Minnie's

face but rather the elderly woman's back as she shuffled her way over to the inn's front door. "I understand. But could I ask one quick thing before you go?"

At the door, Minnie turned and nodded ever so slightly in Tori's direction even though everything else about her demeanor screamed no—her hooded eyes, the rigid set to her narrow shoulders, and the sudden clenching and unclenching of her vein-ridden hands.

"I was hoping maybe you could tell me what Opal was doing when you went in to get your apron from the project room that afternoon." Tori closed the gap between them with several long strides. "Like, for starters, was she *okay*?"

Minnie's throat jumped with a noticeable swallow. "I left that room at the same time as everyone else."

"And then you went back in . . . later on . . . Rose saw you."

All color drained from Minnie's face just before it disappeared from Tori's view completely. Her back to Tori, Minnie pulled open the door and stepped inside. "I'm not feeling well, Victoria. I really must go to my room now and rest for a while."

Tori wanted to call after her, to ask the question one more time in the hopes Minnie would answer before officially heading up the stairs, but that was silly. Minnie wasn't tired, she was simply dodging Tori's question.

Frustrated, Tori backed away from the door only to stop, mid-step, as the sensation of being watched hit her with a one-two punch.

Chapter 19

"Tell me I'm not seeing you *a-gain*."

Tori sank down below the top of the computer monitor. "You're not seeing me again."

"Oh yes I am." Nina crossed from the doorway to the side of Tori's desk with hurried steps. "Didn't you finally leave here about an hour or so ago?"

"I did. But now I'm back." She finished keying the bus driver's name into the *Jasper Falls Courier*'s search bar and hit enter.

Nina's hands moved to her hips. "I see that. I just can't figure out why."

"I got a really bad vibe a little while ago."

"A bad vibe?"

Her eyes ran down the limited hits now listed on her screen while her mind narrowed in on each one. She clicked on the fourth from the top. "Travis Beaker was watching from a window while I talked to Minnie."

"Who is Travis Beaker and why was he watching you?"

Tori gestured toward the screen as an article dated three months earlier popped up. "That's why I'm back here, Nina. Trying to see if I can figure that out."

"Does this have something to do with what happened at Rose's store over the weekend?"

"I'm not sure. Maybe it does, or maybe this guy being at the window meant nothing at all." But even as the words left her mouth, she knew the latter part didn't feel right. In fact, if hair could truly stand on end, Tori's would have been doing just that as she scurried off the inn's porch and made her way back to her car.

For several long moments, she'd sat behind the steering wheel, staring up at the window that had started everything, looking for any indication of who'd been listening in on her conversation with Minnie. It was only when she finally gave up and slipped the key into the ignition that the same sixth sense that had washed over her on the porch sent her eyes upward to the second floor half a moment before Travis ducked out of view.

Sure, she'd entertained the possibility that his presence at that window was a complete coincidence, but that notion had disappeared as she placed the car into reverse and the outline of his body remained just behind the thin white curtain he'd hastily drawn closed.

Travis Beaker, according to the article now on the screen, had organized a picket in front of the Jasper Falls Town Hall. Curious, Tori read on . . .

Spurred by the death of his wife and daughter at the intersection of Route 5 and Market Avenue, Beaker has demanded the high-traffic area move from a stop sign to a traffic light for months. And slowly but surely, his cause has garnered support from Jasper Falls residents who, like Beaker, are concerned about safety.

His latest picket, which included fifty-five residents and a petition of nearly a hundred more signatures, has netted the issue's placement on the agenda for next month's council meeting.

"It's a step in the right direction," Beaker said.

"Oh. Wow," she whispered. "He lost his family."

"Who did?"

"Travis Beaker. The bus driver with Rose's tour group." She skimmed the rest of the article and then looked up at her assistant. "His daughter was only fourteen."

Nina's hands moved to her cheeks. "I—I can't even imagine that. I just can't."

A child's squeal from down the hall sent Nina scurrying toward the office door. "It sounds like my momentary lull in patrons is over. See you day after tomorrow?"

"Assuming I actually leave, yes, I'll see you day after tomorrow."

She listened for a moment as Nina greeted their young visitor and then turned back to the computer screen. Anxious to know if Travis's efforts had worked, she exited out of the current article and scrolled up to one dated a month later.

LOCAL MAN LOSES FIGHT

"Oh no."
Tori right-clicked on the link and began to read . . .

Travis Beaker of Jasper Falls lost his crusade to increase
safety at the intersection of Route 5 and Market Avenue
Tuesday night. Council members voted three to one
against adding a traffic light to the troublesome thorough-
fare, citing a need to keep commuter traffic flowing during
rush hour.

"Commuter traffic?" Tori mumbled. "In Jasper Falls?
Oh, c'mon . . ."

Beaker, still reeling from the unexpected defeat, refused
to comment. His biggest opponent, however, did not.
    "Part of the appeal of Jasper Falls is its simplicity.
Erecting a traffic light at an intersection that should simply be navigated with caution would take us one step
further from that simplicity," said Jasper Falls native—

"Opal Goodwin," she read aloud.
Her heart ached for the man who'd lost his wife and
daughter in what essentially amounted to a split second.
While so many people would have lost themselves in
grief in the aftermath of such a tragedy, Travis had tried
to make sure the same fate didn't befall anyone else.
    A buzzing sound from the top drawer of her desk
diverted her attention from the screen long enough for
Tori to fish out her phone and hold it to her ear. "Hey,
Charles, what's going on?"

"I wish I could answer that with something truly fabulous, but I can't."

"Is Leona on a date or something?" She made herself turn away from the computer in order to focus on her friend, but even as her eyes moved to the library grounds, she found her thoughts straying back to Travis and the powerful motive his defeat provided.

"Paris had an appointment to get fluffed and, since I wasn't supposed to even still be here at this point, I insisted Leona go."

Tori glanced over her shoulder just long enough to read the clock. "You just figured she'd be back before *The Stern and the Sensuous* ended, didn't you?"

A beat of silence was followed by a whiny *no*.

"Liar, liar, pants on fire."

"I *am* wearing my red jeans . . ."

She laughed. "See?"

"When do you get off work, sugar lips?"

"I've been off all day."

"Ooooh . . . the possibilities. Why didn't you call me? We could have done Debbie's and then followed it up with a stop at Shelby's Sweet Shoppe."

"I needed my brain to be sharp," she said, half joking.

"And sugar doesn't make it sharp?"

"No, it makes it loopy. You know this."

"True. So where are you now, love?"

"At the library. In my office."

"But you said it was your day off," Charles protested.

"It is."

"I'd reprimand you, Victoria, except I do the same thing with the bookstore. Only when I'm there on my day off, I'm holding court in the café."

It was a description she knew was dead-on and one that made her smile. "I needed to do a little research on the computer, which turned into a little *more* research on the computer after stopping out at the inn to talk with Minnie."

Charles gasped. "You're investigating? Without me?"

Uh-oh.

"I just wanted to check a few things in the *Jasper Falls Courier* is all. You know, to save us a few unnecessary steps."

She could almost hear the internal battle raging on the other side of the phone, and it took everything in her power not to laugh. Laughter would only add insult to injury. Instead, she weighed her options and decided on feather smoothing. "We need to talk. Motives are popping up all over the place."

One sniff was followed by another and then, "What kind of motives?"

"Ones I shouldn't say over the phone," she said, casting the line and slowly reeling him in.

"They're that good?" he whispered.

"I'll be there in ten minutes."

Her feet had barely hit the welcome mat outside Leona's door when a thin arm reached through the opening and pulled her inside. "I thought you'd never get here."

She returned Charles's hug and then stepped back for a head (now covered with green spiky hair) to toe (bare and freshly manicured) inspection. "Green?"

"I know. Not my best look." Charles linked his arm

through Tori's and walked with her down the hallway and into Leona's living room. "So, did you bring it?"

"Bring what?"

"The notebook."

She dropped her bag onto a nearby ottoman and pulled out the object of Charles's fascination. "I did."

Snatching it from her hands, he opened it, flipped through the pages, and then turned an accusatory eye in her direction. "You didn't add anything."

"I know. I was waiting for you to do that." It was a slight fib, of course, but a painless one. Reality had had her too busy to make any additions. She reached into her purse one more time and extracted a pen. "Here."

Charles squealed as he took the pen and dropped onto the couch in his favorite crisscross pose. "So who has the motive?"

"Gracelyn."

His eyebrow hiked upward. "Really?"

"Uh-huh."

He flipped to her page and prepared to write.

"Travis."

Snapping his head upward, he stared at her. "Sugar lips, you just said Gracelyn."

"You're right. I'm also saying Travis."

His mouth gaped and closed and gaped again. "They *both* have motives?"

"They sure do."

Charles leaned forward, the excitement on his face luring her down to the couch, too. "This is getting good, isn't it?"

"It's getting interesting, that's for sure." Sinking into the corner of the couch, she, too, hiked her legs up, only instead of imitating Charles, she bent hers at the knee and shifted her feet toward the armrest. "Opal didn't just keep Gracelyn's kids from opening businesses. She made them take their dreams elsewhere—the daughter to California and the son to Texas, I think."

"Meaning?"

"Meaning Gracelyn is now living in Jasper Falls all by herself."

She rested her left cheek on the back of the couch and waited while Charles dissected her words. When he caught up, he spread his hand and began to fan himself. "Oh, Victoria. A mama lion separated from her cubs can get mighty angry—I've seen it myself. Many, many times."

"You have?" she asked.

"Yes. At the Bronx Zoo."

"Okay, then there you go. Confirmation that Gracelyn has motive."

Holding her off with his hand, he made notes on Gracelyn's page and then flipped to Travis's. "Okay, now proceed with Travis . . ."

In a flash, she was back in her office, reading the articles that had left her head spinning and her heart aching. "Travis had a wife and a fourteen-year-old daughter."

"*Had*?"

"They were killed in a car accident in their town about six months ago. Since that time, Travis has tried to get Jasper Falls officials to put up a traffic light at that intersection. He picketed the town hall, collected signatures on a petition, and built up a nice little army of supporters," she explained. "But it appears as if Opal waved her magic wand and convinced the board to vote Travis's request down."

Charles sucked in his breath so hard, she actually worried, briefly, that he'd somehow managed to swallow his tongue. But just as she was leaning across the cushion to check, he spoke. "How did you find this out?"

"I did a little research on him after I discovered he'd been eavesdropping on a conversation I was having with Minnie out at the B and B."

"You were investigating *Minnie* without me, too?"

"Gracelyn mentioned some strange behavior on the part of Minnie that I thought should be checked out. So I drove out to the inn and talked to her. Only, Minnie wasn't having any part of my questions." She recovered her position in the corner of the couch and pulled the closest throw pillow onto her lap. "As she was heading inside in a blatant move to dodge me, I had this weird feeling that I was being watched. I didn't see who it was until I was starting to back out of the parking lot. That's when I noticed Travis."

"Why do you think he was watching you?"

It was a question she'd asked herself more than a few times on the drive from the inn to the library. "I think, originally, he was listening as much as watching. Then, when he moved up to what I imagine is his room, I think he was watching—to make sure I was leaving."

"Why would he care?"

"Maybe because he wanted to make sure my sights were on someone other than him for Opal's murder?" It was the only thing that made any sense. Especially in light of what she'd just learned about him in relation to the victim.

"But they *were* on him, right?" Charles prodded.

"Not at that moment, they weren't. But it was after I

caught him watching me like that that I did a little checking and uncovered this power move of Opal's." She traced her finger along the pillow's delicate pattern and then tossed the entire thing onto Leona's favorite chair. "My heart aches for this guy, you know? I mean, instead of wallowing in his pain, he tried to make sure the same thing won't happen to someone else."

Charles returned his attention to the book just long enough to add the information to the bus driver's page. When he was done, he looked up, his chin jutted outward with his trademark attitude. "Now it makes sense why that woman spent so much time yakking about signatures. She had a built-in one."

"Whoa. Slow down. By 'that woman' you mean Opal, yes?"

His nod was barely discernable as he continued. "Being *nasty* was her signature. In sewing and in life."

Chapter 20

With a potato chip bowl in one hand and a pile of napkins in the other, Tori stopped behind Milo and lingered a kiss on the back of his neck. "Thank you for this, honey."

"For what?" he asked as he turned around, pulled her in at the waist, and returned the gesture with a kiss on her lips.

"For this," she said, gesturing around the kitchen with the chip bowl and toward the back deck with her chin. "I know it was incredibly last minute of me to ask six people to join us for dinner the way that I did. But, in my defense, I was kind of desperate for a night off from reality."

"And I don't provide that with my endless supply of questions about your day?" he joked as he turned back to the counter to finish stacking hamburger patties for their trip out to the grill.

She tucked the pile of napkins under her opposite elbow and used her newly free hand to guide her husband's eyes back onto hers. "Hey. The fact that you care enough to really ask about my day is one of the most beautiful gifts you give me on a daily basis. Don't think, for a minute, that I don't treasure that time together each evening—because I do. But sometimes, when my mind has too many threads going at one time, a complete change of pace helps me figure things out in a way talking doesn't."

"Hey, I'm kidding. You don't need an excuse or a reason to want to spend time with your friends." Milo added the salt and pepper to the tray and lifted it off the counter. "Besides, I adore these people, too. So let's go spend time with them, shall we? Last I left Charles, he was discussing the finer points of the moisturizer Leona let him try."

"I love you, Milo. You know that, right?"

"You show me that every day." He kissed the tip of her nose and then waited for her to lead the way out to the deck.

She held the door for Milo and the tray of burgers and then threaded her way through her friends to the table Beatrice was quietly organizing. The youngest of her sewing circle sisters, Beatrice's preferred role at a party or gathering of any sort was that of the observer and the helper. "I got the chips and the napkins," Tori announced as she placed the bowl on one end of the table and the napkins on the other. "Milo is putting the burgers on the grill as we speak."

"Oooh, I love crisps." The British nanny scampered

over to the bowl of chips and helped herself to one. "I didn't realize I was even feeling peckish until I saw them."

"Have as many as you'd like; there's two more bags inside."

Leona sidled up alongside the table, inspected the offerings thus far, and then lifted a nose-twitching Paris until they were eye to eye. "I'm sorry, my precious baby. Aunty Victoria doesn't have anything for you to eat, does she?"

"Don't mind my twin none, Victoria. She's so persnickety, she wouldn't be happy in a diamond mine."

Leona returned Paris to her holding spot inside the crook of her bejeweled arm and made a face at Margaret Louise. "I'd be plenty happy in a diamond mine, dear sister of mine."

"And that is why Mama says if she tossed you in the river, you'd float upstream."

"Mama doesn't say that!" Leona hissed.

Margaret Louise waved at her sister like a bothersome gnat. "Aw, don't go gettin' your tail up and your stinger out, Twin. I just think you're takin' the long way 'round the barn just to get a carrot for that rabbit of yours. Why don't you just try askin' instead of guiltin'?"

"Amen," Tori muttered just loud enough for Beatrice to hear.

Or so she thought.

Leona's glare widened to include Tori. "What was that, dear?"

"I'll get a carrot for Paris right—"

"Never fear, Charles is here." Charles glided over to the table, pulling a carrot from his pocket as he did. "I grabbed one from the fridge just now, Victoria. I hope that was okay."

"No, no, that was perfect. Thank you, Charles." Tori took in the status of the hamburgers she could see from her vantage point and then leaned against the deck railing, content to do nothing for a few brief shining moments. "Those burgers are smelling mighty good, aren't they?"

"Things always smell better when someone else is cooking." Rose shuffled her way across the deck until she, too, was part of the growing circle around the picnic table. "Leona, did you tell Victoria about your friend? The one at that TV station in New York?"

Charles stopped picking at his nail long enough to swap glances with Leona. "So you called her?"

"I did. She's marvelous just like you said, darling."

Nail picking turned to preening as Charles rolled his head around on his neck. "I told you, didn't I?" At Leona's nod, he continued. "So? Is she going to do it?"

"Do what?" Tori and Beatrice asked in unison.

"A feature piece on SewTastic!" Rose beamed as she, too, helped herself to a chip. "Can you believe it?"

"Wait." Tori looked from Leona to Rose and back again. "Why would a television station in New York want to do a feature on a sewing shop in Sweet Briar, South Carolina, of all places?"

"Margot is a features editor for one of the national morning programs," Charles explained. "Their home base is out of New York but they cover things all over the country."

"Okay. But Rose and Leona don't need any more coverage about what happened there on Saturday. They need positive, upbeat stuff like Miranda is trying to secure with stations around here."

Charles called for a momentary pause in the conversation to rearrange the various condiment bottles and then took up where he left off. "Margot can make a cemetery look like the kind of place you want to hang out in for hours. Trust me, SewTastic will be in good hands with her."

Milo flashed the five-minute warning, alerting Tori to the need to gather the buns and side dishes. Before she headed inside though, she posed one last question to Rose. "But what about Miranda? I thought *she* was helping you."

"And she is, dear." Leona held Paris's carrot steady while the rabbit nibbled. "Around here, anyway. But if there's a chance to get the shop some national news, why not take it? Besides, our website means people can order from us no matter where they live. This kind of coverage just means more of those folks will know we exist."

Leona was right. Anything that could give SewTastic a push was good news.

She excused herself to get the rest of the food and then shuttled it back out to the table with Beatrice's help. Moments later, Milo transferred the burgers from the grill to a plate, added them to the rest of the offerings, and declared dinner ready.

When everyone's plate was full and seats were secured, they dug in, the pockets of chatter and laughter that rang up around the backyard bringing a smile to Tori's mouth if not her heart.

Yes, having her friends around had served as a temporary distraction from the stress of the day, but it hadn't lasted. Try as she might, she couldn't keep her thoughts from straying back to Gracelyn and Travis. Both had been burned, and burned badly, by Opal. The key was figuring out which one felt compelled to slip into SewTastic's project room and strangle the woman with a power cord.

"Hey, are you okay?"

Tori pulled her burger away from her mouth and turned her attention on her husband. "Sure, I'm okay. Why?"

"You're mighty quiet. Is the burger okay?"

"The burger is fantastic, Milo. Truly. I guess I'm having a harder time ignoring those threads than I thought I would."

He took a bite of his potato salad and settled back in his chair. "Maybe ignoring them isn't the answer this time. Maybe talking through them *is*."

"I'm sorry if I'm interruptin' but sometimes I can't help myself. 'Specially when I'm noticin' the same things Milo is noticin' 'bout your mood." Margaret Louise polished off her burger and moved on to her pickle. "Maybe more 'n a barbecue, you need a day off."

"I had that today," Tori said.

"A day off you didn't take, sugar lips." Charles winked at her from across the deck before turning his attention on Margaret Louise. "Our Victoria spent her day investigating."

Tori tried to wave Charles off but all she succeeded in doing was spattering her blouse with ketchup from her burger.

Great . . .

Margaret Louise stopped en route to the table for a second burger and spun around. "Investigatin'?"

"I just read a few more articles from the *Jasper Falls Courier* is all."

"Is that all?" Margaret Louise shrugged off that development and continued toward the table. "Why I already did that."

"But Victoria has a motive now."

"Motive?" Margaret Louise looked up from her empty plate, her eyes wide.

"For two different people—Gracelyn and Travis." Charles finished picking off every bit of hamburger bun overhang and then took a bite, his eyes rolling back in his head. "Oh! Oh! Milo, this is truly the best burger ever."

Milo set his empty plate on the armrest of his Adirondack chair and puffed out his chest with pride. "Thank you, Charles. It's a gift."

Charles snapped out his reply. "Yes. It. Is."

She tried to focus on the laughter around them, but the profound silence from the vicinity of the table made that impossible. There was something about everyone on that deck that Tori loved. With Beatrice, it was her sweetness. With Leona, it was her fierce belief in herself. With Charles, it was his all-in personality. With Rose, it was her quiet strength. And with Margaret Louise, it was her normally endless smile.

Excusing herself from the group, Tori stood and carried her plate of food over to the table and her clearly wounded friend. "Help yourself to seconds of anything you want." She pointed at the pasta salad in the center of the table and then to the spot it had once taken on her own plate. "Your pasta salad was amazing, Margaret Louise. I'll need to get the recipe from you sometime."

"It's in my head, but I imagine I can try jottin' it down."
Margaret Louise helped herself to another hamburger bun
and then topped it with a burger and an assortment of
toppings. "What's mine is yours, Victoria. I'm not 'bout
keepin' secrets from anyone, least of all a good friend like
you."

"I wasn't *looking* for a motive for Travis and Gracelyn." Tori shifted her plate to her opposite hand and
watched as Margaret Louise made her way from one
serving plate or bowl to the other. "I mean I was and I
am, but when I sat down at my computer I was really
just looking for a little bit more on all of them."

"But I did all that readin' yesterday."

"I know you did. I just figured it couldn't hurt to try
to learn more about Opal. I mean, all we really know is
that she was nasty."

"And that she's dead," Margaret Louise reminded.

"You're right. But I couldn't shake this feeling that
knowing more about Opal might lead us to her killer."

"And that knowin' led you to Gracelyn and Travis?"

"No. Gracelyn showed up at the library and it was
while talking to her that a possible motive emerged."

Margaret Louise's hand paused above the baked
beans. "You didn't mean to learn what you did 'bout
Gracelyn? You mean it just happened?"

She shot out her free hand. "Yes! Exactly! It just
happened!"

"I reckon Travis was with Gracelyn?"

Tori felt her shoulders slump as the battlefield length-
ened. "No. I saw him out at the B and B."

With nary a word, Margaret Louise dumped a large
spoonful of beans onto her plate and moved on to the

cheesy potatoes Rose had brought. "There ain't no reason for you to be at the B and B unless you're investigatin', Victoria."

"Okay, I won't deny that. I *wanted* to talk to Minnie, but she scurried off to take a nap the second I brought up Opal. That's when I realized Travis had been listening to our conversation from a nearby window. And that he didn't want me to know he'd been listening." She searched for something to say that would make Margaret Louise understand and then proceeded ahead. "Have you ever had a bad feeling about something? Like your gut knows something your head hasn't fully grasped yet?"

Margaret Louise looked up from her plate. "Just the other day, in fact. I was cleanin' my kitchen when I had this feelin' that Jake Junior forgot his lunch. I called Melissa and had her check in her refrigerator. And guess what? As sure as rats run rafters, Jake Junior's lunch sack was sittin' right there on the second shelf."

"Wow."

"I know." Margaret Louise started to walk away from the table but stopped and went back for another scoop of beans. "These beans are so good it makes me want to swallow my tongue so I can eat my taste buds."

She reined in her answering laugh and hurried to make her closing argument while the iron was hot. "Something about Travis's actions made me want to know more about him. So I went back to my office and plugged in his name, never expecting to find what I found."

"Is that the truth, Victoria?"

"One hundred percent."

"You workin' tomorrow?"

Tori nodded.

"Nine o'clock?" Margaret Louise asked.

"Yup."

"Then we'll meet at Debbie's at seven thirty."

Seven thirty?

"And don't you worry none, Victoria. I'll swing by and pick up Charles on the way."

Chapter 21

Once she was sure Margaret Louise was out of earshot, Tori pointed at Charles's still-untouched cinnamon roll. "Hey. Are you okay? You haven't eaten so much as a crumb since you sat down."

Charles took a moment to assess Margaret Louise's proximity to the table and then slumped forward, narrowly missing his plate with his elbow. "I adore that woman, I really do, but she shouldn't be allowed behind a steering wheel." He lifted his head upward like a periscope and, when he was sure their friend had stopped to chat with someone over by the napkin dispenser, he brought his focus back on Tori. "We blew through two stop signs, ran over three curbs, and missed a squirrel by less than a centimeter . . . all before we left Leona's street."

She knew it was wrong to laugh at someone else's misery, but with any luck the pat on his still-pasty-white hand helped soften any resulting sting. "If it helps, she's never had even so much as a single accident."

"Says you." Again, Charles looked at the counter, only this time, instead of talking, he followed it up with a quick inhale into the to-go bag Debbie had handed him on the sly.

"No, says everyone." Tori nudged his plate closer to his chair. "When you're done hyperventilating, you really should take a bite. Debbie's cinnamon rolls cure all ails. Ask anyone."

He took a few more breaths and then stuffed the bag underneath his thigh. "Last night was really fun, Victoria. Living in the city, I don't really get to many barbecues. Unless you count the hibachi my next-door neighbor uses on the fire escape every Fourth of July. But I'm not a fan of Polish sausage."

"Noted." Tori took a bite of her blueberry muffin and then raised the remaining muffin between them for emphasis. "You know there *is* a way you can go to more barbecues if you're so inclined."

"Do tell, sugar lips . . ."

"You could move to Sweet Briar. Permanently."

"Leona said the same thing to me last night. But as I said to her while we were eating popcorn in our jammies, McCormick's needs me."

She swapped her muffin for a sip of hot chocolate. "McCormick's is a bookstore, Charles."

"It's my job, Victoria. And one I'm rather good at, if I do say so myself."

"I'm sorry I kept you two waitin' so long. I was just

talkin' to Lulu's teacher, Miss Applewhite." Margaret Louise hoisted herself up onto the lattice-backed stool and then quickly handed out the napkins she'd gone back to the counter to fetch. "Seems Miss Applewhite is lookin' at Lulu for the spellin' bee this year. Makes a Mee Maw mighty proud, I tell you."

Tori smiled at the mention of Margaret Louise's fifth grandchild. While she loved all eight, there was something about Lulu that had captured her heart from the moment they met, a bond that had only deepened as Lulu's love for reading grew. "That's great news, Margaret Louise! Does Lulu know yet?"

"Not yet. Miss Applewhite is plannin' to tell her sometime after Thanksgivin'. Why, our Lulu is going to be tickled."

"I was in a spelling bee once," Charles offered across his still-steaming mug of coffee. "I was in sixth grade. Lost to Rickie Meanypants Rogers in the third round."

Tori laughed. "Rickie Meanypants Rogers?"

"You. Know. It." Charles pushed his plate to the side and leaned forward. "He stole my meatloaf sandwich when I was in second grade, my favorite eraser in third grade, and chipped my tooth in fifth grade by pushing me into the water fountain . . . See?" He hooked his index finger into the side of his mouth and pulled, pointing to his top front tooth with the index finger from his other hand.

"Least he left you alone in fourth grade." Reaching over, Margaret Louise helped herself to a bite of Charles's cinnamon roll and then moved on to Tori's blueberry muffin.

Charles pulled his finger out of his mouth and dropped

it onto the table. "He moved away the summer before fourth grade only to move right back the next summer."

"So what was the word?" Tori asked.

"Word?"

"That you lost with in the spelling bee."

"Refrigerator. R-e-f-r-i-g-e-r-a-t-o-r." Charles ran his finger across the cinnamon drizzle on his plate, inserted it into his mouth, and then popped it out again. "Looking back now, I realize Rickie Meanypants Rogers had the same signature as Opal Goodwin. They were both mean for the sake of being mean."

"Only instead of stealin' 'n' pushin', Opal was more 'bout throwin' her weight 'round 'n' yankin' people's legs out from under 'em."

"The thing I can't figure out though, is why," Tori said between sips of her drink. "I mean, why would she buy a building she wasn't going to use just to make sure no one else would use it? And why would she stick her nose in someone else's personal crusade? It makes no sense."

"She did it, because she could." Charles took one last finger swipe of the drizzle and then slid the remaining roll in front of Margaret Louise. "It's the same reason why Rickie Meanypants Rogers did all of that stuff to me. Because he knew I wasn't going to fight back."

"But *I* know you're not going to fight back and *I* don't push you into a water fountain." Tori swished the rest of her hot chocolate around in her cup and then finished it off. "Metaphorically speaking, of course."

"That young man was striking out against somethin'," Margaret Louise mused over her newly acquired breakfast treat.

Charles leaned forward on his elbows. "Yeah—me."

"I'm talkin' 'bout the thing that stirred up all that meanness in him. There must've been somethin'."

"No, his father was mean, too," Charles said. "He came by it honestly as you're always saying, Margaret Louise."

"He may have come by it honestly, but that don't mean he was just takin' notes. Maybe he was at the receivin' end of that kind of meanness."

Charles teed his hands in front of his chest. "Time out! *I* was on the receiving end of his meanness and I didn't turn around and do it to someone else."

"Did you have a lovin' family, Charles?" Margaret Louise asked.

"The best."

"What did they say when you came home tellin' them 'bout what this young boy did to you?"

"My mom sat me down at the kitchen table and told me I was special. And that nothing anyone else can ever do or say will change that. Unless I let them."

"Somethin' tells me, no one was sittin' Rickie Meany-pants on any chair, tellin' him to believe in himself."

For several long moments, Charles said nothing, his gaze moving from Margaret Louise, to Tori, and finally to the empty space in front of him at the table. Eventually, Tori broke the silence. "I hear what you're saying, Margaret Louise, I really do. And I suspect it has merit in some cases. But so, too, does the fact that two wrongs don't make a right."

"That's why teachers like your Milo are so important, Victoria. Because he can be the positive role model kids like Rickie don't get at home. That's the only way some of 'em can ever taste the difference between right and wrong."

It was conversations like these that made Tori a better person. They made her think. Yet even knowing there was a measure of truth in Margaret Louise's words, they weren't a one-size-fits-all kind of thing, either. "Some kids are treated like gold and they're still mean," she said. "I see it in the library sometimes."

"That's 'cause folks who spend their time spoilin' their kids don't see how they act when they're not lookin'. Kids who grow up with spoilin' expect the rest of the world to spoil 'em, too. I love my grandbabies with all my heart and that's why I avoid spoilin'. Because spoilin' only hurts them in the long run."

"You need to write a book on raising children, Margaret Louise. And it needs to be required reading for anyone even thinking about procreating." Charles wiped his mouth with his napkin and then pointed it at Tori. "Penny for your thoughts, sugar lips?"

Slipping off her stool, Tori gathered up the empty plates and tossed her own dirty napkin on top. "If Margaret Louise is right, and there's a reason for a person's meanness, I guess I'm wondering what Opal's reason was."

Chapter 22

Tori placed the last book back on the shelf and tried to resist the urge to change her squat into a full-fledged sit. Then again, wasn't that why she'd saved a bottom-shelfer for last?

She glanced over her shoulder, noted the absence of any patrons in her aisle, and rocked back onto her bottom for what she promised herself would be a momentary break. The morning had been nonstop busy with a mom and me reading group, an assisted living field trip, a book delivery, and the standard duties that came with checking in and shelving the night depository's take.

"Sitting on the floor is not at all ladylike, dear."

Leona?

Pushing off the ground, Tori took a moment to brush off any lint she'd accumulated from her painfully short pit stop on the floor and headed in the direction of the information desk. Sure enough, Leona and Paris were waiting. "Leona. I didn't hear you come in."

"I'm not sure *why*. I came through the door just like that gentleman that's over by the computers now."

"Gentleman? What gentle . . ." The words died away as she turned toward the computer bank and the lone figure tapping away at the first of six desks. "Wow. I didn't hear him, either."

Leona carried Paris over to a nearby table and sat down. "This is what happens every time you decide to play Nancy Drew. You become distracted and ornery. Ask anyone. Especially that handsome man you're married to."

"Milo doesn't think I'm ornery."

Dipping her head forward, Leona pinned Tori across the top of her glasses. "Oh? Have you asked him?"

"No. Because I'm not ornery."

"If you say so, dear." Leona stilled her hand midway down Paris's back and sniffed. "I don't want Charles to leave."

Lulled by the empty chair to Leona's left, she wandered over to the table, verified that the man at the computer was doing fine on his own, and then dropped onto the chair with a thump. "Oh. Wow. You have no idea how good this feels."

"Where's Nina?"

"It's her day off. Yesterday was mine." She propped her elbow on the table and rested her chin atop her palm. "So what's this about Charles? Did Chief Dallas give him the all-clear to go home or something?"

"No, but it's only a matter of time. Even *Robert* will have to figure out what happened to that old hag at some point." Leona smiled down at Paris and then turned the bunny so she was facing Tori. "Unless that's why you're taking so long to figure this out, dear . . . so we can keep Charles here as long as possible?"

"While that's a wonderful by-product, it's taking a long time for several reasons. First, I have three viable suspects at this moment—two with actual motives, and one who is acting oddly. Second, I don't know any of these people. This means I have to do a little snooping around to figure out things about each person, including Opal herself."

"As the owner of SewTastic, I wish you'd hurry. As Charles's biggest fan, I'm hoping you hit detour after detour."

Without really thinking, Tori dropped her hands down to the table and reached for Paris. When the rabbit accepted her offer, she took over petting duty. "We met Charles less than six months ago, Leona, and he's already been to Sweet Briar twice."

"And both times I've felt more culturally satisfied than I have since my sister talked me into moving here seven years ago."

"Culturally satisfied?" she echoed.

"When Charles is in town, I go to plays and attend concerts. We seek out all the best restaurants within an hour's drive, try their most popular items, and then critique them all the way home in the car."

She circled her fingers around the base of Paris's left ear and slowly followed the soft, velvety feel all the way to the top before repeating the same motion on the opposite ear. "You and I have done those same things, Leona."

"Once in a great while, yes. But with Charles, we do those things nearly every day. And on the days we don't, we go to the spa or the salon or wherever else we choose to go to better ourselves."

"It's easier for Charles to do those things because he doesn't live here, Leona. If he did, he'd have to turn down some of your suggested outings because of work, too."

Leona reached over, plucked Paris from Tori's arms, and stood. "Must you rain on my parade, dear?"

"Rain on your—wait. I'm not saying I wouldn't love to have Charles living here, too. Because I would. Very much. I'm just—"

"Then help me find a way to convince him, dear."

"How? He loves his job at the bookstore."

"I don't know, I—oh good heavens, who is calling me?" Leona slipped her hand into her purse and pulled out her phone. When the Caller ID screen revealed a New York phone number, she handed Paris back to Tori and took the call. "Yes? Yes, this is Leona Elkin . . . oh yes, Margot Pritchard, Charles has told me so many lovely things about you . . . A TV crew? Of course, we can accommodate that. I don't know if Charles told you, but I have my own television show on our local cable station, so I'm quite familiar with the things your crew will need . . . yes, yes. Your former co-anchor? No, no I'd not heard of that . . . What a shame . . . Trust me, knowing how to sew doesn't make a person a saint . . . yes, yes, exactly. What? . . . Oh. Well I can't speak for other areas of the country, of course, but I can say that sewing is not becoming obsolete in this area. In fact, there's a whole museum devoted to the craft in Jasper Falls. Yes, Jasper Falls is here in South Carolina, as well. It's a little over ninety minutes north of us here in Sweet Briar . . . no, I've never been . . . okay, yes, I'll pencil off Monday for your crew . . . Will you be coming as well? . . . oh how lovely. I look forward to meeting you . . . thank you, Margot . . . Charles sends his love."

Leona ended the call and set the phone down on the table. "Charles is right, she has a very whiny voice. Between that and that odd little cowlick she has in all her pictures, it really isn't any wonder why she can't keep a man."

"I think a man could overlook a cowlick, Leona."

"If there aren't any better prospects, perhaps . . ."

"Sheesh. No wonder I've stopped looking in mirrors since I moved here." Tori scratched Paris between her ears and handed the rabbit back to Leona. "Anyway, moving on . . . It still strikes me as odd that a morning news program—even a national one—would have any interest in spotlighting a small sewing shop in Sweet Briar, South Carolina. Don't get me wrong, I think it's fantastic. But the unbiased side of me is left wondering *why*."

"I have experience on camera, dear," Leona reminded.

"On a small cable television show, yes. But even that's not enough to explain this interest."

"Maybe they simply want to help a little guy—a mom and pop, so to speak." Leona pulled a tube of lipstick from her purse, read the color on the bottom, and tossed it back into her bag. "Is there a reason why you're trying to look a gift horse in the mouth, Victoria?"

"My antenna is just up a little, I guess."

Leona rolled her eyes. "I see that, dear. But why?"

"Because I'm afraid all it's going to do is put an even bigger spotlight on what happened at the shop on Saturday afternoon." Tori pushed back her chair and stood. Her yawns were starting to multiply, and she still had a solid five hours left in her workday. "It just seems counterproductive to what Rose and Miranda are trying to do."

"Rose is all for a national feature story," Leona said.

"And Miranda?"

Leona waved Tori's question aside with an air of boredom. "I haven't told her. I'm every bit as capable of enticing media coverage as she is. And as for this notion that all they want to do is sensationalize what happened to Opal, you're wrong. Margot was asking me whether I know any statistics concerning the craft of sewing and whether it's more prevalent here in the southeast or not."

"Hmmm . . . okay, then maybe there isn't anything to worry about. If they can build a feature story around sewing alone, that could be really good for you and Rose."

"Did you hear that, my precious angel?" Leona asked, lifting Paris up to eye level. "Victoria has given us her blessing."

Tori stifled yet another yawn, shaking her head as she did. "It's not about giving my blessing or not giving my blessing, Leona. It's your shop. I just didn't want to see a bad situation made any worse, you know?"

"Miss? I think I might have messed up the printer somehow."

Bobbing her head to the left, she met the eyes of the only other patron in the library, and smiled. "I'm on my way." Then, to Leona, she pointed in the direction of the computers. "It's time to get back to work. Talk later?"

"Charles and I are going to a movie this evening if you'd like to join us."

Retracing her steps back to the table and the now-standing Leona, Tori planted a kiss on her friend's cheek. "I have plans with Milo tonight, but I'd love a raincheck if that's okay." At Leona's shrug of indifference, she moved on to kiss Paris and then hooked her thumb toward the computer bank and the man patiently waiting for her assistance. "Anyway, I better go. Enjoy your movie."

"Victoria?"

She stopped mid-step and turned back to Leona. "Yes?"

"What does a bell have to do with sewing?"

"Why Leona, are you finally showing interest in sewing after all these years?" Tori teased.

This time when Leona rolled her eyes, it was accompanied by an exasperated groan. "Is it asking too much to get a simple answer to my question?"

"Miss? The printer?"

"Leona, I'm sorry, I have to help this gentleman. But to answer your question, Bell sewing machines were designed primarily for use by tailors in the nineteen fifties, I believe. You can still find them on some of those bidding sites on the Internet. Why? Do you have a customer who wants to track one down?"

"No. It's just something Margot mentioned that I didn't quite pick up." Leona secured Paris inside the crook of her left arm and then looped her free arm through her purse. "Last question. Could you kill someone with a sewing machine?"

Confused, Tori drew back. "You mean like whoever just killed Opal?"

"Touché, dear."

Chapter 23

The second their waitress stepped away from the table with their orders, Tori rested her cheek on Milo's shoulder and exhaled the last of the day's busyness once and for all.

"I take it today was Nina's day off?" His breath was warm against her skin as he draped his arm across the back of their booth and pulled her close.

"It was." She knew she should say more, but at that moment, all she really wanted to do was listen to the beat of his heart in time with the music being pumped through a handful of speakers scattered throughout the popular eatery.

"She's back tomorrow, right?"

"She is."

"Well, the good news is, Bud is doing the cooking

tonight. That means we don't have to lift so much as a finger between now and when our food arrives."

"A heavenly thought if there ever was one," she managed to eke out between yawns.

"Hey!" Milo set his tea glass down on the table and turned just enough to afford a view of her face. "Speaking of Heavenly, any word on whether Nina can cover you for a few days between Christmas and New Year's?"

She breathed in his nearness for a few more glorious seconds and then straightened up on the vinyl bench seat. "Actually, she called me this afternoon and said those days might be a little tricky with some of Duwayne's out-of-town family members coming in for the holidays, but she did say she could cover me over the long Presidents' Day weekend in February."

His answering shoulder slump was fleeting, but still, she caught it. "I know it'll be too late to coincide with our first Christmas together," Tori said, "but it sure will make a great belated Valentine's Day getaway."

"Wait, that's right! Valentine's Day is just a few days before that, isn't it?" At her nod, he took a brief sip of his tea and then returned the glass to the table with a triumphant thud. "We can work with this. I'll call and make a reservation during my free period tomorrow."

"For what it's worth, I'm already looking forward to it," she said, peering up at him. "In fact, I suspect it will be the carrot I use to get through days just like today."

He reached across her lap and covered her wedding ring with his. "Me, too. After today, of course."

"After today?"

"Yup. *That's*"—he pointed at the vanilla milkshake

making its way across the table in her direction—"today's carrot, remember?"

She unwrapped the straw and popped it into the shake. "It's *a* carrot, yes."

"Did you want a chocolate shake instead?" he asked.

"No. Vanilla is perfect." She took a sip of her shake and then held it out to Milo to sample. "The most motivating carrot that got me through the day was getting to see you."

"Watching you two almost makes me want to get married." Jolee, as her name tag read, set the hamburger platter in front of Milo and the French dip sandwich platter in front of Tori and then lowered the tray to her side. "And, judging by the way that fella at the bar keeps looking at you two, I'm not the only one who thinks that way, either."

Curious, she followed the waitress's gaze across the smattering of tables in the center of the dining room to the line of stools bordering three sides of the rectangular bar. There, on the fourth stool from the left, she found an all-too-familiar pair of eyes looking back at her.

Travis.

Her every instinct told her to avert her eyes, but for some reason she held his gaze until he looked away.

"Tori? Do you know that guy?"

The part of her that was desperate to make things right for Rose was sure she'd seen guilt as he looked away, but the part of her that ached for his loss was certain she'd seen something far more raw and tortured . . .

"Tori?"

"If there's anything else you need, just give me a holler." And then Jolee was gone, heading back through the kitchen's swinging door in search of another table's order.

"Tori? Are you okay?"

Unsure of what she was feeling, she turned back to her husband. "I'm sorry, I didn't mean to check out on you like that."

"I take it you know that guy?" At her nod, he led her gaze back to the bar and the man who, once again, was watching them rather than the sports program on the television above the bar. "Who is he?"

"His name is Travis Beaker. He's the guy who drove the tour bus to Rose's shop on Saturday and to our house on Monday evening for the sewing circle meeting."

"Okay. So what's with the staring? He looks almost . . . *sad*."

Milo was right. Guilt would have him averting his gaze from the start. Pain would make it difficult to look away.

"His wife and fourteen-year-old daughter were killed in a car accident six months ago."

Milo raked his hand through his hair and leaned his head against the back of the booth. "Aw man, I—do you mind if I invite him to sit with us? Maybe he could use a friend or two right now."

Again, she followed her husband's eyes back to the bar, Travis's head now hung low over a half-empty glass of beer. She couldn't completely rid herself of the unease that came from the memory of his odd behavior at the inn, but the sadness that oozed from his body stirred something inside her she couldn't ignore, either. "I'm okay with that if he wants to."

"I'll be right back."

She watched as Milo slid out of the booth, weaved his way through the maze of tables, and then tapped Travis on the shoulder. What was said, she could only guess at, but after a few minutes of back and forth, Travis picked his glass up off the bar and followed Milo back to the table.

"Hi, Travis," she said as she motioned to the empty bench on the other side of the table. "I'm glad you can join us."

He hesitated beside the table for a moment before taking a half step backward. "I really shouldn't interrupt. You're eating dinner."

"So I'll call Jolee over and you can get some food, too." Milo motioned to the waitress and then slid into his spot next to Tori. "FYI, the burgers here are really good."

Travis nodded, handed the menu back to Jolee, and placed an order for a hamburger with the works. When Jolee left, he drummed his fingers on the table briefly before abandoning the gesture in favor of an awkward shrug. "I'm sorry if my staring at the two of you made you uncomfortable or made you feel as if I was looking for something. I was really just remembering back to the beginning is all." He pointed to Milo's wedding band and then took a quick pull of his beer. "When did y'all get married?"

"Six weeks ago." At Travis's insistence, Milo finally gave in to the allure of his burger and encouraged Tori to start on her meal, as well. "Oh. Wow. This is good . . ."

"My wife and I got married in October, too. Only our wedding was eighteen years ago." With one hand still on his beer glass, Travis leaned back against his seat, his words delivering him to a place he was obviously already visiting in this thoughts. "And boy was it good. We could lose ourselves in each other just like you were doing over here a little while ago. She was my wife and my best friend all rolled up in one. She made the good times sweeter, and the bad times a whole lot more tolerable, that's for sure."

"I know all about that," Milo said, lowering his burger momentarily. "Victoria does the same for me."

"Ginny—that was my wife—was positively glowing when she told me she was pregnant. We'd been married almost three years at that point, and she was waiting for me at the door when I got home from work. She took me by the hand and led me through the house and out to the patio where she had a box all wrapped up like a present. When I reminded her it wasn't my birthday, she just laughed and said it didn't matter, that some presents couldn't wait." Travis's eyes fixed on a spot somewhere far beyond the half wall that separated their booth from the next one. And as they did, a wistful smile played at the corners of his mouth. "I pulled off the ribbon, the tape, and the wrapping paper, and there, inside the box, was a slip of paper made up to look like a coupon. Across the front, in her best handwriting, were the words 'redeemable for a mini-us in twenty-four weeks.'"

He blinked and then lolled his head back against the top of the booth. "Would you believe it took me a few seconds to get it? I could be so dense at times. But when I did, I'm pretty sure our neighbors three streets over could hear me whooping it up."

Milo's gentle laugh was met with one from Travis as well before the man continued. "Twenty-four weeks later, our mini-us arrived in the form of a baby girl. We named her Rachel Renee, and she stole our hearts with her very first breath."

Unsure of what to say, Tori simply pushed her barely eaten sandwich to the side and waited for the rest of what she knew to be a heartbreaking tale. Travis did not disappoint—his words, his tone, his pain bringing tears to Tori's eyes. "Rachel was brilliant, funny, and caring. She made Ginny and me proud each and every day. Even that last morning, before Ginny left to take Rachel to school, Rachel told us her English teacher wanted to submit one of her poems to a national high school poetry contest.

"I have the certificate she would have won. It came in the mail two months ago—addressed to her."

Jolee reappeared beside the table and quietly placed the last plate of food in front of Travis. If he noticed though, he gave no indication. "I told them to be careful when they left that morning. But I always did. It was part of the routine. But so was them coming back home at the end of the day . . ."

"What happened?" Milo asked as he, too, pushed his plate to the side, unable to concentrate on anything but Travis and a story poised to take a decidedly different turn.

"According to the driver in the car behind them, Ginny stopped at the stop sign, looked both ways, and then proceeded to pull out onto Route 5. By the time she saw the car racing around the bend, it was too late. For both of them."

Tori disengaged her hand from Milo's and reached across the table for Travis's. "I'm so sorry, Travis."

"I've always hated that intersection, hated it with a

passion. I knew it was dangerous. Everyone with half a brain in their head did. But I didn't do anything about it. I just accepted it as the way it was like everyone else in Jasper Falls did." Travis parted company with the back of the booth, flipped the top bun off his burger, and stared down at the mountain of condiments he'd requested, his tone becoming wooden. "For months I blamed myself—if I'd only said something sooner . . . if I'd gone to the town council, to the state, to any number of agencies tasked with roads or safety or some combination of the two . . . if I'd only done this, or only done that, maybe Ginny and Rachel would still be here. Those thoughts were there all day long, and all night, too. But I couldn't have changed a damn thing. And you want to know why? Because money and power trump safety in Jasper Falls!"

Travis smacked his fist on the table so hard several diners at surrounding tables turned to stare, prompting him to lower his voice. "Or at least it did up until five days ago . . ."

Chapter 24

"Is he coming back?" Jolee asked, pointing at Travis's plate. "Do you think he'd like me to box his up, too?"

"No, he's gone." Milo looked from the waitress to the still topless burger and back again. "Does anyone have a pet they can bring it home to? Are you allowed to do that?"

Securing the plate with her fingertips, Tori shook her head. "Actually, why don't we box it up after all? We could swing by the inn on the way home and drop it off for him there."

"You know something? That's a really good idea." He turned back to Jolee and handed her the plate. "When you're done and you've got a chance, could we see a dessert menu?"

"Sure thing."

Tori watched Jolee disappear through the swinging door with Travis's plate in her hand and then gently jabbed Milo in the side with her elbow. "Dessert? Are you serious? I already had a milkshake and neither one of us finished our dinner."

"Who are you and what did you do with my wife?" He captured her hand in his and held it against his grin.

She poked him in the side again, this time following it up with a kiss on his cheek. "Hey! It was a logical question, mister."

"Since when have logic and dessert ever gone hand in hand for you?" He extricated his fingers from hers and picked up the menu Jolee had quietly dropped off on her way to another table. "Besides, we were a little distracted, you know?"

"I do." She tried to focus on the dessert options highlighted by Milo's passing index finger, but her thoughts kept returning to the man who'd sat across the table from them less than ten minutes earlier, the anguish he'd carried still lingering in the air around them. "Do you think he'll ever feel joy again?"

Milo's finger stopped moving as he swung his attention back to her. "You mean Travis?"

"Yes."

"I think I'm living proof of that, don't you?" Releasing the menu back onto the table, he wrapped his arm around her shoulders and pulled her close. "When Celia died twelve years ago, I thought I was down for the count. At twenty-five. But God obviously had a very different plan because, when He felt the time was right, He sent me you and a level of joy I didn't know existed."

She swallowed over the rising lump in her throat and

tried to frame her next question in such a way as to get the answer she sought without forcing Milo into revisiting a painful time in his past. "I know, from conversations we've had, that you were angry when Celia died. Did you ever act out?"

"Sure. I punched walls, I yelled, I screamed, I went on punishing runs for miles on end. But eventually I got through the anger." Hooking his finger beneath her chin, he lifted her gaze to meet his. "Are you asking this stuff because of Travis?"

"I guess, yeah." She pulled free of his hand to take a sip of water. When she was done, she set the glass back on the table and hiked the side of her knee onto the vinyl-covered bench between them. "Do you think your anger might have taken a different form if Celia's death hadn't been health-related?"

"If you're referring to the anger that made Travis hit the table the way he did, that's normal. Trust me, sweetheart, I smacked a few tables myself in those early months."

She took a deep breath and waded in the rest of the way. "I'm thinking more about what he *said* when he smacked the table."

"What did he say? I don't really remember."

"He said something about money and power coming before safety in Jasper Falls—until five days ago."

"Okay . . ."

"Opal was murdered five days ago, Milo."

"I know that. But what's that have to do with Travis getting upset?"

She took another sip of water and then filled him in on everything she'd uncovered regarding Travis's fight to make the intersection where his family was killed safer. When she got to the part about Opal essentially squashing his fight, Milo held up his hands. "Wait, wait, wait. You're not implying Travis killed Opal to get a traffic light in place, are you?"

"No, of course . . ." The protest segued into a resigned nod. "Okay, maybe just a little. I mean, you saw his anger and his hurt just now. Those are both powerful emotions capable of messing with a person's head, you know?"

"He didn't kill that woman."

"How can you be so sure?" she asked. "You just met Travis no more than thirty minutes ago."

"Don't get me wrong. I suspect you're dead-on that he had intense anger for Opal. But his request was formally shot down a month ago, right?"

"Maybe five weeks ago, but something like that."

"The rage would have come *then*. By now, the sadness has seeped back in." Milo traced his finger around the outer edge of the dessert menu and then looked back at Tori. "He didn't kill her, Tori. He may have *wanted* to five weeks ago, but not now. Nothing dulls the sadness except time and"—he smiled—"one helluva second chance."

"But he was watching and listening while I was talking to Minnie the other day. And when he knew I'd became aware of him, he moved," she protested.

"He told me that there's something about your cheekbones that makes him think of Ginny."

"I didn't hear him say that!"

"He told me when I went over to him at the bar. I think he thought I was taking issue with the way he kept looking over at you." Milo picked up the menu and gave it a little jiggle. "The brownie à la mode is calling my name. Want to share?"

It wasn't that she wanted Travis to be guilty of murder, because she didn't. She wanted him to heal and find joy one day just like Milo did with her. But, at the same token, someone had killed Opal and was walking around scot-free . . .

"Victoria?"

She abandoned the menu's offerings for the pair of women waving at her from a few steps away. "Samantha, Lucinda, hello!" Tori motioned them closer, turning to Milo as she did. "Milo, you remember Samantha and Lucinda from my sewing circle meeting the other night, don't you?"

"Yes, of course." He extended his hand to each woman and then invited them to sit, an invitation they quickly turned down.

"We're picking up to-go orders to take back to the inn. Miranda is paying for them right now."

Tori followed the path forged by Samantha's finger and found a waving Miranda at the other end. She returned the wave and then turned her attention back on her own table and Travis's now-boxed meal. "Hey, if it's not too much trouble, Samantha, could you take this box back to the inn with you for Travis? He left it behind, and it's a shame to see it go to waste."

"Sure, we can do that."

Samantha took the box while Lucinda's finger came to rest on the fifth line of Milo's dessert menu. "When I was here on Sunday, I tried the salted caramel bundt cake and it was unforgettable," Lucinda gushed. "Truly. It's why there will be two of those going back to the inn with us in a few minutes."

"You like the salted caramel bundt cake, as well, Samantha?"

"Oh no, the second one isn't for me, Victoria. It's for Minnie. Call it a last-ditch attempt to cheer her up. She's far too sweet to be in such a state."

"Wait. What's wrong with Minnie?" Tori asked.

A series of concerned looks passed between the women before Samantha finally answered. "We don't know, Victoria. We just know that the crying has to stop. Soon. It's not good for Minnie, and it's not good for the rest of us who can't sleep through all that sniffling and crying."

"She's *crying*? When? Why?"

"At night."

"*Every* night," Lucinda corrected Samantha. "At first we thought she was just upset about having to stay here in Sweet Briar longer than expected, but she seems to really like the inn, and the owners—Hannah and Nathan—have developed a real fondness for her that is most definitely reciprocated."

Samantha returned Travis's box to the table and lowered herself onto the very corner of the opposing bench. "Yet every night, like clockwork, she cries in her room. So, last night, I decided someone needed to talk to her. But as I got within earshot of her door, I realized that in addition to the crying, she was also talking."

"Talking? To who?"

"To herself. About Opal."

"*Opal*?" Tori repeated. "Are you sure?"

Samantha fingered a piece of red hair away from her blue-green eyes and nodded. "I was stunned, of course.

But everyone deals with things differently, I suppose. Some people resort to tears, like Minnie, and some even to not-so-quiet celebrating like Gracelyn. In the middle between the two, you find me and Lucinda. We swing back and forth between being angry we can't go home, and downright ecstatic that we don't have to yet."

Jolee returned to the table to check on their status, but all Tori could really focus on was the rewind feature being utilized by her brain at that exact moment. "Gracelyn has been *celebrating* Opal's death?"

"If you thought it would bring your family back, wouldn't you?" Lucinda glanced toward the front counter and then back at Samantha. "Looks like Miranda has everything, so we probably should be heading out." Then, turning to Tori and Milo, she smiled warmly. "It was nice to see both of you again. And really, the caramel bundt cake is a must-get."

Tori waited until Jolee took their dessert order before grabbing Milo's arm and squeezing a wee bit harder than she'd intended. "It's got to be one of them, don't you think? Either Minnie or Gracelyn? I mean, the one who was treated abominably by Opal is crying—which could signal guilt, and the one who lost day-to-day contact with her family because of Opal is celebrating her death."

Milo grinned down at her hand and then relocated it to the table with the help of his own. Interlacing their fingers, he let out a half sigh, half laugh. "When we retire, maybe you should give some thought to becoming the first-ever granny PI. And maybe *I* can be your assistant."

"Ha. Ha. Very funny." She stuck her tongue out at him and then followed it up with an apologetic kiss. "But seriously. Doesn't it make sense it's one of them?"

"I suppose. But crying could just mean Minnie is sad, couldn't it?"

"Over Opal? A woman who humiliated Minnie at every turn in the hours leading up to her demise? Um, doubtful."

"And your reason for the other one?" Milo prodded.

"You mean Gracelyn? Oh, that's easy. Gracelyn has reason to celebrate Opal's death. With that one out of the mix in all things Jasper Falls, those buildings Gracelyn's kids wanted to lease for their respective businesses will be available again. Voilà, welcome back, family!"

Milo sat back as Jolee neared their table with his brownie sundae and Tori's salted caramel bundt cake. "Not necessarily. Opal could have a kid or a spouse who gets everything upon her death, thus changing nothing in Gracelyn's world."

"Ughhh! I hadn't thought of that."

Chapter 25

Tori hit the power button on the computer tower underneath her desk and waited for her monitor to spring to life. All night long she'd tossed and turned, mentally trying to counter the holes Milo had poked in her remaining who-killed-Opal-and-why theories. Try as she might, she couldn't discard his comments.

Then again, she couldn't discard her theories completely, either.

Yes, Minnie's incessant crying could simply be about sadness. That's what crying usually meant. But *usually* didn't necessarily mean *always*. In fact, if Tori were a betting person, she'd place good money on the fact that prisons were probably littered with inmates who cried on occasion—some because they simply wanted to be free, and others, perhaps, because of guilt.

Minnie had no reason to be sad over Opal's passing.

Opal had been awful to her, humiliating her over everything from the way she shuffled her feet to her sewing-related questions that, to anyone truly listening, had been more about making conversation than needing an answer. So even if Milo's summation on crying was right 99 percent of the time, sadness didn't fit as the reason in Minnie's case.

As far as whether Opal's death could really change anything for Gracelyn's children, that would take a little research . . .

A peek at the monitor showed the aging computer was slowly springing to life, and she took advantage of her remaining downtime to work on the apple Milo had stuck in her lunch sack as they were parting ways in the driveway that morning. Not an apple eater by nature, she made herself eat one on occasion, especially if it came from her husband. They tended to taste better when they did.

A red light out of the corner of her eye distracted her from a second bite, and she picked up the main library phone. "Yes, Nina?"

"Hey, I'm sorry to bother you on your lunch break, but there's a call for you on line two. I think it's Rose, but I'm not positive."

"Thanks, Nina." She switched from intercom to the second phone line and set her apple down on her napkin. "This is Tori."

"Nina says you're on your lunch break."

She did her best to place the raspy whisper and decided Nina was right. "Rose? Is that you?"

"Yes."

"Why are you whispering?"

"Because she's here."

Grabbing her apple off the desk once again, she leaned back in her chair and took a loud bite. "Who's . . . there? Wait . . . one . . . minute. I'm a mess." She swapped her apple for the napkin and wiped the spray of juice from her chin. "Okay, I'm back. Sorry about that. Anyway, who's there? And where, exactly, is there?"

An exasperated sigh filled her ear as the whispering became a little less whisper-like and a lot more irritated-like. "I'm talking about Minnie. And she's here, in SewTastic. At this very moment."

"And?"

"And I thought maybe you could stop by. After all, according to Nina, your break just started. That means you have a few minutes to get here, about ten minutes to do a little snooping, and a few minutes to get back. It's perfect."

She fought the urge to remind her elderly friend of the thought process behind a lunch break, but kept it to herself. Instead, she opted to focus on the fact that Rose—a woman who rarely asked anyone for anything—was asking Tori to stop by the shop. "Do you think she'll still be there in ten minutes?" she asked.

"I see no signs of her hurrying to get anywhere."

"Then I'm on my way. Keep her there." Tori took one last look at the fully booted computer and switched between the outside and inside phone lines once again. When Nina answered, she told her where she'd be and when she'd be back and then headed toward the door with her apple in hand.

Down the hall, out the back door, and across the grounds she went, the slight chill to the air a welcome change after being inside all morning. She vacated the library grounds and headed toward the town square and its array of matching business shingles, including the one belonging to SewTastic.

Sure enough, when she stepped inside, Minnie was at the counter looking through a sewing book with Rose. "Oh, that is a beautiful blouse, isn't it?"

Rose acknowledged Tori's entrance with a wink and then waved her over to the counter. "Victoria! Isn't this a nice surprise . . ."

She made a mental note to praise Rose on her acting ability at a later date and focused, instead, on Minnie's lack of skills in the same area when it came to Tori's presence.

"Hi, Rose. Hi, Minnie—it's good to see you out and about and feeling better."

Rose took Tori's unintentional cue and ran with it. "You were feeling poorly, Minnie?"

"No, I've been—"

"It was the other day, at the inn. You had to cut our conversation short because you were feeling tired." She'd known it was a ruse at the time, but now, with Minnie's reaction, there was no doubt whatsoever.

"I—I don't sleep well when I'm not in my own bed," Minnie said weakly.

Seeing her opportunity, Tori stepped forward, placing a reassuring hand on Minnie's shoulder as she did. "I heard about your rough nights this past week. Is there anything I can do to help?"

"Hot milk always helps me settle down at night." Rose removed the book from possible distraction range and slid it to the opposite side of the counter. "I'm sure Hannah will make you some if you ask her."

"Minnie has been upset, Rose."

Minnie's mouth gaped. "H-how do you know that?"

"From a few of your fellow tour members. They're concerned about you, Minnie." She stepped even closer to the elderly woman and hoped it didn't send the woman straight for the door. "We all are. What happened here on Saturday was awful. I know the difficulty *I've* had processing it, and you spent all that time on the bus with her that morning, too."

Minnie's lip quivered and she looked away.

"Minnie?"

"I wasn't nice to her," Minnie whispered. "My parents raised me to be a kind person and I wasn't that day."

Rose shuffled her way around the counter and then led Minnie toward the hallway that linked the main room with the rest of the building. Halfway there, Minnie came to a standstill.

"I—I can't go in there again."

It took a moment for the meaning behind the woman's words to register with both of them, but as soon as they did, Rose rushed to correct the impression she hadn't meant to give. "I want you to go sit down in my office. It's small, but it's private. And you can sit down for a spell."

"Sitting down sounds good," Minnie half whispered, half mumbled.

The telltale jingle of an arriving customer detoured Rose back to the counter while Tori took over as hallway escort. There was no denying the way Minnie's gait slowed as she neared the project room, but by the grace of God, she kept walking until she was in Rose's office.

"Sit here." Tori moved Rose's favorite chair into the

center of the windowless room and held it steady as Minnie lowered herself onto its edge. "Can I get you a glass of water? Or a cracker? Rose keeps a supply of crackers in her drawer. She says it gives her a boost when she's feeling tired."

"No. I'm okay. I just need to clear my head, I think."

She pulled a folding chair from the narrow closet, opened it across from Minnie, and tried to ignore the ticktock of the clock on the wall behind her head. "Minnie, I think you're being awfully hard on yourself. I never heard you say so much as one unkind word to Opal the entire time you were here on Saturday. She poked at you all day long, and you took every shot with grace. If kindness was important to your parents, I'm quite sure they'd have been proud of you a million times over."

Unless you killed her . . .

She started to shake the troubling thought away but kept it close, instead. After all, Minnie was a suspect.

"Just because no one heard the things I said to Opal, doesn't mean I didn't say them. *I* know I said them and so, too, does . . . Opal." Hunching forward in Rose's chair, Minnie began to cry, her shoulders shaking back and forth as her cries turned to sobs and finally petered off into hiccups. "I . . . don't . . . know . . . why . . . I couldn't . . . let . . . it . . . go. Everyone knew she was . . . mean. But I guess it was . . . watching her be so nasty to Rose . . . got to me."

Repositioning her chair so they were side by side rather than across from each other, Tori sat down and began to quietly rub Minnie's back. In time, all lingering effects of her sobs disappeared, leaving a completely spent woman in their wake.

"Minnie, I didn't like the way Opal spoke to Rose or anyone else, either. That's nothing to feel bad about. Nice people generally don't gravitate toward mean-spirited people. Not when that mean spirit is on full display as it was with Opal on Saturday."

"Did you yell at her?"

"No. But neither did you."

Minnie's chin dropped to her chest. "Yes, I did. When everyone was enjoying those lovely treats Rose and Leona put out for us, Miranda offered to get my project on her way back from the restroom. I thanked her but said I'd get it myself. I followed her down the hallway and then headed into the project room while she went on to the bathroom."

Unsure of what she was about to hear, Tori pulled her hand from Minnie's back and waited. On one hand, she wanted closure for Rose. On the other hand, she didn't want Mrs. Claus to be guilty of murder.

"I didn't have any intention of speaking with Opal. I just wanted to get my holiday apron and return to the main room to try one of Margaret Louise's hushpuppies. But the second I walked into the room, Opal got mean. She said it was people like me who gave old folks a bad name."

"People like you? Are you kidding me? Did she not see how every one of us gravitated toward you from the moment your group arrived?"

If Tori's words registered in Minnie's head, it didn't show, as the woman continued her story in the same defeated tone. "I tried to ignore her just like I had to that point. I even hummed a little song my mother used to sing to me as a small child. But while I hummed, she started quizzing me on sewing terms. Most I knew, but a few I didn't recognize. When I would say I didn't know one, she'd roll her eyes and laugh. She even brought up that signature thing again. Only this time, she started quizzing me on famous designers and asking me if I'd know their label by sight. A few I knew and a few I didn't. Those I got, she ignored. Those I didn't, she hung over my head as yet another example of how I was letting my generation down. By the time she was done, I was shaking. And that's when I snapped."

Uh-oh . . .

"I told her she was a mean, nasty woman and that no one cared about her any more than they cared about some stupid bell on the label of a shirt. I told her if I had the choice between knowing everything and being liked, I'd take being liked any day of the week." Minnie stopped, took a deep, shaky breath, and did her best to power through yet another round of tears. "And that's when I said it, Victoria."

She started to brace herself for the inevitable confession, but stopped as Minnie's choice of words hit her with a one-two punch.

That's when I said it . . .

"Wait. That's when you *said* it?" she clarified in her own shaky voice.

Minnie's gaze dropped to the floor. "Yes."

"Said *what*?"

"I told her that when she died, no one would attend her funeral."

Chapter 26

Tori stood in front of her window and waited for the inner calm that usually came whenever she looked out at the moss-draped trees canopying the library grounds like an old southern plantation. She tried to help it along by imagining a sprinkling of children—some reading under trees or at picnic tables, and others engaged in a spirited game of duck, duck, goose. But none of it made any difference. The unease that had settled over her the moment she realized Minnie's big secret wasn't so big after all showed no signs of going away.

She was back to square one with the exception of Gracelyn Moses. And while part of her wanted to believe that meant Gracelyn was the killer, the other part—the part that had waded into similar waters before—couldn't shake the feeling that she was missing something. What that something was though, she had no idea.

Tap. Tap. Tap.
Tap. Tap. Tap.
Tap-tap-tap-tap-tap . . .

Yanking her eyes to the left, she spotted Charles between the shrubbery and the window, looking down at the ground and using his finger on the glass to complete his chosen song: "Jingle Bells." Recognizing the tune, she took care of the next line for him.

Tap tap tap tap tap tap tap tap tap tap tap tap tap t-app.

Charles's head snapped up to reveal the infectious smile she'd grown to love as much as the man who sported it. "Can I come in, sugar lips?"

She considered feigning an inability to read lips as a joke, but when she finally found her calm, the last thing she was going to do was risk sending it away in a huff. Instead, she nodded and pointed him toward the back door that would serve as their meeting place.

When she reached the door, she made sure to push it open slowly thanks to past complaints from Leona that still echoed in her ears. "Charles?" she called, looking around. "Where are you?"

"I'm. Right. Here." She turned toward the triangle of snaps and motioned her friend inside, meeting his lips with her cheek as he passed. "Another week and your choice of songs will be spot-on."

"'Jingle Bells' is spot-on no matter what time of year it is, love." He waved a manila folder in the space between them and then marched ahead of her into the office. "So why are you still here? Shouldn't you be home spending time with Milo?"

She pointed him toward Nina's desk chair and sank

down onto her own. "Well, let's see. First up, I cheated Nina out of her lunch break, so I made up for it by letting her go home an hour early. Second, I had to make up for all the work I didn't get done because of my extended lunch break. And finally, I didn't get to what I wanted to do during my break, so I figured I'd do that now, only I'm not."

"I know I shouldn't have followed that, love, but I did." He wiggled his fingers between them and let loose a little squeal. "I'm on fire today."

"Dare I ask?" she said, grinning.

"How about I just show you, instead?" He held out the manila folder and waited for her to take it. "I'm quite sure my genius will speak for itself."

"Genius, eh?" She set the folder on her desk and flipped it open to find a pile of single-sheet questionnaires. "What are these?"

"Only personal information about each and every one of the people on Miranda's tour."

"Are you serious?" She liberated the pile from the folder and laid each page across her desk so she could see them side by side. "Okay, wait, I sort of recall you mentioning something about these before the bus showed up that morning. Only I thought you were kidding."

"Nope. Leona wanted to make sure no one was allergic to Paris so when we talked on the phone two weeks ago, I proposed adding it to the questionnaire Miranda was drafting for the tour participants. Which is why, if you look at the fourth question on the sheet, you see the specific question regarding known allergies. Unfortunately, because Lucinda noted an allergy to cats, dogs, and rabbits, Paris had to stay back at the condo under my constant video surveillance."

"Ah yes, I remember. I'm surprised Leona didn't have Lucinda thrown off the tour the moment that questionnaire came back in."

"She thought about it, but, in the end, she decided to let it slide this one time." Charles rode Nina's wheeled chair across the floor to Tori's desk and pointed at the series of papers. "I'm not sure any of the questions or their corresponding answers can help fill in any real blanks for us, but I figured it's worth a look, don't you?"

"Absolutely." She read the first question regarding everyone's sewing experience and found that virtually everyone had picked up the craft during their teenage years except Opal. Opal hadn't picked up a needle and thread until her forties—an interesting curiosity considering her attitude toward Minnie . . .

"I like the question regarding their commitment to the craft. Lucinda and Samantha both say they make time to sew because it grounds them. Minnie and Gracelyn say they sew because they like making things for other people. And Opal pointed to the sewing museum she opened in Jasper Falls as her testament to a dying craft."

"Sewing is *not* dying," she argued.

"Opal was dramatic. We know this, Victoria."

"True." She leaned in for a closer look at Opal's sheet. "What else do we know about her from this?"

Charles's finger moved down the row of questions while his mouth narrated. "She reported no allergies. Her favorite sewing project thus far was a blouse she sent to her friend—the governor's wife—and she visited Sweet Briar one time about twenty years ago. So, in answer to your question, we still know nothing." He slumped forward on the desk in a classic pout, lip and all. "I'm sorry, Victoria. I was hoping there'd be something useful here."

"It was worth a try." She glanced at the answers on the rest of the questionnaires and then inserted them back into the folder. "We could do what I was planning to do when Rose dragged me off to talk to Minnie."

Charles rescinded his lip and stared at Tori. "You talked to Minnie?"

"I did. And she's officially off our list of suspects."

"I could have told you that."

"Ha. Ha."

"No, I'm serious. I did a lot of thinking over the last few days, and I remember seeing Minnie come back from the project room, too. And yes, she looked a little shaken as Rose described, but I knew she couldn't have killed Opal because I checked on the old bat after that, and she was alive and well when I went in. Just ask Miranda."

"But why didn't you say something sooner?" she asked.

"Because I didn't want to be wrong in the event she slipped back in when I wasn't looking. And when you mentioned that book she checked out, I had to consider the fact I was wrong on the timing."

"The book was a mere curiosity. She felt so guilty— and still does—over the last few things she said to Opal, that she wanted to know how it could have happened. How someone could kill Opal like that and get away with it." She swiveled the chair around to the computer monitor but stopped short of actually turning it on. "You know what? I need a treat—something chocolaty."

"You're speaking my language, sister."

"Debbie's?" she teased.

"Is there any other choice even worthy of consideration?" He raked the folder over to the edge of the desk but left it there for a moment as he double-checked the knot in his accessory scarf. When he deemed it acceptable, he grabbed the folder but remained seated. "You sure about this, love?"

"About needing a treat? Absolutely."

"No, I was referring more to wrapping things up here prematurely."

"I'll get it done. I always do. Right now though, I just want some fun time with you before you have to head back to New York. After all, Chief Dallas can't keep you here forever."

They were about a bite away from finishing the sampler plate Emma had put together for them when Debbie dropped a stack of color travel brochures on their table and kept walking.

"Hey, what's this?"

"Excess."

Charles craned his head around his extra-tall coffee and helped himself to half the pile, cycling through the material in record speed. "Did it, did it, did it, didn't do it, did it, did it."

She took his stack back and looked down at the top brochure. "When did you go to the Tom's Creek Butterfly House?"

"Tuesday."

"And the Jackson Family Ice Cream Factory?"

He sucked in a breath and let it out with his answer.

"Tuesday afternoon, on the way home from the butterfly house."

"You've really done all of these things?" she asked, holding out his stack.

"Everything but the ziplining. I don't look good in ropes."

"But you've only been here twice . . . for less than two full weeks in total."

He started to shrug but got distracted by a hangnail on his left thumb. "Leona is a wonderful hostess, what can I say?"

She separated his pile into two separate piles—one for those attractions that fell in the must-do category, and one for those that didn't. When she reached the end, she moved on to the second stack.

"Kayaking on Reiner Lake—must do. Wolf sanctuary—must do. Jasper Falls Sewing Museum—must . . . wait. This has to be Opal's place, right?" She turned the brochure so Charles could see it, too, and then took a good hard look at the cover. A collage of colored pictures filled the top half of the front page while the museum's address and hours claimed the space underneath. Inside, they saw more pictures and a list of fourth-quarter exhibits.

THE YESTERYEAR OF SEWING:
A LOOK BACK AT THE TOOLS OF THE TRADE
THROUGH THE DECADES.

SEWING TO LIVE:
FOR SOME, SEWING IS A PASSION.
FOR OTHERS, IT'S A WAY OF LIFE.

SIGNATURES DON'T LIE:
THE HISTORY OF THE PERSONALIZED LABEL.

When she came to the end of the last line, she doubled back and read it a second time. "Ahhh, so that's why she was so horrid over the whole label fingerprint thingy. She was preparing an exhibit and wanted to fling her knowledge around."

"I wonder if I could talk Leona into going to this with me," Charles mused. "Maybe if I bill it as a way to reach more customers for the shop, she'll consider it."

"If she doesn't, you and I can go the next time you're in town. We could make a whole day out of it with lunch on one end, and a stop for frozen custard on the other. Maybe some of the others might want to join us."

Charles's gasp was faint but still noticeable. "You mean like a real live sewing circle field trip?"

"Sure. Can't you see Margaret Louise and the others lapping something like that up?"

"Please, please don't let her drive," Charles pleaded. "Please?"

"We'll need a few drivers to get everyone there."

"I get that, Victoria. I'm just calling dibs on any car she's not driving."

Her laugh filled the space between them and she reveled in the moment, the stress of the past few days evaporating like water droplets on a hot day. "You know there's a movement under way to keep you here permanently, yes?"

"I know. You mentioned it the other day."

"Okay, but did I also happen to mention the beat is getting louder and louder?"

"Trust me, sugar lips, I hear it, too. Leona is becoming downright relentless on the subject. Her latest tactic, you ask? Using Paris to guilt me into making the move."

"She's used Paris to guilt you? How?"

"Well, she likes to drop the fact that my departure after your wedding upset Paris so much she had to see a therapist for a few weeks."

"Is—is that true?" she stammered.

"She showed me the bill."

Chapter 27

She grabbed her laptop from its temporary resting spot atop her vanity and climbed into bed beside Milo. "So? How's the book?"

"I keep telling myself just one more chapter, but then I can't stop." Lowering the thriller to his lap, he took in her computer and the brochure resting on its keyboard. "I thought you were caught up with work for the day."

"With library stuff—yes. With this whole who-killed-Opal thing—not so much. But I'll quit when you quit, deal?"

"Deal."

She waited for him to return to his book and then settled against the headboard with her computer atop her lap. Positioning her hands on the keyboard, she entered the website address located on the back of the brochure into the search bar and hit enter.

"What's that?"

She followed her husband's eyes back to the computer screen and the exterior shot of the Jasper Falls Sewing Museum. "I thought you were reading."

"You're a bit of a distraction."

"I could go into the living room with this." She scrolled halfway down the welcome page, only to find herself staring at a professional headshot of Opal.

"Don't you dare." He flipped his book upside down across his own lap and pushed up on his hands until he was sitting more than reclining. "Who's that?"

"The building is a sewing museum located in Jasper Falls. And this woman?" She pointed at the screen. "That's Opal Goodwin, the woman who was murdered in Rose's shop on Saturday."

"May I?" At her nod, he lifted the computer off her lap and took a closer look. "She looks a little younger than I imagined."

"It's a headshot, it's been airbrushed—a lot." When he was done inspecting the photo of the woman he'd only heard about until that moment, he returned the machine to its starting point. "So that's her museum at the top? The one you say she started?"

She scrolled down to the bio beneath the picture and began to read aloud.

"'Opal Goodwin, founder of the Jasper Falls Sewing Museum in Jasper Falls, South Carolina, has never taken anything at face value. Guided by a curiosity about sewing, Opal sought to learn every nuance of the craft. When she was done, she realized she'd pieced together a historical trail her fellow sewing enthusiasts would love.

The Jasper Falls Sewing Museum is the very embodiment of that trail—stretched out for all to enjoy.'"

"Wow. Sounds like that place is right up your alley." Lowering himself back down to his reading pillow, he resumed control of his book. "Maybe we should check it out some weekend."

"That's sweet, and I appreciate the offer, but I wouldn't subject you to that. Besides, Charles and I think it might make a really fun field trip for the sewing circle one day." She leaned over, kissed Milo on the top of his head, and then settled back into place.

"If it interests you, it interests me, Tori. But yeah, you're probably right. A field trip sounds like it's definitely in order with this place, assuming, of course, it doesn't fold now that its founder is gone."

It was a point she hadn't necessarily considered before, but that didn't make it any less valid . . .

With Milo's attention back on his novel, Tori returned the cursor to the top of the page and clicked on the heading devoted to interior shots of the museum. When the page appeared, she scrolled down to the first picture and the assortment of antique sewing tools it featured.

Sewing shears . . .

Wooden thread spools . . .

Real china and ceramic buttons . . .

A once white but now yellowed measuring tape . . .

A delicately carved wooden box with a pincushion top . . .

A sterling silver thimble . . .

"Oh, Milo, my great-grandmother would have loved this."

He looked up from his book and squeezed her hand. "That's why you're going to make the time to go. So you can enjoy it for her."

"And I will." She scrolled down to the next picture and sucked in her breath. "Oh. Wow. That's an antique Singer sewing machine. It has to be almost a hundred and fifty years old!"

Her gaze strayed down to the next shot. "Oh, and look at that one. It has golden-colored details. Wow. Surely that belonged to someone with wealth . . ."

"Why is that one in a case?"

She followed his finger to the next picture and the mint green sewing machine packed neatly into a handled case with additional storage for thread and other assorted sewing needs. "Oh, that's a vintage Bell sewing machine like Leona was asking about the other day. It was predominantly used by tailors."

Slowly, she made her way through the rest of the pictures designed to entice visitors to the museum. When she reached the bottom, she returned to the menu and clicked on the page devoted to special exhibits, both past and present. A banner near the top heralded the upcoming label exhibit, while smaller banners beneath it paid homage to past events.

Again, she scrolled her way down the page, stopping periodically to read an occasional tidbit or visitor-relayed quote. The final quote, from Opal herself, accompanied a picture depicting a half dozen hand-sewn labels. She recognized two of the signatures from outfits she herself had worn as a child, before scrolling back to the exhibit's banner and its teasing nod to "the labels of the famous and infamous."

"Infamous, huh?" She clicked on the next page, read through the museum's hours and pricing, and then exited off the site completely. "Opal may not have been a very nice person, but there's no doubt she's put together an amazing tribute to something that's been a huge part of my life, as well as that of my friends. I hope someone finds a way to keep it going without her."

"Is there someone you can call and ask?"

"Not at ten o'clock at night there isn't." Leaning over the edge of the bed, she set the computer on the floor and then rolled into place next to Milo. "So, you still finding that book impossible to put down?"

He met and held her gaze for all of about two seconds before he tossed the book onto his nightstand and pulled her close. "Not anymore, I'm not."

The smell of bacon frying pulled her from the bed at eight thirty. Her hair was tousled and her eyes were still hazy with sleep, but it didn't matter. There was bacon to be had.

Maneuvering her way around an unfamiliar box in the middle of the living room, Tori headed toward the kitchen. "You do realize you've hit upon the second-best way to wake me up, don't you?"

She stepped through the kitchen doorway and stopped as the man she expected to see turned out to be a sixty-something woman in a polyester running suit and an apron. "Margaret Louise?"

"Good mornin', Victoria. Don't you look all cute in your nightie and slippers." Margaret Louise picked up the tongs she'd placed on the counter beside the stove and carefully flipped each of the seven crackling strips of bacon. "The French toast is finishin' up, and we should be sittin' down to eat in 'bout two or three minutes. You want orange juice or milk?"

"Milk." She liberated her empty glass from the carefully set table and headed toward the refrigerator before reality made her stop. "Um, Margaret Louise? I love you to pieces, but why are you here? Making me breakfast?"

"Oh, I'm makin' it for Milo and me, too, Victoria. That's why there's three places set at the table."

She glanced back at the table and noted the three forks, the three knives, the two glasses . . . Unsure of whether she was dreaming, she rubbed her eyes.

Nope, Margaret Louise is still here . . .

"Do you happen to know where my husband is, by chance?"

Margaret Louise stopped pushing bacon strips around the pan and pointed the tongs at Tori. "Your *husband*. Ain't that a mighty fine thing to say, Victoria?"

She continued on her path to the refrigerator but detoured toward the counter at the last minute thanks to Margaret Louise's tongs. Still confused and a little bit tired, Tori filled her glass under her friend's watchful eye and then carried the carton back to its preferred spot on the top shelf of the refrigerator. "Milo? Do you know where he is?"

"He's outside, fetching the last of the two boxes from my station wagon."

"Oh, so that box out in the dining room is yours?" She took a sip of milk and tried not to think about the bacon-induced hunger pains that were making it hard to completely focus.

Margaret Louise stepped away from the stove long enough to remove the perfectly cooked French toast slices from the griddle and transfer them onto Tori's favorite serving plate. "I'm hopin' you'll go through them and decide to keep 'em yourself, but if you don't, I'll take 'em on to Goodwill."

Shaking off her lingering confusion, Tori accepted the serving plate from Margaret Louise's outstretched hand and carried it to the table. "You brought me clothes?"

"I brought you some clothes. The rest I brought over to Melissa's last night." With a flick of her wrist, Margaret Louise shut off the burner and carefully removed each piece of bacon from the skillet to a secondary serving plate. "She sure was tickled 'bout them clothes. You'd have thought I'd given her a million dollars in gold the way she carried on."

The screen door smacked open against the pantry, and Tori turned to find a box-holding Milo smiling back at her with a mix of surprise and pleasure. "Oh, hey there sweetheart, you're awake?"

She stole a piece of bacon from the serving plate as Margaret Louise passed by en route to the table. "I smelled *this*."

"Yeah, I know. It got me, too."

Margaret Louise stepped back, stole the piece of bacon right out of Tori's hands, and placed it back on the plate. "I let myself in with that key you gave me. But don't worry none, I brought all of this food from home so I wouldn't be emptyin' your cupboards."

Shifting his arms from the sides of the box to the bottom, Milo made his way through the kitchen, stopping to kiss Tori as he passed. "You want me to just put this with the other one, right?" At Margaret Louise's nod, he disappeared into the dining room.

"He's mighty accommodatin', Victoria. I think you should keep 'im." Margaret Louise waited for Milo to return and then motioned them both to sit down. "Orange juice or milk, Milo?"

"I can get it." He started to stand up again, but his progress was thwarted by Margaret Louise's pudgy hand.

"No. Sit. This breakfast was my idea." The woman crossed to the refrigerator, held both choices up for Milo to see, and then filled his glass to the top before doing the same with her own. When she was seated beside them, she handed the bacon plate to Tori and smiled broadly. "*Now* you can have your bacon, Miss Impatient."

"That's Mrs. Impatient now." Milo dodged Tori's playful swat and then helped himself to a few pieces of bacon, too. "This was awfully nice of you to do, Margaret Louise. Especially when I have to head out of here in less than fifteen minutes to help John Peter pack up Calamity Books' entire inventory."

Margaret Louise beamed. "It's my pleasure. I just know how hard you two are always workin', and I wanted to do somethin' special. Uncoverin' all them boxes in my attic yesterday just gave me the nudge to do it now rather than later.

"I reckon I would have been here even sooner if I hadn't run into Charles at the grocery store. When that one gets his gums a-flappin' it's hard to get away." Margaret Louise took a momentary pause from eating to point her fork at Tori. "So tell me 'bout this sewin' circle field trip that's got that boy happy as a calf in clover . . ."

Chapter 28

Tori was just opening the first box when Leona breezed into the living room with her favorite cameraman in tow. "Charles told me my sister unearthed a few boxes of clothing in her attic and that she was on her way here to foist them on you, dear."

"I ain't foistin' nothin' on anyone," Margaret Louise protested. "I'm just seein' if Victoria wants anythin' before I head to Goodwill."

Leona shuddered, once, twice, and then pinned Tori with a stare capable of melting flesh. "Tell me I've at least gotten through to you regarding the horrors of hand-me-downs."

"I—I . . ."

Something that looked a lot like disappointment dulled Margaret Louise's smile as she turned her nearly identical brown eyes on Tori. "We don't have to go through this stuff if you don't want to, Victoria. I just thought maybe you'd like to see if there's somethin' you might want to keep is all."

"And I do." She threw out her hand in anticipation of Leona's reaction and reached into the box with the other. "Your sister went to a lot of effort to bring these things to me, and I'm going to look at them."

"As long as looking doesn't lead to wearing, we're fine." Leona snapped her fingers in the direction of her cameraman and summoned him to come closer. "Skip, I want you recording all of this. It may spawn a future episode of *Leona's Closet*."

Skip's wink disappeared behind his shoulder-mounted camera. For a moment, Tori considered jockeying for Skip's removal, but she let it slide. Skip was only doing his job, and she could always demand the tape be deleted at a later date.

Outfit by outfit they made their way through the box, with Leona coaching Skip to pull in tight on anything she found to be extremely appalling. Halfway through the box, however, Leona gave the cut sign and lowered herself onto a chair for a closer look.

"Is that French silk?"

Margaret Louise nodded. "It sure is."

"Since when have you ever owned a scarf made out of French silk?"

"Since you gave it to me for Christmas a few years ago."

Leona gasped in horror. "You're getting rid of a gift I *gave* you? How—how *could* you?"

"I told you, when you called me that day, that I didn't need nothin' so fancy. But you didn't listen. Not that you ever do."

"I listen, Margaret Louise. I just choose to do what I know to be best." Leona reached into the box, pulled out the scarf, and spread it carefully across her lap. "Which, in this case, was to gift you with something that could make you look less like a hillbilly."

"I ain't ashamed of bein' a hillbilly, Leona. Never have been, never will be."

"But you should be."

Tori leaned across the empty chair between them and ran her hand across the scarf. "Did you get this in Paris, Leona?"

"No. I purchased it in a specialty shop when I was in New York one year. In fact, truth be told, I bought one for myself, as well."

"You mean you and me could have been matchin', Twin?"

Leona glared at her cameraman until his smile disappeared, and then waved off her sister's notion with a flip of her freshly manicured fingers. "No. That's precisely why I got mine in royal blue."

"Well it sure is purty, Twin, but it's collectin' dust in my attic when it could be makin' someone else feel fancy."

"Victoria?"

"Yes, Leona?"

"I can count on you to give this a good and appreciative home, can't I?"

It was Tori's turn to gasp, and gasp she did while holding a hand to her throat. "Leona? Are you encouraging me to wear a hand-me-down?"

"I ain't never worn it, Victoria. See? It still has the price tag my twin left on it so I could see how much money she spent."

"But it was yours first," Tori protested. "Which makes it a dreaded hand-me-down. I've been warned about such horrible atrocities."

"Oh, shut up, dear." Leona carefully folded the scarf and then held it to her cheek. "So lovely. Makes me want to wear mine again."

Tori tried not to laugh when Skip winked in her direction, but she was grossly unsuccessful. She, in turn, tried to pass it off under the guise of happiness. "You know what, Leona? You should wear your scarf when that news crew from New York comes to the shop on Monday. You look fabulous in royal blue, and it'll really make you pop."

"They're not coming, dear." Leona reluctantly pulled the scarf from her face and handed it to Tori.

"Not coming? Why not?"

"Because I told them not to."

Tori looked for all of Leona's tells to see if her friend was kidding, but none of the usual suspects were there. "Why would you do that? I thought you were all excited about the boost that kind of coverage could give to SewTastic's online presence."

"I was. But, in subsequent conversations with Margot, I began to realize they were looking to exploit the shop, and we simply can't afford that after what happened there on Saturday."

"Ah, so you think they were going to zero in on Opal's murder after all?"

"No. Margot was far more interested in her late co-anchor's murder."

"What are you talking about, Leona?"

Leona pulled a few more items from the box and held

them up for Skip to film. "This skirt is dreadful, Margaret Louise. Please tell me you never actually wore this in public."

"I didn't, Twin. *You* did."

Leona dropped the skirt onto the table as if it were diseased, and leapt to her feet. "I did no such thing!"

"You're darn tootin' you did. Mama even has proof in her photo album. You wore it to a dance when we were in ninth grade. No one danced with you."

"I did no such . . ." In a flashback evidenced by the slow draining of all color from her face, Leona's words trailed away.

"Now you're rememberin', ain't you?"

Seconds turned to minutes as Leona said nothing. Eventually, she cleared her throat and turned to Skip. "If you breathe a word of this to anyone, I will blackball you in this industry, do you understand?"

He peeked at Leona over the top of the lens and then lowered the camera down to his side. "I'll get rid of the proof the second I get back to the station."

"No, you'll sit down on that chair and you'll get rid of it now." Then, as if nothing happened, Leona dropped the skirt back into the box and pushed it to the side. "Now, Victoria, where were we?"

It took a moment to get back on point, but with a mumbled cue from Margaret Louise, she found her way. "Yeah, you mentioned something about Margot's former co-anchor having been murdered?"

"Oh, yes, that's right. Bad fashion always throws me." Leona sat up tall and took a deep, cleansing breath. "Anyway, the co-anchor. Yes, from what I was able to gather during my conversations with Margot, her former co-anchor at the station was murdered by his wife six months ago."

Margaret Louise stopped picking through the second box of clothes. "Was he caught philanderin'?"

"I don't know. Margot didn't address that. Though, if he was, his wife shouldn't have stopped with poison."

"So she's been charged?" Tori asked.

"They can't charge a woman who's disappeared off the face of the earth." Leona reached past her sister for a closer look at a patterned sweater, and then dropped it back into the box with disgust. "But that's not my problem. SewTastic is."

She knew she was missing something in translation, but no matter how hard she tried to figure out what it was, she kept coming up empty. Eventually she gave up and opted to risk the wrath of Leona in order to piece it together. "I realize I'm probably setting myself up for a glare to end all glares with this question, but what does SewTastic have to do with this man's murder?"

"Absolutely nothing."

Well, alrighty then . . .

Halting the conversation with a bejeweled hand, Leona stood and made her way over to Skip. "Did you erase that last little bit of tape, handsome?"

Skip's Adam's apple gave away his swallow. "I sure did."

"Excellent." Leona playfully walked her fingers along the cameraman's shoulders and then motioned to the camera. "I'll be sure to let the station manager know what an asset you are to me."

"Thanks, Leona."

"No, thank *you*, Skip." Leona peeked around the

table at the second box and then batted her false lashes at the man. "You've done such a fine job this morning, Skip, I think you should head home. If something comes up, I'll give you a ring."

He gathered up his camera and his bag but remained seated. "Are you free tonight, Leona? Maybe we could catch a movie or something?"

"I'm sorry, Skip, but I have plans."

Defeated, he stood, hooked the camera bag strap over his arm, and disappeared into the kitchen. Seconds later, the screen door banged shut.

"One of these days, Twin, I'm gonna figure out what you're doin' to make men swoon."

"It's quite simple, Margaret Louise." Leona slowly ran her hands down the edges of her body. "*This* makes men swoon."

"Leona?"

Holding her pose, Leona's eyes narrowed on Tori. "Yes, dear?"

"I'm not trying to sound dense here, but I'm still stuck on the thing about Charles's friend—the TV reporter."

"Margot."

"Right, Margot. Why did you turn her coverage down?"

"Because I know how people think, dear, and I don't want people coming away from a feature story associating SewTastic with yet another murder. One is more than enough, don't you think?"

"No, I agree with that completely," Tori said. "You've just lost me on how this Margot woman could possibly tie a sewing shop in Sweet Briar, South Carolina, with the murder of a morning show co-anchor in New York City. It doesn't make any sense."

"It's not SewTastic, per se, dear. It's the fact that SewTastic is a sewing shop."

"And that matters because . . ."

"His wife was a gifted seamstress."

Chapter 29

She was on her third lap around the Green when she felt Milo's arms circle her midsection. "Hey, pretty lady, did you miss me?"

"Every minute." Turning, she rose up on tiptoes and met his kiss. "Did you get John Peter all moved out?"

"We did. We got the last box of books into the truck about fifteen minutes ago, and he pulled out of Sweet Briar for the last time about five minutes after that." He captured her hand in his and pointed toward the gazebo. "Could we sit for a while before we head home for dinner?"

"Of course. Are you okay?"

He led her through the closest break in the picket fence and across the expanse to the gazebo they'd helped to paint during one of Georgina's annual Let's Spruce Up Sweet Briar campaigns. "I'm fine, just a little beat,

I guess. Apparently every one of John Peter's rare first editions is a hardcover."

"Oh, yeah, I see where this is going."

"A couple dozen of those in one box makes for some heavy lifting, that's for sure."

She sat down on the gazebo step and patted the vacant spot to her left. "I hate seeing Calamity Books close, but Sweet Briar is more of a read-for-fun kind of town, you know? A shop stocked solely with rare first editions doesn't really fit."

Angling his body toward her, he linked his fingers behind his head and leaned against the gazebo's frame. "So how'd the clothes stuff go with Margaret Louise? Was anything salvageable?"

"There were a few things I considered, but Leona nixed every single one of them."

His laugh was tired but no less perfect. "Leona showed up?"

"With Skip."

He scrunched his face. "As in the cameraman from her cable show?"

"One and the same."

"Why?"

"Because she found out Margaret Louise was bringing me hand-me-downs and she wanted to: A, make sure I didn't take any; and B, get some footage for possible use in a future episode of *Leona's Closet*."

"So I take it you're keeping nothing?"

"Leona allowed me to keep one particular scarf. But when she wasn't looking, Margaret Louise put a really pretty skirt and blouse I liked onto one of the dining room chairs for me."

He shook his head slowly, chuckling as he did. "Leona really is a piece of work, but I don't have to tell you that. I'm curious though, why was the scarf okay?"

"Because it had been a gift from her to Margaret Louise a few years ago."

"Ouch," he said, cringing.

"I know." Reclining her back against his chest, she looked across the Green to the shops that comprised the town square, and tried to imagine what Rose was doing at that moment. "Leona turned down that news crew from New York."

"The national one? Why?"

"It seems they just wanted to use the store as a way to give new life to a very different tale."

"Hey, you two."

Tori and Milo looked to the left to find Travis standing just a few steps away. Instinctively, she sat up, allowing Milo to do the same. "Hey, Travis, how are you?"

"I'm doing okay. I wanted to thank you for the other night. Talking about Ginny and Rachel felt good."

Milo accepted the man's hand and shook it firmly. "I'm glad. Did you get the dinner we had wrapped up for you?"

"I did. Thank you. Miranda brought it up to my room later that evening." He stopped, looked across his shoulder, and waved over a pair of familiar faces. "The three of us were going a little stir-crazy hanging around the inn this evening, so we decided to come down here and walk around for a while."

Miranda stopped beside Travis and smiled first at Milo and then Tori. "We went to the shop before this so I could share some good news with Rose, but she didn't get as excited as I'd hoped. Do you know if she's upset about something?"

"I don't think so . . ."

"Maybe she's a little disappointed about that news show," Milo suggested.

"That's why I stopped by. To tell her I got it." Miranda tucked a strand of hair behind her ear and sat down on the edge of a nearby bench. "There will be a crew at the store just before lunch on Monday. And if we do a good job giving them something fun and lighthearted, I'm quite sure they'll find a spot for it on the six thirty news that night."

"Oh, wow, I thought that one was off the table. Are they coming by plane?" Tori asked.

Miranda's eyebrows dipped. "No, they're driving. They're only coming from Tom's Creek."

"Oh. I'm sorry, I thought you were talking about Margot Pritchard and that crew from New York."

"Mar-Margot Pritchard?" Miranda echoed. "As in the *Wake-Up America* anchor?"

"Yes, that's the one. It was a connection Leona had that didn't pan out in the end, but really, it's probably for the best."

"So they're not coming?"

"No. Leona felt there was simply too big of a difference between what *they* hoped to accomplish and what *you* hope to accomplish."

Miranda drew back. "What *I* hope to accomplish?"

"On behalf of the store . . . And honestly, I think Leona made the right call." Tori heeded the pull of Milo's hands and leaned back against his chest once again. "As for Rose, she'll come around. She's going to be pleased as punch to see SewTastic on television no matter where the station is based."

Samantha came around to the step and sat down. "Hey, I wanted to tell you I'm going to try my hand at making a pillow like yours. I mean, if I have to stick around another day or so, I might as well be productive, right? And of everything in the store, that spoke to me the loudest."

"*My* pillow? I don't understand."

"It's right here." Samantha reached into her back pocket, extracted a glossy card, and handed it to Tori.

"Hey, that's your envelope pillow," Milo said, pointing at the card. "And look, that's what it's called, Victoria's Envelope Pillow."

Tori skimmed the instructions for making the pillow and then held the card up to Miranda. "Do you know about this?"

When Miranda didn't answer, Tori gave the card a little shake. "Miranda?"

"Huh—what?"

"This project card," Tori said. "Did you have something to do with this?"

"In so far as suggesting the concept, yes. But that's it. I know absolutely nothing about sewing."

Milo laughed. "And you're sure you should be marketing a *sewing* shop?"

A buzz from Tori's purse pulled her attention off Miranda's shrug and sent her riffling for her phone. She located it at the very bottom, under a package of gum and the paperback mystery she carried around in the event a sliver of time opened up in her day.

"Hello?"

"It's me, dear."

"Oh, Leona, hi." Excusing herself from the steps, Tori moved to the other side of the gazebo so Milo and the others could continue talking. "I thought you and Charles were going to a movie this evening."

"We are."

She waited for more, but nothing came. "Um, is everything okay?"

"I'm still traumatized from this morning, dear, but I'll recover. In time."

"Lots of people wear hand-me-downs, Leona."

"I shudder at the thought." Leona's voice faded out and back in again as Tori imagined her switching the phone from one ear to the other. "I located my French silk scarf when I got home from your house today. It was in the second drawer from the top on the right-hand side."

Unsure of what to say in response, she hoped the grunt she settled on would suffice. The fact that Leona didn't stop to chastise her for the nonverbal response was a positive sign.

"I showed it to Charles and he gushed over the quality and the color, as I knew he would. When I told him where I purchased it, he got even more excited. It turns out a former neighbor of his worked at that exact shop around the time I was there."

She wandered around the gazebo's interior, listening partly to Milo and the tour folks, and partly to the ramblings in her ear that seemed to have no discernable point.

"Anyway, when he left to take a call, I unfolded the scarf and compared it in my head to the one that's now in your possession. I prefer the royal blue, of course, but the emerald green would work well with my eyes, don't you think?"

She stopped in the center of the gazebo and stared up at the roof. If it had been Dixie's name on the screen, the rambling would make sense. If it had been Margaret Louise's name on the screen, the rambling would make sense. But Leona's name? It didn't fit.

"Leona, I hate to ask this, but is there a point here that I'm missing?"

A potpourri of odd noises that sounded a lot like hemming and hawing faded away as Leona's normally strong voice returned. "I'd like my scarf back."

"You mean the one I got from Margaret Louise?"

"Who got it from me," Leona reminded.

Tori shifted her gaze back to Milo and the others but remained transfixed in the center of the gazebo. "You want the scarf back."

"Yes."

"O-kay . . . sure. I can bring it to you tomorrow if you'd like."

"That would be lovely. Thank you, Tori. I'll make it up to you at a later date."

"That's not necessary." She wandered over to the railing and watched the early evening sun sink lower in the western sky. "I am confused though as to why you didn't want to take it when you first saw it."

"Because I didn't look at the label until I got home."

"I don't understand."

"They're Lily Belle Originals, dear. I'd forgotten that."

"*Lily Belle Originals*?"

"An exquisite line of handmade clothes and accessories that appears to have gone belly-up."

"What happened to it?" she asked.

"Probably the same thing that happens to *all* the little guys these days—they simply couldn't compete."

She wanted to argue, to point to any number of stores along Main Street as examples to the contrary, but she wasn't on the inside like Leona was. Some shops—like Debbie's Bakery—seemed to thrive no matter what, while others—like SewTastic—had to fight for every single customer. Still, she believed in positive thinking and its propensity to germinate into truth.

"Things are going to get better for you and Rose. I feel it in my bones."

"I wish I could say my bones were saying the same thing, Victoria."

"Maybe this TV news crew Miranda landed for Monday will do the kind of piece that'll make people sit up and notice."

"We don't need them to sit up and notice, dear. We need them to sit down and sew."

Chapter 30

Tori tried not to fixate on Rose's need to return to the front window again and again throughout the day, but it was difficult. Yes, it was a chilly day and yes, the filtered sun helped in that regard, but there was more at play with the elderly woman than November's indecisiveness.

Rose was struggling, plain and simple. Her shuffle was more shuffle-y, her arthritic winces were more wince-y, and the smile she normally had for her customers was a lot less smiley. But every time Tori found the courage to ask her friend if everything was okay, something came along to ruin the moment—a passerby stopping to ask for directions, a phone call from any assortment of newspapers asking for information on Opal, and last but not least, a pessimistic phone call from Rose's majority partner.

Abandoning the safety of the thread display she'd been using as her vantage point for the past hour, Tori wandered over to the counter. "So have you picked out what you're going to wear yet?"

"Probably a variation of what I'm wearing right now." Rose flipped a page in the same catalogue she'd been looking at off and on since she'd propped the open sign in the front window that morning.

"I think you should wear that beige suit you like to wear for special occasions. You always look so sharp in that."

"But it's *not* a special occasion, Victoria."

Tori rocked back on her kitten heels and crossed her arms. "Yes, you're right. Having your pride and joy spotlighted during the evening news *is* rather ordinary."

"Don't be sarcastic, Victoria. It doesn't become you."

"Then *talk* to me, Rose. Tell me what's bothering you so I can help. *Please.*"

Several beats of silence ticked by before Rose finally let go of the catalogue and sighed. "I can't shake this feeling that this place is done—that all the joy I felt leading up to Saturday is gone forever."

"Hey, you were happy before SewTastic!"

"At times, yes. But nothing compared to the way I felt in the weeks leading up to and immediately following our opening. People asked my opinion on fabric they were buying, tools they were using, and projects they were thinking of trying. I haven't had that kind of validation since I retired from teaching."

Tori felt the pain emanating from deep inside Rose's soul and the answering helplessness from inside her own. "It's only been eight days, Rose. I'm going to figure out who did this, and once I do, you're going to be able to put all of this craziness behind you once and for all. In the meantime, Miranda is working overtime trying to polish the store's image. And when you consider the fact she knows nothing about sewing, you have to admit she's come up with some neat ideas."

Rose lifted her bifocal-enlarged eyes to Tori's and made a face. "What are you talking about, Victoria?"

"The project cards, the video instructions for the elderly, the crafty weekend tour—even if this first one didn't go exactly as planned. She's very, very clever."

"I mean the part about her knowing nothing about sewing."

A pile of butterscotch candies in a jar beside the register caught her eye, and she reached over the counter and took one. "What about it?"

"It's incorrect."

"I'm not saying that should have kept you from hiring her." She unwrapped the candy and popped it into her mouth. "I mean all you have to do is look around the shop to know she's a marketing genius even if she doesn't know a button from a snap."

"Oh, she knows a button from a snap every bit as well as she knows how to sew," Rose argued. "Don't you remember me telling you this, Victoria? Miranda helped me fix that decorative stitch in my kitchen curtain once and for all."

She tried to rationalize what she was hearing from Rose with what Miranda herself had told her the previous evening, but it didn't fit. "You're *sure* she can sew, Rose?"

"I may be getting frailer with each passing day, but

I'm not stupid and I'm certainly not blind. Miranda can most definitely sew. In fact, she designed a tag I can attach to the inside of my curtain if I want. Would you like to see it?"

"Of course."

Rose opened a drawer to the left of the register and pulled out a small plastic case with a satin tag inside. In the center of the tag was a simple red embroidered rose.

"She made this for you?"

"It's like I told you a minute ago. Miranda can indeed sew."

So why tell me otherwise?

Shaking the thought from her head, she forced herself to remain in the present. With Rose. "What about your normal label? The one with your initials?

"The rose is prettier."

She wasn't sure if she agreed or not, but she opted to let it go. "How did you find her, by the way?"

"Find who?"

"Miranda."

"She came to me. Said she'd seen the ad I talked Leona into placing on one of the big sewing sites, and she wanted to know if I'd be interested in hiring her to grow the business. At first, I said no, but when she followed it up with a proposal of things she could do for the store, I agreed."

"And she does this for other businesses?" Tori asked.

"She said she did. And with everything I've seen from her these past few weeks, I've no reason to doubt that." Rose shuffled out from behind the desk with a large envelope in her hand. "Charles brought this by for you when you were picking up our lunch. I said he could wait, but he said he had an appointment, and off he went."

"An appointment, eh? Sounds mysterious." She opened the envelope and spread its contents across the top of the counter. In the center of the mix was the same brochure she'd all but memorized a few nights earlier. She tapped her finger on its front page. "Have you seen this? It's a *sewing* museum. In Jasper Falls."

"You mean Opal's?"

Tori scanned the rest of the material Charles had assembled and recognized most of it as having come from the museum's website. "She's listed on the website as its founder, yes."

"I have some flyers for it up by the door, but that's it. Why?"

"Charles and I want to take the entire sewing circle on a field trip there sometime soon," Tori said. "I saw a few pictures on their website the other night, and they looked so good they actually helped move it to the top of my short-term must-do list."

The quick but unmistakable jingle of the door-mounted bell brought an end to their discussion and sent Rose shuffling to the door with a hint of hope inching her mouth upward into something resembling a smile. But as quick as the hope appeared, it faded as Leona breezed into the shop's main room with Paris under her arm. "Hello, Rose. Hello, Victoria. Have we had a better day?"

"It was the same as it's been all week," Rose said. "*Dead.*"

"Maybe that will change after the evening news tomorrow." Leona removed her sunglasses and pointed at Tori. "Did you bring it?"

"I did. It's in my purse." She hurried down the hallway to Rose's office and returned with her purse and the emerald green scarf that had been Tori's for all of about half a day. "Here you go."

Leona rested the scarf against her cheek for a moment and then held it out for Rose to see. "Have you seen this?"

"It's lovely, Leona," Rose said. "Did you get it on one of your trips?"

"I got it in New York a few years ago—at a specialty shop on West Sixty-Eighth Street." Leona unfolded it across the top of the counter and pointed to the silk tag depicting an embroidered lily draped across a delicate silver bell. "It's a Lily Belle Original!"

"I always imagined her as such a lovely person, but I was wrong."

Leona stopped caressing her scarf and turned to Rose, hands on hips. "Just because she stopped sewing doesn't mean she isn't a nice person anymore."

"True, but killing one's husband certainly does."

She wasn't sure whose gasp was louder—hers or Leona's—but it was close. Leona, however, recovered faster. "What are you talking about, you old goat?"

"Leona!"

Rose quieted Tori's protest with a hand to Tori's back. "I actually *asked* Leona to call me that from time to time.

"Why?" she asked.

"This past week has left me craving a little normalcy."

"And Leona calling you an old goat qualifies as normalcy?"

"Yes."

Pinning Tori with a death glare, Leona addressed

Rose once again. "What is this about Lily Belle killing her husband?"

"She poisoned him, I believe."

"Why?"

"There was speculation by the media that he was having an affair with a co-worker—a young woman who worked at the television station with him."

"*Television station*?" Leona repeated. "Lily Belle is who Margot was hoping to turn a spotlight on via our shop?"

Rose ran her hand along Leona's scarf, stopping as she reached the off-white satin tag. "I'm confident Lily Belle's sewing ability will be her downfall one day. A person with that kind of talent can't hold it at bay forever."

An odd chill skittered down Tori's spine as she looked again at the embroidered lily atop the embroidered bell. So simple, yet so memorable . . .

Like Rose's.

Gripped by a sudden yet intense unease, Tori looked from Rose to the Lily Belle tag and back again. "Rose? Could I use the computer in your office for a minute? I want to look something up real quick."

"Be my guest. While you do that, I'll finish the thread display and then start to close everything down before Margaret Louise shows up to drive me home."

She was pretty sure she nodded but when she saw Leona eyeing her strangely, she wasn't so sure anymore. "Leona? Would you join me at the computer for a minute? This shouldn't take long."

"If I must, dear." Leona glanced down at Paris, explained where they were going, and then led Tori down the hallway and into the small office she shared with Rose. "So what are you looking up?"

"Lily Belle."

"I can probably tell you just about anything you want to know." Leona claimed the chair next to Tori's and settled Paris atop her lap. "Her clothes and her accessories always had an elegant intricacy about them."

"Did you ever meet her?"

"No."

A little voice inside her head disputed that claim.

She typed *Lily Belle Originals* into the search bar at the top of the screen and pressed enter. Scrolling past the links pertaining to the death of the seamstress's husband, Tori found and clicked on the link that would take her to images of the once-lauded seamstress. Instantly, the screen changed to reveal countless pictures of a woman Tori guessed to be in her late thirties—a woman with reddish blonde hair and a narrow nose dusted with a tiny smattering of freckles . . .

"Victoria, that's her! That's . . . Miranda!"

Oh, how she wanted to believe Leona was wrong, but she couldn't. The woman smiling back at her from Rose's computer screen was Lily Belle, aka Miranda Greer. Miranda's hair was now brown and curly but the nose and the freckles were exactly the same.

And as she continued to stare at the images lined up in rows from one end of the screen to the other, the puzzle pieces that had been there all along suddenly slid into place—

Miranda's familiarity with the inner workings of a television news station . . .

Her ability to help a seasoned seamstress such as Rose with an unfamiliar stitch . . .

Her noticeable discomfort at the mention of her late husband's co-anchor in relation to SewTastic . . .

And the simple yet elegant flower she'd made for Rose's curtains—a label eerily similar to Lily Belle's . . .

The only thing that didn't make any sense was why Miranda had killed Opal, unless—

"I suggest you shut that off, or I swear I'll kill her right here and right now."

Tori and Leona turned as one, the sight of Miranda's hands around Rose's throat bringing them both to their feet.

"I said turn it off, not stand up."

Reaching behind her back, Tori did as she was told while Leona pleaded with Miranda. "Please, I'm begging you, let Rose go."

"Yeah, that's not going to happen. For any of you." Miranda forced Rose to take a step forward and then yanked her to a stop. "Opal hadn't even officially put the pieces together yet, and I knew she had to go just like I knew Dirk had to go the second I found that note from Margot in his pocket. You snooze, you lose, as my dad always said."

A sound from somewhere just over Miranda's shoulder caught Tori's attention a split second before a familiar voice took center stage. "See, now I'm thinkin' *our* daddy said it better, don't you think, Twin?"

Miranda's surprise was short-lived, but it was enough for Leona to pull Rose to safety as Tori rushed forward and knocked Miranda to the ground.

"He said two apples don't make no bushel." Margaret Louise pulled her phone from the pocket of her polyester jacket and lowered herself onto Miranda's stomach. "I'm thinkin' it's 'bout time we put in a call to the chief so all those nice folks from Jasper Falls can finally go home . . ."

Chapter 31

Tori tiptoed out of Rose's bedroom and collapsed onto the couch next to Milo.

"So I take it she finally fell asleep?"

She wanted to answer, she really did, but the emotions she'd managed to hold at bay until that very moment were sure to make speaking difficult. Instead, she nodded and nestled herself against him, waiting for his warmth to chase the pervasive chill from her body's every nook and cranny.

"She's going to be okay, baby. The doctor said so. She's just a little shaken up is all."

Seeing Rose so helpless and so frightened was an image she never wanted to see again, yet she knew it would return for an encore on those nights when sleep proved elusive.

He moved his hand to her face and gently stroked her

cheek. "Leona called for about the fourth or fifth time just before you came out. She's worried about the two of you."

Clearing her throat of the emotional fog lodged around the halfway mark, she made herself speak for no other reason than to try and soften the concern she saw in his eyes. "I'm fine. Miranda didn't touch me."

"That doesn't mean she didn't hurt you, Tori. In fact, Leona told the chief that Miranda threatened all of you."

Had she?

Tori couldn't remember, either way.

All she could remember was Rose's face and that sickening feeling in the pit of her stomach that she wasn't going to be able to save her friend. "I can't believe Miranda didn't hear Margaret Louise. *Everyone* hears Margaret Louise," she whispered.

"Margaret Louise said she had a sense something was wrong the minute she stepped onto SewTastic's front porch to pick up Rose."

"I'm glad." And she was. Truly.

"Do you know if she confessed to the police?" Milo asked.

"She did." Lily Belle, aka Miranda, bared her soul to the department's detective before they'd even reached the patrol car. She poisoned her husband because of a purported affair, and she snuck into the project room and strangled Opal as a way to keep the troublemaking museum founder from identifying her as the acclaimed seamstress and wanted felon Lily Belle. "But do you want to know what's really crazy?"

He pulled his hand from her face and gently interlaced their fingers. "What's that?"

"Miranda's husband wasn't having an affair. The note

she found in her husband's suit jacket was about a diamond anniversary ring he was planning on getting Miranda—a ring Margot was trying to help him find."

"She killed him for no reason?" he asked.

"That's right, and she did the same thing to Opal. She was confident it was only a matter of time before Opal's extensive knowledge of labels would result in her capture. But considering the group was due to head out of Sweet Briar bright and early the next morning, the likelihood Opal was going to figure out Miranda's true identity was growing slimmer by the minute."

"So two people lost their lives for no reason. Wow."

"*Three* people," Tori corrected. "Miranda's life is essentially over now, too. And why? Because she assumed something that was untrue about her husband and then, because of how she handled that falsehood, she felt compelled to make another erroneous assumption—this time about Opal."

"So what happens with the museum and all the other properties that Opal bought up in Jasper Falls?" Milo asked. "Is there a husband or a child who gets them now?"

"No. Opal lived alone. All she had was her money and her power. It's why she was all over the place in what she did with that money. Sometimes she did good things, sometimes she wielded it like a weapon because it was the one place in her life she felt she had control." Tori pulled her legs up and onto the couch. "It's kind of sad, you know?"

He rested his lips against her head. "You're right, it is. All the way around. But we can't change any of this. All we can do is learn something from it, I guess. "

Milo was right. It was time to pick up and move on.

"I think I should check in with Leona and make sure she's doing okay, too. Watching Rose being handled like that upset her deeply."

She took a step back and surveyed the cake. The purple sugar from Charles's favorite Pixie Sticks added a nice splash of color, as did the M&M's he now loved thanks to Leona.

"It's getting' harder 'n harder to keep sayin' good-bye to him, ain't it, Victoria?"

"Yes, Margaret Louise, it sure is." Tori slipped her hands under the cake and led the way across the kitchen and over to the back door. "It's like Rose always says, Charles is a breath of fresh air. When he's here in Sweet Briar, everything is just a little lighter and a lot more sparkly."

"Sparkly? What's sparkly?"

Margaret Louise jumped in front of Tori and shielded the cake from Charles's prying eyes. "Don't you worry your head none 'bout what we're sayin' in here, Charles. Just scamper over to the other side of the deck and don't peek."

"But I like to peek!"

Channeling her inner Charles, Margaret Louise snapped out her reply in a slightly misshapen triangle. "That's. Too. Bad."

Charles squealed and turned away. "My work here is done, people."

"Not even close, peeker." Tori hipped her way through the door and then stopped on the other side to try to get a handle on her emotions.

Rose sidled up beside her to get a closer look at the cake. "What's that purple stuff?"

"Sugar crystals from one of his Pixie Sticks."

"Of course it is." Rose pulled the flaps of her sweater more tightly against her body and grinned up at Tori. "That's what makes you so special, Victoria. You pay attention to everyone's likes and dislikes, and you operate accordingly."

"You do the same thing, Rose."

Clearly uncomfortable at the praise, Rose called everyone over to the table and the waiting cake. "As much as we don't want to see Charles go, he does have a plane to catch."

"Just this one last time I do."

Every head on the deck turned in Charles's direction with Leona's voice leading the verbal charge. "You're not coming back?"

He took a moment to appreciate the cake and then ran his finger across the purple sugar crystals with the reckless abandon of a six-year-old. "Oh I'm coming back. I'm just not *leaving* again."

"Quit your sneakin' and start spillin'!"

Rising onto the balls of his feet, Charles let off a series of happy claps. "I know a few of you are probably wondering where I was on Sunday afternoon when Hurricane Miranda exploded her wrath all over my friends. If I'd known what was happening, I'd have been sitting on top of her right next to you, Margaret Louise. But since I didn't know, I was busy signing some papers— lots and lots of papers."

"Papers?" Tori echoed.

"That's right." Charles pointed to the cake and then

looked around at each and every person circled around him. "Who wants a piece of cake?"

Leona stepped forward, pulled the knife from his hands, and put it back down on the table. "Finish your story, Charles."

"Actually, I think I'd rather show you instead." He flounced across the deck to his favorite backpack and pulled out a sheaf of papers bearing the McCormick's Books & Café logo of his New York employer. "For the past six months or so, my boss has been trying to persuade me to help him open another store location. I was flattered, of course, but I liked where I was better than the location he was considering."

Rose pilfered a red and a brown M&M from the side of the cake and handed one to Leona. "What's this got to do with you not leaving anymore, young man?"

"Well, when Leona mentioned that Calamity Books was closing up shop for good, I got to thinking. A shop with rare first editions might not be able to make it here in Sweet Briar, but a store like McCormick's might."

Tori held her hand over her mouth, afraid to breathe, afraid to move. "And?"

"I asked my boss if he'd consider Sweet Briar as a place to put another location."

Eight bodies leaned forward. Waiting.

"But he said no. He said Sweet Briar was too far."

Eight sets of shoulders slumped.

"But the more I thought about it, the more I realized he was right. Sweet Briar *is* too far away for another McCormick's Books & Café. But it's an absolutely perfect spot for *Snap. To. It.* Books & Café, don't you think?"

Reader-Suggested
Sewing Tips

~Taryn L.

🪡 For those leftover thread snippets: Buy a glass ornament. While sewing, anytime you have an extra piece or just a snippet of thread, place it in the ornament. When it gets full, you have a wonderfully colorful ornament that you can hang on your Christmas tree. I even like to add a little bit of shiny silver or gold thread at the end for a bit of flair.

~Julie S.

🪡 When working with silky fabrics, it's best to use a round-point needle instead of a sharp needle. It keeps the fabric from getting little runs in it.

~Judy G-L.

* When doing appliqués, I put HeatnBond Lite on the back of my pieces. It helps with fraying, and you can iron down the piece before you do the final stitch.

~Debra W.

* For those last-minute needs, I keep about four to five sewing needles threaded on a spool of white thread and the same on a spool of black thread. I grab the last needle, unwind what I need, cut the thread, and knot the end for next time. I keep them in the junk drawer with an empty bottle to keep needles in. When I use the last one, I rethread a batch and put it away for the next emergency.

Sewing Pattern

A Simple Holiday (Dishcloth) Apron

~SHARED BY READER LYNN D.

Dishcloth Apron Supplies

A festive holiday (or otherwise) dishcloth
4 to 6 feet of sturdy ribbon
Pins
Sewing machine (or needle and thread)
Scissors

Adult Apron Instructions

Cut a length of sturdy cloth ribbon that will go all the way around your waist and tie comfortably into a bow.

Fold the ribbon in half lengthwise and mark the middle of the ribbon with a pin. Then, fold the dishcloth in half lengthwise. Match the middle of the ribbon with the middle of the dishcloth, and pin the centers together at the top of the towel.

Continue to pin the ribbon to the top of the towel.

With your sewing machine, sew from one end of the pinned ribbon to the other end.

**Note: If using needle and thread,
do a sturdy stitch such as a backstitch
to secure the towel to the ribbon well.**

Remove pins and clip threads.

FROM NATIONAL BESTSELLING AUTHOR

ELIZABETH LYNN CASEY

-The Southern Sewing Circle Mysteries-

SEW DEADLY

DEATH THREADS

PINNED FOR MURDER

DEADLY NOTIONS

DANGEROUS ALTERATIONS

REAP WHAT YOU SEW

LET IT SEW

REMNANTS OF MURDER

TAKEN IN

WEDDING DURESS

NEEDLE AND DREAD

Praise for the Southern Sewing Circle Mysteries
"Filled with fun, folksy characters
and southern charm."
—Maggie Sefton, national bestselling
author of *Purl Up and Die*

elizabethlynncasey.com
penguin.com

1755

LAURA BRADFORD

Éclair and Present Danger

An Emergency Dessert Squad Mystery

With her rent rising faster than her pie crust, bakery
owner Winnie Johnson had hoped to be rescued by
an inheritance from her wealthy friend and neighbor
Gertrude Redenbacher. Instead all she inherits is the
widow's hostile hissing tabby, Lovey, and a vintage
ambulance, restored by Gertrude's late husband.
As her dream crumbles, Winnie makes her final
delivery—a peach pie to an elderly widower. But
she finds Bart Wagner lying on his kitchen floor,
smothered by a pillow.

To comfort her frightened and grieving neighbors,
Winnie comes to the rescue with her baked goods—
and an idea is born: dessert delivery via her ambulance
and a new business called the Emergency Dessert
Squad. When she's not speeding to the scenes of
dessert emergencies, Winnie is also racing to track
down Bart's killer—before she needs to call a real
ambulance for the next victim...

laurabradford.com
facebook.com/laurabradfordauthor
penguin.com